TUPPENNY HAT DETECTIVE

Brian Sellars

Published by YouWriteOn.com
Sponsored by Arts Council England

Tuppenny Hat Detective is a work of fiction.
All characters in this publication are
fictitious and any resemblance to real persons,
living or dead, is purely coincidental.

TUPPENNY HAT DETECTIVE

Set in the South Yorkshire city of Sheffield in 1951, Tuppenny Hat Detective recalls a time when the UK was struggling to recover from World War 2: bomb damage, shortages, rationing, and the indomitable wartime spirit of the people were still features of daily life. Despite the hardships, many who lived through the fifties recall them with great fondness.

Brian Sellars was born in the Sheffield suburb of Walkley in 1941. The background to Tuppenny Hat Detective recalls a wonderful childhood spent there and scroamin around in Rivelin Valley, probably the most beautiful and underrated river valley in England. A walk from Rivelin Post Office to the Holly Bush Inn is the most entrancing two and half mile stroll you can take. A guidebook to demystify the strange watercourses, grassy bumps, and mossy stone ruins that are found along the way will be useful.

John Ruskin, the nineteenth century writer, artist, and philanthropist, built himself a house overlooking Rivelin Valley. He said it had one of the best views in the country, "Comparable to Brantwood in the Lake District."

Author's note:
The Sheffield accent, with its thee, thou, and thine, can be a bit of a trial for the uninitiated. I have tried to curb my enthusiasm for it in Tuppenny Hat Detective, to help the pace of the narrative. However, there is a glossary of Sheffield-eeze at the back of the book, together with a little exercise piece that you might enjoy.

www.briansellars.co.uk

By the same author

THE WHISPERING BELL

Historical fiction.
Set in 7th century Anglo-Saxon England.
To be published in March 2009
by Quaestor2000 Ltd.

www.quaestor2000.com

www.briansellars.co.uk

For Jeanie

With thanks to Geri and Denis

TUPPENNY HAT DETECTIVE

www.briansellars.co.uk

CHAPTER ONE

The old Star Woman would never return a stray ball. Most kids would rather face a mad dog than risk being eeny-meenyed into trembling on her doorstep to plead for one, but in the early nineteen-fifties even an old tennis ball was a valuable toy and not to be given up lightly.

Eleven-year-old Billy Perks and his pals decided it would be pointless knocking on her door. A daring commando raid was called for. Somebody would have to climb the wall into her back yard and retrieve the lost ball. It would be no simple task, and if Yvonne Sparkes had not been there Billy would not have volunteered. Yvonne believed he could do anything, and would gladly tell the world as much. Such female adulation was in short supply for Billy, and like old tennis balls, was not to be wasted.

With all the gravitas of one of his cinema heroes embarking on a deadly mission, he issued final instructions to Yvonne and his best pal, Michael "Kick" Morley. 'Keep quiet. Don't yell over the wall. She'll hear thee and grab me if you do.' The pair nodded solemnly.

Though towering above him, the sandstone wall enclosing the old woman's back yard offered an easy climb with generous handholds. The return however, would be tougher. Not only because of the fear that she might spring up and turn him into a newt or something, but the far side of the wall was white-washed and slippery, the handholds stuffed with foaming tumbles of flowers.

Billy scrambled over the wall and dropped silently to the ground. Crouching low, he listened for sounds of enemy activity. He found himself in a small yard paved with old stable tiles. It was scrubbed and spotless. On three sides, blue sky was all he could see above its walls. The crooked, whitewashed house completed the enclosure.

The old place bulged like a clenched fist, its walls of crumbling brick and wattle, held together by ancient ivy. It sagged into the yard, as if exhausted by the effort of having been

1

a house for unknown centuries. Darkly ajar, its back door threatened. Billy scuttled to a far corner and crouched beside a stone slab table, crowded with daffodils and crocuses erupting from treacle tins and old buckets. Peering through them, he studied the yard, planning his next move. He knew he must pinpoint the ball, so that he could grab it and dash away safely.

There was no sign of it.

A black cat dropped from the wall onto the stone table, giving him a heart stopping fright. With a malevolent glare it oozed softly to the paving, stalked across the yard, and disappeared into the house. Billy wiped a hand over his sweating forehead, his gaze following the cat into the darkness beyond a donkey-stoned doorstep. He edged cautiously towards the door, his mouth as dry as dust. Sneaking a quick look inside, he spotted the ball. His breath caught in his chest. How was he going to get that? It was at least a yard inside the house, trapped at the dog-eared edge of a coconut fibre mat.

The cat had vanished, but there sat the ball in plain sight, easy for the old woman to spot and confiscate at any second. Or maybe, Billy speculated chillingly, she had deliberately placed it there - bait to draw him to her witch's den.

Taking a deep breath, he ran into the house and reached for the ball. In his panic, he fumbled it. Stricken, he watched it roll out of reach. It bumped into the old woman's bare foot, but luckily, bounced straight back. He grabbed it, his heart fluttering in his ribcage, and made a mad dash to the wall. Scrambling over it blindly, he dropped into the street in a moil of breathless disarray.

'Chuffin eck! I saw her,' he gasped. 'I almost touched her foot.'

'Errrgh! What'd she do?'

'Nowt.'

'Didn't she say owt?' Kick was agog, his mousy blonde hair standing up like corn stooks above his russet face and wide blue eyes.

Yvonne reached out and touched fresh blood on Billy's knee. 'You've cut thee sen. Dunt it hurt?' She swept chestnut curls away from her brown eyes with the back of her hand.

2

Billy saw her concern but said nothing. His mind was on that naked foot. He was beginning to realise that it was not that of a vigilant huntress waiting to pounce on prey drawn to her baited trap, but of someone collapsed and helpless on the floor - maybe unconscious, or worse.

'I've gorra go back,' he said. 'I think she might be hurt or sommat.'

'Tha must be crackers,' Kick Morley gasped, his eyebrows skidding up his forehead to disappear beneath his tangled fringe.

'She were laid out on her floor. She could've fell. Old folk are always toppling over - me mam sez.' Without waiting for their approval, he scaled the wall again. There was no need for stealth this time. He dropped into the yard and marched up to the back door. 'Hello! Hello, are you there, Mrs?'

The black cat's haughty exit between his feet, prompted him to pull up his socks and wipe the blood from his grazed knee. He called out again. 'Are you all right, Mrs?'

Sunlight slanted through the door, laying his shadow across smooth flagstones. The old woman lay across a frayed coconut fibre mat. Billy's stomach flipped. His knees wobbled, threatening to dump him on top of her. Swallowing hard he composed himself and peered into the gloom. He had never seen a real corpse, though he had seen thousands of phoney ones on the cinema screen at the Walkley Palladium. They usually had arrows or tomahawks sticking out of them. This one did not. Even so, he was certain that he was looking at a dead woman – a real one.

Steeling himself, he stepped into a cool, dark room, whose beamed ceiling was barely at head height. Wearing a white night-shift, the old woman lay stretched out on her side, her long silver hair unbound around her face and shoulders. Her thin arms reached out like someone preparing to dive into a swimming pool. Her eyes were wide open as if she were about to speak. Their liquid stare sent a shudder down his spine.

'Are you all right, Mrs?' he asked feebly. 'Are you hurt? I just wanted us ball back.' He felt stupid talking to a corpse, but could not stop himself. Summoning courage, he knelt and touched her wrist, seeking a pulse. He had no certain idea what to do, but

3

mimicked what he had seen done in the films. She felt cold, and wherever her pulse was supposed to be, he was sure she did not have one.

'Dead as door nails,' he mumbled, and immediately thought of his granny. In her younger days his grandmother had been the street's unofficial midwife and mortician, laying out the dead on a lavatory door stretched over a couple of chair backs. He could never touch a dead person - not like that, he told himself. It was a sickening idea, not to mention the practical disadvantages of using the lavatory with a corpse on the door. Though he realised this was not the time for such deliberations, he nevertheless, added mortician to a growing list in his head, of professions he vowed never to enter when he left school.

Looking about, he wondered what he should do next. He felt as if the room was watching him, judging him from its centuries of experience. A scrubbed pine table and a few dining chairs, none matching, occupied the middle of the floor. Corralling a collection of threadbare cushions, a Windsor chair stood close to a shiny black-leaded Yorkshire range. On the wall adjoining the back yard, ivy had forced its way in through the wattle and daub and found a warm welcome. Clipped to perfection, it thrived around a slit of window. A huge Victorian sideboard, her prized possession, so his Granny Smeggs had said, dominated almost an entire wall. Beside it hung a sepia photograph of an infantryman, stiffly posed behind a seated young woman, whose dark, beautiful eyes, gazed out fearfully. Billy felt sick. Those same unblinking eyes were staring from the floor, and just as lifeless.

He needed a drink of water. In the ivy-clad corner, water dripped from a brass tap. He found a cup, drew himself a drink, and sat at the table miserably pondering the situation, and regretting too late his weakness in the face of female adulation.

Gazing around he wondered how she had died. The room appeared undisturbed. Everything seemed neatly in its place. Had she fallen? There was no blood or signs of a struggle. Her arms looked strange, stretched out like that, and no obvious explanation presented itself. He wondered if she had been trying to reach the sideboard. Perhaps it contained something vital to

4

her in her final moments: medicine, an alarm bell, a torch - who could say? Speculation was pointless. Then he recalled how sometimes in films, murder victims struggled in their dying moments to reach some tiny clue, something that would point an accusing finger at their killer, even from beyond the grave. 'Stupid,' he scolded himself. This was not a film. He should concentrate on the real world. His stomach swirled sickeningly, draining his strength as he fought rising panic.

In the gable wall that adjoined the street, a small bay window glazed with old bullions, distorted the images of everything beyond it, including the faces of his two friends now bobbing and craning to see into the house. They tapped on the greenish glass, calling to him. With a final glance around the room, Billy stiffened his shoulders decisively and rose to leave - this time by the front door. There was no longer the need to climb walls. Lifting its heavy iron latch, he pulled open the ancient door. He was relieved to see sunlight and to feel fresh air brushing his face. A few yards along the street his friends had left the window and were now hanging on the backyard wall, calling for him in loud whispers.

He crept up behind them. 'What?' he yelled, making them jump. 'We've gorra ring the cops. T'owd Star Woman's dead.'

'Tha didn't touch her, did tha?' Kick asked, wide eyed.

'Come on, let's ring 'em quick,' Billy urged, keen to limit Kick's questioning. 'Do you know how to do nine-nine-nine?'

'Nein! Nein! Nein!' Kick quipped, assuming a German accent.

Yvonne whacked Kick's ear, merging laughter with groaning disdain.

'We'll go to the cop box. That'll be quickest.' Billy set off at a sprint.

Faded green and cream, the police box perched on precipitous cobbles in a street only a hundred yards away. Usually a couple of bobbies could be found there: making tea, having a smoke, or fixing their bicycles, but not this time. Billy glared at the locked door and tugged on its unyielding handle.

'You can break that glass on the key box,' said Kick, stepping back as if to stress that his role in any such action, however authorised, would be purely advisory.

Yvonne gaped. 'You can't do that!' she cried, her eyes wide and fearful in her small, heart shaped face.

'That's worrits for,' hooted Kick. 'If there're no coppers here, you're allowed to bust the glass and use the special 'phone inside. It's for emergencies. It says so - look.'

All three peered at the lettering on the white enamelled notice screwed to the police box door. A taut silence enveloped them as they read, then read again.

'Chuff it! I'm not busting no glass on no cop box, no matter what. Coppers'll kill thee. Come on, we'll go down to the phone box instead.'

On route, they decided that Yvonne should make the call, because, as Kick pointed out, 'She can do the poshest voice. And anyway,' he added, 'coppers never believe what lads say. They always think we're messing about.'

After placing the call, the walk back to the old Star Woman's house was something of an anticlimax. It was a steep, wearying climb, which they completed in thoughtful silence. Back at the Star Woman's cottage a little crowd was forming, including Billy's Grandmother Smeggs. Kick Morley's mother was there too, hipping his perpetually food-stained infant sister. She and her neighbours were whispering and pointing curiously as they assembled beneath the crooked gable.

Built in Tudor times the row of cottages had once been a public house. Long before the war, it was converted into three dwellings: bikes, runner beans, and washing lines took over its outdoor skittle alley. It stood, gable end to the road, its ancient stone roof sagging like a wet tent. A single window punctured the whitewashed gable. Behind its thick bullions, the Star Woman had lived for more years than most could remember: a solitary eccentric, named for "The Star" newspaper she had sold on Sheffield's streets between the wars.

Billy's deadly enemy, Stan Sutcliffe, appeared at the back of the crowd. He barged to the front to join his sour faced bruiser of a father. Billy shuddered as he eyed the pair. Only the Sutcliffe

6

females were scarier. Sutcliffe senior was as big as a church door, and could loom up suddenly on people, much like a bread van in fog. His snarling glare, challenged anyone foolish enough to return it. Billy avoided eye contact. The old man had planted himself firmly at the best vantage point, shoving others aside like a jack through skittles. No one had objected. Billy confined his rebellion to thinking how the old man lacked only a handle, to make of himself a piratical Toby jug. His swaggering son, a miniature in the set, thrust his knotty body beside his father. Even his apprentice snarl was enough to chill a vet.

'I thought there might be something wrong,' Granny Smeggs was saying to nobody in particular. 'I've not seen her around this morning like usual.' Billy slipped his hand in hers and concentrated on not looking at the Sutcliffes.

Beside him, with a display of alarming facial acrobatics, a wheezing gossip put in, 'I always knew she'd be trouble in the end. You could smell her.'

Billy took an instant dislike to the woman. He had never thought the old lady smelled, though nobody seemed surprised to hear of it. True, she was far from pristine, and never seen in hues but dun and dingy: a tatty fringed shawl, a black full skirt down to the ground over button boots, and a fitted high-necked bodice behind a grey apron. She was a relic from the past, and of course, looking as she did, most children felt she might easily be a witch.

The urgent clanging of a police car's alarm bell interrupted speculations. A shiny black Wolsley saloon approached, followed by a cream coloured Daimler ambulance. Bells down, the vehicles swerved into the street, slowing at the last moment, scattering folk in every direction. The Sutcliffes vanished like steam. Billy looked for them but they were gone. It was no surprise. The police and the Sutcliffes invariably had unfinished business.

Police Sergeant Burke, a towering man with a ramrod back, and a chin that seldom broke contact with his sternum, unfolded himself from the car and eyed the crowd. He fitted his helmet, pulling it down over his eyes like a guardsman's peak. 'Where's

Billy Perks?' he bellowed, his baritone resonating on the hushed air.

A general buzz arose from the bystanders, suggesting that it was no surprise to find Billy Perks at the centre of this drama. After all, was it not Billy Perks, who on his bike had demolished the herbalist's shop window, wiping out centuries of sun-bleached window dressing and a new electric Vimto sign? And was it not Billy Perks who had borrowed Mrs Seaton's commode for a wheel-chair for his "Penny-For-the-Guy Fawkes dummy"? The poor woman had only placed it outside her door to dry it off after scrubbing it with carbolic.

Summoning defiance in the face of such a hostile, faithless group, Grandmother Smeggs stuck out her chin and proudly pointed to her grandson, though inwardly dreading the shame she feared might at any moment deluge the proud names of Smeggs and Perks.

Billy stepped forward, a tousled, copper-headed figure, looking as though he had just wrestled a spaniel in a haystack, and lost. A concerned frown had banished the normally cheerful grin from his open, freckled face. Steeling himself for the worst, he approached the policeman.

'Well done, lad,' said the sergeant, placing his huge hand on Billy's narrow shoulder. 'Wait here a minute. I want you to talk to the young constable and make your statement.'

In the crowd, the pendulum of opinion had swung and Granny Smeggs fielded compliments as though she had never doubted her grandson's virtue for a second.

Sergeant Burke turned his attention to his young constable who was squaring up to shoulder in the Star Woman's front door. A voice from the crowd pointed out that the door was seldom locked, and that he needed only "the nail" to gain access.

'Nail, what nail?' Burke queried.

'The sneck nail. It's a six inch nail she uses to lift the latch,' chorused his audience.

'Where are we going to get a six inch nail in a hurry?'

'Off'n her windowsill,' they told him.

The sergeant searched, making much of his efforts, but eventually found the nail, which he handed to his subordinate.

The constable stuck it into the latch, no doubt pondering the contorted logic of having a nail for a key and then hiding it where everyone knew it was.

Billy however, was distracted by quite another question that had popped into his head. Why was the sneck nail not already in the latch? The old woman was at home, so surely she would have used it to let herself in. When he had opened the door from the inside to let himself out, he had simply lifted the latch. There had been no nail sticking through from the outside. The mystery had not occurred to him then, but now, he realised, the nail should only be in its hiding place on the windowsill when she was away from her house. Whenever she was at home it should be in the door during the day, or taken inside at night where perhaps she kept it on her sideboard until morning.

Two ambulance men and the sergeant were now inside the house. The crowd speculated wildly as to what they would find. 'She weren't right in her head,' one said. 'I always knew sommat like this would happen.'

'She's got gold tha knows,' another said, 'sovereigns, lots of 'em in a mucky sock.'

The young constable joined Billy beside the police car and took out his notebook. Billy leaned proudly against the shining vehicle, enjoying the celebrity that permitted such familiarity with expensive civic equipment. It was not long however, before he began to feel that some of the constable's questions were misguided and even irrelevant. He decided that the young man must be new to his job. He patiently tried to explain to him the point of the sneck nail clue. The officer was not interested. Instead, he insisted on giving Billy a telling off for climbing over the backyard wall in the first place. The sneck nail clue went unrecorded. Billy regretted that it was not Sergeant Burke asking him the questions. He knew the old sergeant would not need important clues explaining to him - as if he was an idiot. He decided to seek him out later.

As the crowd waited for the ambulance men to re-emerge, speculation ran wild. The Star Woman's so-called life story, wild inventions of the fancy free, ranged from tales of an escaped Russian aristocrat, to a deranged ex-suffragette with a house full of gold coins – in a mucky sock. Wild stories flitted like moths, gathering nonsense at each telling.

'I want to talk to you, grandson,' said Mrs Smeggs, nailing Billy with her pale blue eyes. 'Have you done with him, young man?'

'Yes thank you, Ma'am,' replied the constable. 'Any road up, if we need him we know where to come.'

Granny dropped an arm around Billy's shoulders and started to move away. 'Come on love, let's go indoors. This wind is cold enough to break tripe.' She paused, distracted by the sedate arrival of a gleaming Rover Six saloon car. It drew up behind the ambulance, bringing a hush to the crowd's excited burble. It was old Doctor Greenhow's car. Beside him, in the passenger seat, sat Doctor Hadfield, his new locum, a young man said to be a heart breaker. When Billy had heard this, he had failed to see why being a heart breaker was such a good thing for a doctor. Surely, a heart fixer is what is called for?

A respectful silence fell on the gathering. People nodded and smiled deferentially as the two men alighted and strode through their midst to the door of the old woman's house. Billy watched the older man raise up an ebony walking stick, richly handled with a silver horse's head, and wield it like a sabre, carving a path through the throng.

Sergeant Burke, who had been called to speak on the police car's radiotelephone, was unable to greet the pair. He glared at them from his car, seeming stressed and annoyed by their arrival. With a series of nods, ticks and facial gestures, he mimed instructions to his constable to escort them inside, while he dealt with the radio.

Doctor Greenhow entered, posting his nervous assistant at the door to fend off intruders. Mrs Seaton, the Star Woman's next-door neighbour, seeing the young doctor trapped and defenceless, evidently saw this as an opportunity not to be missed. With a rancid glance at Billy, no doubt recalling the commode episode, she set off to consult the young doctor. The stricken locum gazed about helplessly as Mrs Seaton rolled down a thick, tobacco coloured stocking and showed him a battered, blue and white, lumpy shin. Billy cringed, feeling sick at the sight of it, and mentally added physician to his list of rejected professions.

The locum was saved by the re-emergence of his boss, who angrily disposed of Mrs Seaton. 'You know where my surgery is, madam,' boomed old Greenhow. 'If you need treatment - visit it!' Gathering his sheepish assistant, he strode back towards his car.

Sergeant Burke finished his radio call and intercepted him. The two men whispered in a huddle for several minutes, the sergeant, scribbling in his notebook all the while. Billy watched them, thinking how sour and resentful the doctor seemed towards the Sergeant's questioning. Surely, he cannot have been surprised. He must have expected it.

When the Sergeant had what he wanted, he abruptly turned from the doctor and strode off. Billy suspected they might have had harsh words about something, though he could not tell what.

Doctor Greenhow headed for his car, but paused, evidently on an afterthought. 'Oh Sergeant, before your man locks up I need to go back in there. I left something inside.'

Sergeant Burke called to his young constable, who was now attempting to screw a padlock hasp to the cottage door. 'Let the doctor back inside, Handley. And don't forget the back door too. I've got to go. That was the Super on the radio. Can you finish up here?'

Pink and sweating from his exertions, the constable nodded, and stood aside for Doctor Greenhow to re-enter the house. After a moment or two, the doctor gloomily re-appeared. He trotted to buttonhole the sergeant once again, before he could drive away in the police car. As Billy watched all this, standing beside his grandmother, he was surprised to see the sergeant point him out and call him over. 'Billy my lad, come here a minute. The doctor would like to speak to you.'

Meanwhile, Mrs Seaton had by no means given up on getting some attention for her gruesome limb. She was hopping after young doctor Hadfield, her skirt hem held above her cauliflower knees, like a demented dancer.

Spotting this, Greenhow turned on her suddenly, and with surprising fury. 'Damn it woman, are you stupid?' he bellowed.

'Did you not hear what I said? This is not the time, nor the place. Come to the surgery at the proper hour. Now go away!'

Shocked and cowering, Mrs Seaton scuttled into her house, badgered at every step by the old doctor waving his walking stick and shouting at her. After seeing this, it was with some trepidation that Billy approached him.

Dabbing his brow with a Paisley handkerchief, Doctor Greenhow turned suddenly to Billy. His anger fell away like water and he smiled genially. 'Well done, young man,' he cried, grabbing Billy's hand and shaking it firmly. 'You handled this nasty business like a true champion. Now tell me, Old Stick, how d'you feel?' he asked, steering Billy slowly through the open yard and away from the crowd. 'Will you be frightened, do you think? Will you have nightmares?'

'No sir. I don't think so. I wasn't scared.'

'Good lad. Good lad. So you don't feel the need of a magic potion from my bag eh?' he joked. Billy shook his head. 'Now tell me, did you move anything in there? I mean when you found Annab – err - Mrs Loveday, did you touch anything?'

'I took her pulse,' said Billy, then, remembering added, 'Oh, I had a cup of water because I felt sick.'

'Yes well, I'm sure you did, Old Stick. Bit of a shock, eh? I mean to say - dead body and all. But you didn't touch any - err - anything?'

'No sir, nothing.'

'Now think hard, Billy. This is very important for my report. Was the room disturbed? I mean such as - were the cupboards open or closed?'

Billy thought for a moment, remembering the old lady's eyes gazing at him from the floor and from the photograph on the wall. 'Everything was - err - orderly,' he said, the word popping unexpectedly into his head. 'Her eyes were open, but the cupboards were shut.'

'Orderly hum, orderly you say. Very well, thank you. If I may, I shall shake your hand again. You did an excellent job, very well done indeed.'

Billy's hand was stinging when the doctor finally released it and he wondered casually when the pain of congratulation might fade. He watched the old man join his colleague in the Rover. Both men beamed and waved as they drove off.

Billy waved back half heartedly, shuddering as he wondered how his father would react when he heard about all this. Should he even tell him, or would it be better to keep quiet? Billy knew he would certainly not be as generous with his praise as the old doctor had been. At times, it felt that nothing he could do would please him.

Better to say nothing, he decided.

. . . .

CHAPTER TWO

Billy loved trams. He thought of them as friendly and as comforting as old gloves. How the rickety old double-deckers could climb up and down the city's switchback of mountainous streets astonished him. Even just to see one careering past down the steep cobbles thrilled him.

He attended a Catholic school a mile or so from his neighbourhood, and might have envied Yvonne and Kick who went to the local "Proddy", but for his tram rides on the top deck, on bad weather days.

The day after he had discovered the Star Woman's body, he was riding the tram home from school when Stan Sutcliffe jumped aboard. Billy's heart sank. Stan had been after him for weeks, boasting that he would "get him". Billy knew this was no idle threat.

Stan Sutcliffe was seventeen, almost a man. Constantly in trouble with the police, he was a notorious thug and bully. Stupidity magnified his violence; he seemed incapable of understanding its possible consequences. In happier days with his dad, Billy remembered him joking that all the Sutcliffes were as "thick as dubbin". One of his father's pet jokes was that the Army had tested old Mr Sutcliffe and rejected him. "They gave him a shovel with which he felled ten oak trees before somebody explained its proper use."

Stan sat across the aisle from Billy, glaring and mouthing threats. He was neither subtle, nor lacking persistence. He was after him, because Billy had spotted him and his father stealing tools on the garden allotments. Old Sutcliffe had amassed a shed full of them. The pair would clean them up with a wire brush, paint them with red lead and sell them back to the very gardeners they had stolen them from. Some dim-sighted old gents had bought their own spades and rakes several times over. Billy had told his uncle Bert Smeggs about their caper. Uncle Bert had gone straight round to old Sutcliffe's shed, forced the

14

door, gathered up all the stolen tools, and returned them to their rightful owners.

Stan was still sporting a black eye, though now faded to a pale, yellowish colour. Billy knew it would not have been his Uncle Bert's handy work. Uncle Bert read the Observer, and in Billy's estimation could bewilder even a crazed bull with logic and rational argument. Billy had heard that you could tell about people by the newspapers they read. Uncle Bert did not need to punch people, and Billy suspected his own father might be the author of Stan's facial decoration. Dad read the sports pages.

Huddled in his seat Billy planned his escape. To get off the tram and escape a beating, he would have to bail out suddenly and run like crazy. He would need to jump off, well before the tramcar stopped, and hope to catch Stan napping. He knew the route very well. Walkley tramcars invariably built up speed as they clattered down past the Yorkshire Penny Bank, and on to a straight, level run along the main shopping street. Being so close to the end of the line, there were seldom people waiting to board at the tram stops, and providing there were none on the rear platform waiting to alight, drivers would open up the throttle and enjoy themselves. They would lurch along past Saint Mary's church, banging and swinging. Billy wanted to be a tram driver when he grew up. They had so much fun.

His was the last stop before the terminus, past Binks' the barbershop and the Ebenezer Chapel. Of course, Stan Sutcliffe knew this too. He was grinning and brandishing his fist. Billy tried not to look at it, but as big as a tin loaf, and as knobbly as a sack of clog irons, it was hard to ignore.

The conductor rang the bell for Billy's stop. It was just before the cinema. Billy pretended not to notice; he sat coiled and ready to spring off as soon as the driver began cranking down on the power. When the moment arrived, he sprinted down the aisle, clattered down the narrow stairs and leapt off the rear platform, hitting the ground running. He did not look back to see if Sutcliffe was following him - he knew he was.

Highton Street is a very steep climb from the tram stop. Only the fit could climb it, let alone run up it. Billy had noticed that few people could run up Highton Street without wearing shorts.

15

A third of the way up, a right turn into Orchard Road offered a merciful respite to the winded. They would lean, puffing and gasping, against a low wall, as they pretend to be enjoying the view over the Don Valley, an unlovely vista choked with steel mills, smoke, and factories.

Billy's granny lived on Orchard Road. Hers was the end cottage of a pretty, stone terrace of three, standing in neat gardens, behind a wall. Billy's mother would still be at work, so his own house, though closer, was locked and empty. Granny's therefore, offered his only refuge. If he could get there before Sutcliffe mangled his bones, he would be safe for another day.

A narrow gate, taller than Billy, served all three cottages. A recycled industrial spring, strong enough to fend off a battleship, kept it firmly shut. Sutcliffe was gaining as Billy reached the gate; barely a yard separated them. He threw his weight against the spring and forced through to safety. Like a mousetrap, the gate snapped shut behind him, whacking Stan hard enough to make him yelp. He doubled up, hopping around with his hands between his legs, as if he had hit his thumb with a hammer.

Breathless, Billy clattered into Granny's house and ran to the window to goad and grimace at Stan. He stuck out his tongue and vigorously wagged the two fingered vee-sign at him with both hands, completely forgetting that behind him his granny would be sitting, gently rocking in her old chair.

'And where did we learn that, pray tell?' she asked, with stiff disapproval.

Billy blushed with shame, staring at his offensive fingers, as if they had suddenly sprouted from his hands and tricked him into such vulgarity.

'Do you know where that gesture originates?'

Billy knew she was about to tell him. She seemed to know everything, and he loved her endlessly fascinating stories. She was the perfect granny, in his opinion, and looked exactly as a granny should: neat silver hair fastened with a shiny nacre comb, delicate, gold sleeper rings in her lobes, and round tortoiseshell spectacles sitting on faint blue marks on the bridge of her nose. She played the viola: baked bread, made jam from incongruous

16

combinations of fruit, and sewed all her own clothes on an ancient, Singer treadle sewing machine.

As usual, he found her wrapped in her thick brown cardigan. A lace trimmed handkerchief peeked from one pocket, a large iron key on a weary loop of string from another. The handkerchief was for show, the key was for the lavatory up the yard at the back.

Billy's chores at Granny's, included breaking the coal in the cellar beneath her cottage, polishing her copper coal scuttle with Brasso, and keeping it filled with coal. As he watched at her window and waited for Stan to lose patience, the chink of china cups announced apple cake and tea. Stan finally gave up and left. Billy relaxed, safe for another day. Granny began her story of the two-fingered V-sign and English longbow-men after the battle of Agincourt.

*

Easter at last, Billy's spirits were soaring; no school for two weeks. On Maundy Thursday, his mother sent him to collect the family's bread order from Mr Bradshaw's bakery. As usual, she threatened him with worse than death if he nibbled the corners off the loaves, but this time she also said that he should ask the baker if he had anything for him.

'You'd better look in the window, m'lad,' the baker told him later.

Being Easter, the shop window displayed a tableau of hot cross buns arranged in pyramids, surrounded by mobs of raisin eyed, gingerbread rabbits. The centrepiece was a display of chocolate Easter eggs arranged in furrows of crumpled, blue sugar paper. Candy flowers decorated some; others had sugar footballs, cricket bats, pianos, and marzipan violins. Billy particularly admired one with a blue and white striped image of Sheffield Wednesday's star footballer, Redfern Froggatt. He was so taken by the sugary detail of his hero that he failed to notice his own name piped across it. The baker had to bang on the window and point it out. 'It's for thee – tha wassock!'

Billy realised that the chocolate bars his mother had mysteriously been depositing with Mr Bradshaw for weeks, had become a sumptuous confection, an Easter football fantasy.

Nibbling bread corners held no interest now. For once, the warm crusty loaves would reach the Perks' bread bin, intact. Billy skipped home, admiring his Easter egg, and nibbling the boots off Redfern Froggatt. He had never seen so much chocolate all at once, and had certainly never possessed so much. The sweet-ration was only four ounces a week, an amount soon eaten, and ration points were better spent on pear drops, or Mintos which outlasted chocolate by many hours.

As he passed the Star Woman's house, he saw that an official notice the police had pinned to her door had fallen off and was now blowing about the skittle yard. He chased after it. It was a brief instruction to anyone seeking the old woman on business to contact them, or the firm of solicitors, whose address appeared at the bottom of the notice.

He caught the note, trapping it beneath his foot, and bent to pick it up. Pain exploded in his head, and beat him down like a torrent of boulders. Blows fell on him, crashing into him like a relentless cataract, an avalanche of kicks and punches that continued unabated until he passed out.

The face he saw when he came to was his mother's, bending over him, gently coaxing him back from the blackness. 'Billy! Billy what happened, my love?' she cried, frowning with worry. 'You were so long, I was worried. I went looking for you. What happened? Where's the bread?'

Beyond his mother's face, he saw the sky and the towering blind gable of the house adjoining the skittle yard. Pain jabbed at every rib and limb. He was lying in the narrow space between the gable and Mrs Seaton's row of rabbit hutches, a creaking terrace of little shanties devised from old boxes and tarpaulin. Nettles stung his bare legs. The taste of blood was in his mouth.

Mrs Seaton had joined them. 'I never heard a thing, Marian,' she gushed apologetically, bending to peer at the boy. 'I've been in all morning. I even came out to feed my bunnies and I still never saw nowt. Then I heard that Mr Pearce shouting - you know, him from the chemists. He was out here yelling at somebody. I came out to see what all the fuss was about and I saw him go chasing off after a man. That's when I found your Billy, bless him - and then you came. I feel such a fool.'

'Never mind Madge, I think he's all right now,' said Marian Perks, gingerly touching her son's bruises.

The bread and his Easter egg were gone. So too was the one-n-tuppence change he had had. His mother was too busy fussing about his injuries to think about it right then, but Billy knew she would soon ask for it. She watched every penny and she would not be pleased at losing her bread and her money too, let alone the hard-earned chocolate egg for which she had saved several weeks' sweet ration.

What had happened, Billy wondered, staggering groggily as he was helped up. Everything hurt. Congealed blood from a wound in his hair glued one eyelid shut. His lips felt blubbery and sore.

Marian Perks fussed, dusting him down and pulling at his limbs, working each joint in search of other injuries. At last, she pronounced him a survivor. 'You seem all right. You've a cut on your scalp, but I think it looks worse than it is.' She hugged him gently, kissing his forehead. 'Thank goodness you're all right. I was searching for you for ages. A strange tramp came and told me where you were, but he was so weird, with horrible scars on his face, it put me off. I didn't know whether to believe him.'

Billy watched her groggily, and waited for her news to worsen, certain it would. 'What tramp?' he mumbled.

'Oh some scruffy man in an old air-force greatcoat,' she said, at last seeming satisfied that he was not too badly injured. 'You'll do I think. You look like the wreck of the Hesperus, but you'll survive. What on earth were you doing, Billy? Were you climbing?' She turned her face up to the house gable towering above them. 'What on earth were you climbing up there for?'

'No, Mam, I never,' protested Billy. 'I was trying to get this,' he explained, showing her the crumpled notice, which had somehow survived intact. 'It's blown off that door. I was gerrin it to put it back. It's official tha knows.'

'Don't thee and thou Billy,' she scolded mildly. And taking the notice from him gave him a quizzical stare. 'Well how did you get into this state then?'

'I was picking it up and somebody hit me. I never saw a thing.' He bent to demonstrate his recovery of the fluttering notice and found a builder's nail bar lying at his feet. Picking it up he inspected it carefully. 'Is this yours, Mrs Seaton?'

'No love, what is it?' she said, peering at the crow bar and running a podgy finger along its surface of freshly painted red lead.

'It's a jimmy. It's for pulling nails and levering things.'

'I've never seen it. There shouldn't be owt back here,' she said, with a regal wobble of her head. 'I'm always clearing rubbish out. It's kids what chuck stuff in. It's endless keeping it clear. Well, I mean to say, you don't want rats do you, Marian?'

Marian Perks nodded, frowning at the idea. 'Did they hit you with that? It could've killed you. Didn't you see anybody at all?'

'I never saw nowt,' he moaned, quickly correcting himself before his mother did, 'I mean - nothing.'

'All right, love. I believe you,' said his mam. 'Come on, I'll take you home. We'll get some Dettol on those cuts. You need to lie down.' She wrapped an arm around his shoulders and steered him towards their home at the end of the street. 'I'll tell the constable when I see him, Madge,' she called back. 'They'll probably come to take a look round. Somebody should pay. It's not right. You were safer in the blackout.'

Mrs Seaton nodded. 'Maybe that Mr Pearce will catch whoever it was.'

'Let's hope so,' agreed Mrs Perks. 'Now come on, Billy love, let's get you to bed. Oh, you had better give me my money back. I'll need to go and get the bread, and you never know - maybe there's a special treat for you.'

Billy burst into tears and clung to his mother, sobbing miserably.

………...

CHAPTER THREE

The next few days drifted blissfully by as Billy reclined on the settee wrapped in a crocheted blanket, which hitherto, the Perks' wire haired terrier, Ruff, had assumed was his bed blanket. Yvonne and Kick visited frequently to marvel at his injuries. His mother cooed and coddled him, doled out double helpings of National Health orange juice and an extra spoonful of malt each morning. Billy's biggest fear was that he would not be able to keep it all going past the Easter holiday and so get time off school, as well as being excused his usual chores.

With his friends around him, he played the invalid, as they pondered the mystery of the Star Woman's death. They drew diagrams and listed evidence and suspicions, mostly suspicions, until they had convinced themselves that she had definitely been, "done in".

Billy's life of ease ended abruptly, when his mother discovered him playing in the coal cellar, wearing a gas mask and his dad's old A.R.P. steel helmet. In a few hectic moments, the dog recovered his bed blanket, and Billy and his friends found themselves booted outside to play – it was raining.

*

As the Easter break wound down and the return to school drew ever closer, Billy saw less of Kick Morley. He'd been called to football practice. The Bole Hills, a cinder pitch high up on a windswept hill above Walkley was the venue for numerous football teams, juniors and adults. Kick spent much of his time up there. A few weeks before Easter, he'd been picked for his school's First Juniors, a challenge he'd risen to enthusiastically.

After notching up five goals in his first two games, he was enjoying celebrity and indispensability in equal measure. Billy tried to be pleased for him, though he was annoyed that Kick's frequent absences did not help their search for old Annabel's killer. Or perhaps, he wondered, was he just envious of his friend's success?

21

Since the police had sealed the house, Billy knew nobody had done a proper investigation. He imagined all sorts of clues lying around inside just waiting for somebody to recognise their significance. But, padlocked and sealed by the police, it was an offence even to go near the place without good reason. The coroner's office was silent, doing whatever coroners did, and the newspapers had not mentioned the Star Woman for more than two weeks. As far as he knew, nothing new had happened in the three weeks since the excitement on Orchard Road. When he tried explaining his frustrations to his father, he was grumpily fobbed off. 'Let the police get on with their jobs. You keep your nose out. You should be doing your schoolwork, not pestering everybody about murders and such.'

*

'Mam, how old is granny?'

'The same age as her tongue and a bit younger than her teeth.'

'Ooh you always say that. What's wrong with telling somebody how old you are? I just want to know if she's older than the Star Woman was.'

'Go out and play, you're getting under my feet. It's nearly stopped raining and I need to beat the peg-rugs before it does. I don't want dust flying all over.' She shooed him outdoors into a gloomy drizzle.

The street was quiet. As if by magic, Yvonne arrived and joined him to swing on the front gate. Apart from a few soggy house sparrows sulking and squabbling, the only movement they saw was Mr Leaper's horse and cart. It approached slowly down the steep hill, its iron tyres grinding chalky lines into the road surface behind the steady plod of a big grey mare. Yvonne gave the carter a half-hearted wave.

'Where's old Leaper going with his cart?' Billy whispered, puzzled by the absence of its usual gay pyramid of fruit and vegetables.

'We could follow him and find out,' she suggested. 'He'll let us gerron for a ride if we want.'

Mr Leaper was a large, amiable man with a beaming red face and a constant line in chat. No matter where or when he was

22

seen, he seemed to be delivering a punch line, or enjoying one. He was a greengrocer whose shop was normally on the back of his cart. He trundled it around the steep streets, stopping every so often. He would put a nosebag on his horse and level his weighing scales with a battered brass spirit level, ready to weigh out fruit and vegetables to his customers. They would gather on the kerb, emerging from their dwellings at his approach, as if in receipt of some telepathic invitation. Today the colourful terraces of fruit and vegetables, the lush swags of cloth vine leaves and flowers strung over artificial grass were gone, stripped away to reveal the bare boards of the wooden float.

As the cart drew near Yvonne stepped up to the horse's big grey head. 'Hello Mr Leaper. How's Beattie today?'

'She's champion, love. And why not? She eats better than me and thee put together. I doubt if'n king's hoss is any better fed.' Mr Leaper pushed back his shoulders nodding and bobbing his head as if acknowledging applause from around the street. His russet face bore testament to a life spent in the open air. An ancient cap, its peak worn shiny where he handled it, covered his head. A faded brown warehouse coat stretched across his broad front beneath a weary leather belt, whose buckle bore the badge of the Royal Artillery.

'Where's yer fruit?' asked Yvonne.

'Well, I'm on official business, tha sees,' confided Mr Leaper, puffing out his chest. 'I've had to clear everything off'n me cart so I can load the old Star Woman's stuff on it. I've been retained.'

'Retained?' queried Yvonne.

'Aye, retained. It's a posh word for saying, "G'en t'job".'

'What job have they g'en thee?' Billy asked.

'Hi ham retained,' he said, adopting his telephone voice, 'to take her stuff to the h-Ebenezer Chapel's bottom 'all. They're gonna sell it to pay for her funeral and everything.'

'Isn't she buried yet?' Yvonne cried, distressed to think that a three week old corpse was waiting for a furniture sale before it could be laid to rest.

'Oh aye, she's been buried a while. No, this's for the solicitors and bigwigs to gerrit it all sorted out. They've lots o' dotting and crossing to do before it's done proper. And tha knows what landlords are like? He'll want to rent her house to somebody else. He's already lost three weeks rent. He'll be sweating soggy pie crusts.'

'But the police have locked it up with a padlock,' Billy said. 'Nobody's been able to gerrin since she died.'

'Well I know that, but I just told thee, I'm retained. It's official. I've gorra key.'

Billy's heart leapt. This could be his chance to get inside the house to do some real detective work.

'I've had to fetch t'keys from the police. I had to show 'em the letter from the solicitor and everything. It says I can remove property for sale or other disposal. That means I can even burn owt that I think is just rubbish and can't go in the sale.'

Billy's gaze bored into Mr Leaper, willing him to ask him for his help. 'But it's a big job for thee – all by thee sen, I'n't it?' he suggested, adopting a strained expression to emphasise the wearying enormity of the task. 'You'll never lift everything by thee sen.'

Mr Leaper looked alarmed. 'Well aye it is. Mind you, I'm used to lifting tha knows. Spuds come in hundredweight seks and I carry 'em all way up me yard to me barn.'

'Well I don't know. I couldn't possibly help you for less than threpenz.' Billy said, frowning as though he'd been strenuously propositioned.

'Threpenz! Threpenz a-piece, does tha mean?' cried Mr Leaper.

'Well go on then, twist my arm, tuppenz,' Billy said.

Mr Leaper's face brightened uncertainly. He knew he had achieved a commercial victory of some sort, but was unable to decide quite how.

It was Billy's dream come true; not only to be invited into the old house by an adult with a perfect right to be there, but also he would earn two pennies for his trouble. 'Yeah, we'll help thee, wont we Yvonne?'

Yvonne, looking pale, smiled weakly. The prospect of poking about in a dead woman's house and belongings was not quite so appealing to her. She felt events were taking her over. Nevertheless, she reluctantly agreed.

24

Five minutes later Mr Leaper halted Beattie at the end of the skittle yard, a few feet short of the Star Woman's padlocked cottage. He put the nosebag on the old mare and rubbed her neck affectionately. Beattie dropped her head and flicked her ears.

'It's stopped raining, thank God,' Mr Leaper observed, squinting at the sun poking from the silver edge of a grey cloud. 'That'll save us having to sheet it all when we gerrit loaded.' He began patting his pockets, and looking about as though he could not remember why he was where he was. At last, finding a key with a brown paper label tied to it with string, he pulled it from his pocket and tossed it to Billy. 'Here, thee get the door undone. I've just to get some cigs and I'll be back in a tick.'

Billy caught the key, delighted. Knowing Mr Leaper's fondness for gossip, he guessed it could be quite some time before he returned from the shop to do any work. He and Yvonne would have the cottage to themselves.

The key turned easily in the padlock, but when he tried to open the door, it wouldn't budge. 'You need the nail,' Yvonne reminded him reproachfully. She took it from the windowsill and handed it to him with a wry grin. 'You, of all people, should know that.'

He looked at it solemnly. It was the sneck nail that had started him on his trail. Inserting it into the sneck-hole, he pressed it down with his thumb to lift the latch. The door swung open slowly, as if trying not to disturb the air inside. 'Don't touch nowt, no matter what,' he instructed Yvonne firmly.

Inside felt cool and musty. The sounds of the trams banging along on South Road seemed distant and muted. A shaft of sunlight leaned in from a slit of window to spear the coconut fibre matting on the stone floor. Flashing sparkles of dust spiralled slowly in its beam.

'Don't touch nowt.'

'Yeah-yeah, you said already. I'm not soft.' Yvonne's patience was worn down by foreboding. She was in no mood for Billy's bossiness. 'What are we going to do first?' she demanded, determined to bring him to heel.

Billy looked doubtful. 'Have a good look round,' he said.

'That's no good,' she snapped. 'You need a plan, and you need to record everything. I suppose you've brought a pencil and a notebook?' She knew very well that he had not.

Billy gaped penitently.

'No, you didn't,' she said triumphantly. 'Luckily there's some paper on the floor over there, and I've gorra pencil in my pocket.'

Trying to look disinterested, Billy glanced at the few sheets of lined paper she had pointed out on the floor in front of the large sideboard. They were like pages torn from a school exercise book.

'When you stop nagging me not to touch owt,' Yvonne went on, 'I can gerrit and start writing notes. Then we'll be doing a proper investigation.'

Slightly chastened, but grateful for the suggestion, he pretended not to hear her. 'It might be a clue,' he said, adding for emphasis. 'Everything could be a clue - for example, where did the paper come from? Why is it on the floor?'

'Trees and gravity,' Yvonne quipped, unwilling to relinquish the upper hand. Bending she moved to pick up the paper. A small flash of reflected sunlight caught her eye. It had sparked out from under the sideboard. She moved her head slowly, hoping to see a repeat of the reflected flash and pinpoint its source. There it was again, a brief spark of brilliance. Fixing its position, she bent close and saw it was a fragment of silver coloured metal. Using one of the sheets of the writing paper, she carefully scooped it up and brought it to the table. 'Look at this, Billy. What do you think it is?'

Billy had found a spent match in the hearth and was staring at it as if it contained the answer to the meaning of life itself. 'I've found a dead match.'

'Was that murdered too?' she growled, annoyed that he was ignoring her discovery.

At last, Billy turned from his matchstick and peered dismissively at the silver sliver lying on the sheet of exercise book paper. His expression changed to one of eager curiosity. Though smaller than a grain of rice, he could clearly see that it had blood on it. 'Chuffin eck,' he breathed.

'There's a hair and some blood on it,' Yvonne said. 'I didn't touch it. I got it up with this paper. If it's her blood they'll be able to tell, as long as we don't touch it.'

Studying the fragment, he pulled the paper carefully towards him. 'We need sommat to put it in.'

'Like an envelope or a jar or sommat?' Yvonne suggested, beginning to search in a cupboard under a stone sink. She found a battered cardboard box containing an assortment of medicine bottles, ointment jars and bandages. She began lifting them out, searching for a suitable container. 'Do you think we can throw these out?' she asked Billy, showing him a little glass jar containing a few mouldy looking pills.

Billy took it from her fingers and stared at the contents. 'Gimbals! They look like mouse droppings.'

'It's some sort of medicine. It's gorra label.'

Billy peered at the dusty label. It looked very old. The words, Three times a day, were just visible in faded ink. There was nothing else written or printed there, no dates or names. 'It looks ancient. I don't think it'll matter if we chuck 'em out.' He handed the little jar back to her. 'But clean it out with sommat dry, we don't want any water left in it. It might spoil the clue.'

'Contaminate it,' Yvonne corrected grandly, earning herself a sneering glance. She shook the contents out into the sink and then blew in to the jar to clean it out.

Billy leaned over the table inspecting the bit of silver metal. 'Can you see what it is?' Yvonne asked, bringing her nose close to the object. 'It's like sommat broke off'n sommat, but what?'

Using the notepaper, Billy scooped up the clue and slid it, with its hair and blood, into the pill jar and refitted the cork stopper. He slipped it into his pocket. 'Bunny Parfitt's gorra microscope. He gorrit for Christmas. We could ask him for a lend of it.'

Yvonne hugged herself excitedly. 'It's a good clue isn't it?'

Billy knew it was. 'Yeah, not bad, but we'll need to find some of her hair so that we can match it. I've seen 'em do it at the flicks. They get a hair from a comb or sommat and look at it down a microscope to match it with another one they got from sommat else.'

Yvonne beamed with satisfaction and arranged the remaining sheets of paper into a neat pad. 'What shall I write?'

'First things first,' he said, scratching invisible stubble on his chin. 'How did she die? That's the first thing.'

'They said she fell down stairs in the night and banged her head on the fireplace. They said there was blood on the fork steady.'

'The fork what?'

'That thing,' Yvonne said, pointing at the hearth. The thing the toasting fork is resting on. They said it made a distinctive mark on her head, like a square shape.'

'Oooh distinctive,' hooted Billy. 'What's distinctive? How d'you know all this? This weren't in the papers.'

'I know, but I heard that young doctor telling our Marlene. He likes her you know. I think he wants to take her out.'

'Huh, he shouldn't have much trouble there then. Your sister will go with any bloke, so long as he can breathe.'

'And just what might that mean?'

Billy turned away feeling it was probably safest not to respond. 'The toasting fork thing,' he mumbled. 'I can't see what's so "distinctive" about it.' Bending close to the hearth, he examined the wrought iron fork steady. It was a plain, functional object, with a clumsy homemade look. It had four little feet, which supported a cross bar with upturned ends to prevent the fork handle slipping off sideways. The toasting fork was a twin pronged twist of black iron, its handle end worn shiny from regular usage. 'That's impossible,' he said emphatically. 'Look at where it is. This kettle trivet is in the way.'

Yvonne peered over his shoulder. Immediately above the toasting fork steady, a round trivet, about the size of a tea plate, was hinged to the stove. It sat like an umbrella over the toasting fork. 'Well they found blood on it so it must be possible,' she argued, though she could not see how.

Billy got down on all fours and tried to put his head on the fork steady. 'Rubbish! Look at it. How can you fall and hit your head on that? It's too far under this kettle thing. I can't even get my head in there if I go on my knees and butt it like a tup.'

'Has somebody moved it?'

'There are no marks in the ash to show it's been moved.'

'But the blood?' Yvonne persisted. 'That's how they knew what killed her. They saw there was blood on it, her blood. They did a blood test and everything.'

'Doctor Hadfield told you this, did he?' he asked, frowning as she nodded. 'Well then, somebody's a liar. Any fool can see she couldn't have fallen on to that thing. It's impossible. And it's not been moved neither. You can see the ash and dust around it has not been disturbed. That shows you it's still in its proper place.'

The friends stared blankly at each other, each trying to justify what they were seeing. Confronting them was evidence that clearly contradicted the official report. Had Doctor Greenhow and the police made a mistake? It looked as if they had. Had they jumped to the wrong conclusion and simply assumed that she had fallen and knocked her head, because she was old and frail? After all, old women had falls all the time.

But, Annabel Loveday was not frail and weak. She might have looked old, but she was even younger than Granny Smeggs, he reminded himself. And his granny was as fit as a flea. The police were wrong to say this was simply another frail old lady taking a fall in the night.

'I don't understand,' Billy said. 'They said there was blood on the toasting fork stand? How did it get there? Where is it now?'

Yvonne chewed her cheek thoughtfully. 'If it was put there deliberately, that means somebody killed her, doesn't it?'

'Yes, and they put her blood on that fork steady to make it look like she fell over. Then, when they came in to inspect it officially – the doctor and the constable, they see the blood and hey presto, they jump to the wrong idea, probably because she always looked so old.'

'We hope,' said Yvonne, cryptically.

'What do you mean?'

'Well if they didn't make a mistake, it means they did it deliberately. That means it's a cover up.'

'Blimey! Who, the police and the doctor?' hooted Billy. 'Nah, why would they lie?'

'I don't know,' Yvonne said, spreading her arms in exasperation. 'But you must admit it's crazy that they could completely misunderstand what they saw. I mean we spotted it straight away. They're supposed to be the experts, not us. It's their job. They're grown ups. We're just kids.'

'Huh, when did being a grown up ever mean owt?'

'Anyway, no matter what else we think,' said Yvonne. 'We can be certain that somebody deliberately put the old lady's blood on that fork steady, or they lied about it. That means somebody wants everybody to think she just toppled over - an accident. But we know different now. We know she was murdered.'

'Write it down.'

'And another thing,' Yvonne said, pointing a trembling finger, 'it's got coal ash on it.'

'So what?'

'Well, I was wondering if she could have been hit with it. You know like, did somebody pick it up and bash her with it?' She paused, staring at Billy, inviting him to see her point. He gaped back at her dumbly. Exasperated she went on. 'Well, if it had been picked up to bash her with, there wouldn't be any ash on it, would there? It would have got knocked off. And you'd be able to tell it had been moved.'

'Write it down,' Billy said, excited by their rapid progress. Yvonne was proving to be an unexpectedly good *assistant* detective, he thought. They made a good team.

'When I found her, I came in through the back door.' He pointed it out to her as if it was some great mystery. 'I guess they've padlocked it on the outside now ...'

'Try it.'

'No point; anyway I'd have to go round and climb over the wall, and we've only got one key. It's not very likely it fits both padlocks, is it?'

'I mean just try it. Pull it from the inside,' she insisted. When he made no move, she marched to the door and tried it herself. It swung open revealing a padlock still locked through a broken hasp and staple. It had been prised from the doorjamb. 'You see?' she cried.

'OK you were right, but now you've put your fingerprints all over it the clue is rubbish. You might as well not have bothered.'

30

Yvonne narrowed her eyes and gently shouldered the door closed. 'It's not rubbish,' she growled through clenched teeth. 'It tells us a lot, and you know it does.'

Billy spotted an iron bar in the stone sink beside the door. With a sheet of the writing paper to protect it from his fingerprints, he carefully picked it up. 'I bet this is what they used to force the lock off. It looks like a car jack handle.'

'You wunt have seen it if I hadn't opened the door.'

Billy groaned. 'Oh chuffin eck! I hope you're not gerrin all mardy about it. Why can't you just gerron with the job and stop moaning? If we're detectives we've got to be more grown up about stuff. It's no good thee gerrin all mardy.'

Yvonne glared at him. 'Mardy? I'm not mardy, but who'd blame me if I were? You never give me credit for nowt.'

'OK, tha were reight,' he conceded grudgingly. 'I were wrong. Now write it down, and take thee mardy face off.'

A smile slid slyly across Yvonne's lips as she began writing.

'She was laid down with her head near the fireplace, and her feet near the back door,' Billy said. He moved to the spot and lay down, demonstrating the position the body had been in when he had found it. 'She had her hair down, so that shows she'd gone up to bed. There was a candle on the table. That's started me thinking.'

'What?' she asked.

He raised his face to her, a puzzled expression furrowing his brow. 'What?'

'You just said the candle on the table started you thinking.'

'Yes because if she'd fallen down them stairs, the candle should have been on the floor, not the table. She'd have dropped it, wouldn't she?'

Yvonne frowned. 'The police could have picked it up.'

'No, I'm talking about before, when I found her - before we rang 'em. Nobody had been in the house by then, except me - and the murderer. 'We'd better look for fresh wax on the floor, or on the stairs. If she fell and dropped it, candle wax would have splashed on to sommat. And that'd prove somebody had picked it up afterwards.'

'Why use a candle? Why didn't she just turn a light on?' Yvonne asked.

'She's only got gas. She never used lectric. Some old folk don't like lectric. My granny uses it but she's always going on about how gas was better.'

After a thorough search, they agreed there were no tell tale splashes of candle wax on the stairs, or the coconut fibre matting. The old lady, they concluded, could not have fallen and dropped a lighted candle.

Billy was now racing around, bobbing up and down to view the room from every angle. Yvonne was silent and still. She was looking at the floor where the old woman's body had lain. 'What's up?' Billy asked, noticing her troubled demeanour.

'She never dropped that candle,' Yvonne replied sadly. 'She never fell down the stairs. She never banged her head on that fork steady.' Her eyes were bright with tears, as she looked into Billy's. 'Somebody killed her, Billy. Somebody killed the poor old lady. Brutally bashed her head in, and left her alone and cold on the stone floor.'

'Well of course they did. I thought you knew that already. What do you think I've been saying for the last three weeks?'

'Yes I know, but somehow it didn't seem real. It felt like a game, but not any more. Now it really is real. This is where it happened. This is where somebody beat a harmless old lady over the head and killed her.' She wiped her eyes and blew her nose.

'But they made mistakes,' Billy told her softly. 'And that's where me and thee come in. We'll find their mistakes and we'll make sure they don't get away with it. That's what'll hang 'em.'

'But we'll have to be careful, Billy,' she cautioned. 'Whoever did it is going to know we're after them. They'll want to stop us. They could even try to kill us.'

'Gimbals!' Billy gasped as the stark reality hit him. 'I never thought of that. Yeah, somebody's going to be watching us every minute; him who forced that door with this jack handle. Maybe it's the same one who bushwhacked me near the rabbit hutches?'

'Stan?'

'Maybe - or his mad owd father.'

'What do we do?' Her voice was tight with fear.

Billy looked forlornly around the room, considering the question. His gaze finally settled on a faded brown photograph hanging on the wall. He had seen it before, but now took time to study it. It portrayed a young woman, stiffly seated before a corporal of infantry, standing with his hand resting proprietarily on her shoulder. He assumed it showed the old Star Woman and her husband, taken sometime before he went off to the front in nineteen-fifteen, never to return. The pair looked sad and already detached. Even faced by her photograph, he found it hard to think of her as such an attractive young woman, and in love. A wave of sadness washed over him, stiffening his resolve to get justice for her. 'We'll get 'em, Wy,' he croaked. 'We've gotta find 'em and hound 'em down until they pay. Write it all down, Wy: all about the candle and the wax and everything.'

Yvonne scribbled feverishly, the pink tip of her tongue visible at the corner of her mouth. 'That clock's another clue,' Billy told her, pointing to a cheap, moulded tin clock, painted to look like a priceless Louis XV ormolu. It was on the table now, but Billy remembered the table had been clear, except for the candle. He could not swear that the clock had been on its sideboard shelf, where it belonged, but he had no doubt whatsoever, that it had not been on the table.

The old lady's sideboard was a magnificent oddity amongst the simple, everyday objects in her low, dark room. Two flame mahogany serpentine doors, each with a drawer above it, seemed to glow with an inner radiance. A curving triangular backboard, edged with carved vine leaves, supported tiers of small cupboards and whatnot shelves. It rose to a peak just below the ceiling. Billy dragged a dining chair up to it and stood on it for a better view of the higher shelves. On the narrow shelf in front of the topmost cupboard door, a faint mark in the dust showed where the tin clock had stood. Billy supposed that someone had moved it, so as to open the cupboard door, but had not put it back. But why? What was in the cupboard? He recalled the old lady's arms stretched out towards the sideboard. Had she been trying to get to it? He opened the little cupboard.

Yvonne scrambled up to join him on the chair and peered. into the cupboard. It contained three school exercise books and some pencils and pens, quivered in a Bovril jar. There was also an inkbottle, and some used leaves of blotting paper.

'Chuffin eck! Look at this,' Billy gasped. He brought out the exercise books, jumped down from the chair, and carefully arranged them on the table. Numbered one, two and three, each bore the title, My Life, Annabel Lillian Loveday.

Yvonne picked up number three. Two pages fell out. 'Somebody's torn some pages out,' she said, and immediately began comparing the loose pages with the blanks she had found on the floor. The tear patterns matched. 'They're all from this book. Somebody must have torn out some written on pages and left these blanks.' She began counting the torn pages. 'There's five missing.'

Billy returned to the fireplace and began examining the ashes in the grate. 'Maybe they burned 'em. We might be able to see what they said with a mirror,' he said excitedly.

Yvonne laughed. 'That's for blotting paper, you dope.'

Blushing, Billy hid his hot cheeks. 'There's paper ash here,' he said, 'but it's completely burned through. You can't tell what it says on it.'

'Let me see.' Yvonne moved in and peered closely at the little pad of cinder wafers resting on top of the coal ash.

'It's no use,' Billy said. 'That doesn't tell us anything.'

'It does. Look at the ashes.'

Billy stared disbelieving. 'I am doing, and you can't read owt on 'em.'

'No I mean the coal ash underneath the burned paper. It's all dropped down and flat, like it was completely burned out. That shows it was a cold grate. Somebody burned them pages after the fire had gone out. They had to set light to 'em.'

'I found a dead match,' cried Billy, delighted to have at last found cause to enter his find onto the growing list of evidence.

'It tells us even more.'

'What more?'

'It tells us when,' said Yvonne confidently. 'It must have been very late, probably the small hours of the next morning, because the fire was out and the grate was cold when they burned the pages.' She eyed Billy critically, annoyed that he did not seem able to grasp the significance of her deduction. 'It could mean that whoever did it was spotted on the street by somebody going to work early - like my dad and yours do.'

Billy was impressed, and secretly had to admit that he had not taken his own advice to regard everything as a clue.

'The thing is what did it say on those pages?' Yvonne asked rhetorically. 'Was whatever it said the reason she was killed?'

'Sometimes they get impressions in paper from when somebody has pressed on hard when they were writing,' Billy said, keen to demonstrate some grasp on forensic examination. Yvonne was not convinced, but held the blank pages up to the light to see if any such indentations were apparent. None were.

Billy examined the blotting paper he'd found in the cupboard. The ghosts of words danced before his eyes, tantalizingly illegible. 'Somehow we need to find out what was on those pages. I think you're right, Wy. The murderer must have torn 'em out because they betrayed him, or sommat.'

'What do we do now?'

Billy was about to suggest a thorough search of the sideboard and the bedroom upstairs when Mr Leaper burst into the house. 'Sorry kids. I got waylaid in the shop,' he gasped, shaking his head. 'I accidentally let it slip that I was, *retained*, and I couldn't get away. I was hoping to keep it quiet until we was all done, but you know what some folk are like. They have to go ferreting for gossip.' He stomped around the room clicking his tongue, picking things up and putting them down again. 'I think we should get all the small stuff on first, Billy. There's some orange boxes on the cart - bring 'em in, there's a good lad.'

Billy slipped the exercise books under his jumper and went to get the orange boxes, secretly fuming that Mr Leaper had chosen that moment to return. Why hadn't he stayed in the shop a few more minutes? Even five minutes would have been enough to search the sideboard's cupboards and drawers. It was a major blow.

With orange boxes teetering above head height, Billy carried them in from the cart. He had decided to persuade Mr Leaper to give him the job of emptying the sideboard. That way he could search it. He would get Yvonne to distract him. That shouldn't be too difficult. All she needed to do was mention his horse and he would talk for an hour and give her a conducted tour of Beattie's harness and brasses.

Despite Billy's best efforts, **Mr Leaper** insisted on doing the job himself. He made them responsible for collecting all the pots, pans, cutlery and cleaning things. Angry and disappointed, Billy resolved that somehow he had to see what had been in the sideboard's drawers. Also, and crucially, there was supposed to be a secret drawer. Its existence had become common knowledge since the old lady's death, together with rumours of gold sovereigns and even Tsarist Russian jewellery.

When they had finished and Beattie strained to get the cart rolling, Billy watched anxiously. Soon the sideboard would be locked in store beneath the Ebenezer Chapel, awaiting the auctioneer's hammer. It would be too late. Already some of her effects were smouldering on a fire in the farthest corner of the skittle yard, rejected as mere rubbish by the *retained* Mr Leaper. Thank gimbals, Billy told himself, he had managed to hide the exercise books, the jack handle and other bits of evidence.

As he watched the cart trundle away, he vowed that somehow he would have to find and search that secret drawer before the auctioneer sold the sideboard and it was lost to him forever.

. . . .

CHAPTER FOUR

On the Monday after the school holiday, with his cuts and bruises faded to hardly more than faint smudges, Billy had little to show for his beating behind the rabbit hutches. A bright purple bruise, or suppurating scab, might have impressed his schoolmates, but pale discolorations that have to be pointed out, even in bright sunlight, would earn no kudos. Disappointed, he hid them away and kept quiet.

Study was impossible. He tried to concentrate, but the Star Woman's death preoccupied him. Throughout the day, his various teachers took pot shots at him with bits of chalk, textbooks, and blackboard rubbers, in an effort to improve his concentration. In history, Sister Clare, who prowled between the neat rows of battered desks like a snarling black panther, whacked him on the head with a wooden ruler whenever she came close. Finally, she dragged him out for four stripes on the hand with the cane, for what she called, "Wasting God's glorious gifts by dilly-dally-daydreaming."

At home after school, with his fingers still throbbing from the cane, Billy took Annabel's exercise books to the bottom of the garden and hid himself in the family's chicken shed to read them. The pages had a cluttered, confusing appearance that took him a while to accept. The old lady's handwriting however, was neat and precise: each word penned with obvious care. But between the lines and in the margins, comments, altered words and extra lines had been pencilled in by a different hand - one more rushed and untidy. Presumably, she had asked someone to read it and suggest the changes. Whoever it was had even marked whole sentences for removal.

Annabel's story sobbed from the pages, unfolding in bursts of disjointed reminiscence. Hers was a shocking world of disappointment and loneliness. Billy read, feeling ashamed and somehow guilty for the old woman's pain. If only he'd known she was so unhappy, perhaps he would have viewed her

37

differently. He might have tried to get to know her better, befriend her, offer her some cheer.

But then, with rising anger, he demanded of the startled chickens around him, 'What good would it have done? She was an old grouch. Some people can't even be happy at Scarborough on a Bank Holiday Monday.'

*

Kick Morley called for Billy at his back door early that evening, a sodden leather football under his arm - then on his left foot - then on his head – then back under his arm again. He wanted to go up to the Bole Hills for a kick-about on the cinders, before it got too dark. Unfortunately, football was the last thing on Billy's mind. Annabel's story had raised many questions, which he felt only a visit to Granny Smeggs would answer. Football would have to wait.

Disappointment scarred Kick's face. 'Thart mardy these days,' he complained. 'Tha never wants to do nowt. All tha thinks about is t'bloody Star Woman. Thart no fun no more.'

Though Billy tried to explain, it was useless; his apologies were swatted aside. Kick was angry and smarting with rejection. He stomped off, grumbling.

Heavy with guilt, Billy watched him head up towards the windy open spaces at the top of the street. 'I'll call for thee tomorrow,' he shouted, attempting consolation.

'Don't shape thee sen,' was Kick's sullen reply.

A few minutes later Billy arrived outside his grandmother's cottage, and pushed against the garden gate, battling its powerful spring. Granny Smeggs reacted to the gate's familiar creak and popped up to her window to see who was visiting her. A smile lit her eyes when she saw her grandson. She was always happy to welcome Billy. He brought lightness and jokes, and even a little mischief into her life, but on this occasion she could see that his leaden gait, and frowning face, signalled trouble.

'What's up, lost a bob and found a tanner?' she asked, as he came in to her tiny house.

'All her furniture's gone. I'll never find out if there worra secret drawer,' he moaned, flopping into the armchair opposite her rocker.

'Why do you want to know?'

'Well I just do. I think it's great having secret drawers in things. You could hide owt in it: diamonds, gold,' he enthused.

'Oh quite right. I keep all my diamonds in mine,' she joked.

Billy scowled and sagged deeper into the armchair, drawing his head into his tank top like a concerned tortoise. If there was a secret drawer in the old lady's sideboard, Granny Smeggs did not seem willing to discuss it sensibly.

'Look, you can forget all that nonsense about gold sovereigns and secret drawers,' she told him. 'The poor soul didn't have two farthings to rub together, let alone sovereigns.' She smiled, sensing his frustration. 'She did have a secret drawer though. It had her rent book in it.'

Billy's head tortoised out from its woolly shell. 'Where is it? Did you see it?'

Granny laughed. 'What sort of secret would it be if everyone knew about it?'

'Well how do you know she hid the rent book in it?'

'Mash us a cuppa and I might tell you. And there's a date and walnut cake in the meat-safe on the cellar head.'

Tea and cake - nobody made cake like Granny Smeggs: fruitcake, coconut cake, apple and bilberry sponge, date and walnut, and seed cake. There was never a day when there was not a cake of some sort in her meat-safe.

Granny's little cottage was at the end of a row of three identical sandstone dwellings. Each had a small ground floor room with a coal cellar beneath, and a bedroom above. For heat and cooking, there was a black-leaded iron range. Cold water flowed from a brass tap over a stone sink in a corner.

'Some of the old sideboards have a false back in a drawer,' Granny said, as she watched Billy balance her kettle on the fire bars. 'Usually you push it in and the drawer pops out. I know she had one, but I don't remember it well. I only saw it once when I paid the rent for her Tommy because of his impetigo.'

Impetigo - rent for Tommy - she's flipped! he thought. What's she talking about?

'I only glimpsed where she kept it – accidentally like,' she went on. 'It was just fleeting. She didn't want me to see it.' She glanced at him huffily, reflecting his disbelieving frown. He forced a smile, and tried to appear uncritical.

'You see, normally she left the rent with her Tommy to give to the rent man when she was out working. But when Tommy went to the skin nurse for his impetigo, she left it with me and I paid it. Well she'd forgotten that it was rent day, and I knew it was her Tommy's skin clinic day, so I went round to remind her. As soon as she saw me coming in through her door she rushed for the rent book. She was just on her way out to work. That's how I saw her secret drawer.'

'Where abouts?'

'Oh crickey, I can't think.'

Billy watched his grandmother, her face a mask of concentration. 'I think it was in her Tommy's old folder.'

'Not the rent book, the drawer, where was the secret drawer?'

'Oh, in the top drawer.'

'There's two – which one?' Billy demanded, excitement smothering courtesy.

'Left. Yes, definitely the left one,' she said, appearing not to have noticed his rudeness. 'The one nearest as you went in.'

Billy released a sigh. Her story was beginning to make sense. Tommy, he had already guessed, was Annabel's son. Granny was not losing her marbles after all.

'And don't think you can bark at me that way, young man,' she scolded, delivering him a sudden clip on his ear.

'Sorry, Gran,' he mumbled, ducking unnecessarily as she followed up with a proffered slice of date and walnut cake.

'You said she kept the rent book in Tommy's folder. What was that?' asked Billy, speaking into his steaming teacup.

'Oh just something he made at school, but she loved it. She thought it was marvellous. It was just folded card and gummed tape, but he'd painted a design on it: a lovely bird and a lion. It was very nice. She kept her gas bill and all her most important papers in it.' Granny gazed reflectively into her teacup. 'He was ever so good at drawing and painting was her Tommy. He could have been a real artist, you know: shop fronts, and signs on things.'

Billy bit his cheek thoughtfully. 'What's a DFM?' he asked.

40

'What d'you mean - the medal? It's a medal. The Distinguished Flying Medal,' she told him, 'It's for them in the RAF.'

'How do you get it?'

'You mun do sommat very brave. They don't give 'em out like liquorice allsorts you know. It's only for the bravest.'

'I think somebody got one cos they lied about sommat,' he told her. 'I can't be sure because it's not all there, but that's what I think.' He handed her book two of Annabel's memoirs.

Mrs Smeggs read the title on the little book's cover, taking it from his hands as carefully as if it had been sculptured snow. She placed it on her lap and gently patted along the edges of its pages with her palms. 'How did you get this? You must give it back, Billy love,' she breathed reverently.

'I didn't steal it. I saved it, Gran. It would've been burned else. Old Leaper would have chucked 'em on that fire he had.'

'Oh but, Billy love, are you sure?'

'Of course I am, Gran, and when we get the murderer, I'll give 'em back. But you've gorra read it first – please, Gran.'

'Where's the other? This says book two, have you got another one?'

'There's three,' he said, pulling the others from under his jumper. 'They're ever so sad. If you don't want to read 'em all - I've marked the main bits with tram tickets.'

'Oh, I know it'll be sad. I know this poor woman's story already,' Mrs Smeggs said. 'I knew her Noah too. We were at the same school. He was a bit older, but I remember him. He went off to the front in 1915. The same year they got married. He was killed on the Somme - him and thousands of other lovely young chaps.'

'It says about her son. That was him – Tommy, wasn't it?'

'He was a smashing boy - a flyer - sergeant in the RAF. Tommy Loveday.'

Billy visualised a scrawny boy with purple ointment blobbed all over his face and shaven head, rather than the smart RAF sergeant his grandmother was seeing in her mind's eye. He prodded impatiently at the exercise book on her lap. 'Did he have a DFM?'

'No, but if he did, it certainly would not be through lying about it.'

'Read what she says.'

The old lady started to read, then stopped to clean her glasses. 'I'll read it later when you've gone. Anyway, I can tell you for sure, even before I read a single word of it, Tommy Loveday would not have lied. He wasn't the sort,' she said emphatically. 'He was a grand lad.' She started reading again, and Billy watched her closely, waiting for her expression to betray her impressions. It did not. She turned the page and stopped. 'I'll read it later - when you've gone.'

*

That evening, with the measured tick of her clock, and the hiss of the coals on her fire for company, old Mrs Smeggs reluctantly opened exercise book one and began to read. She had known Annabel Loveday for most of her life. Her solitary existence in her cottage nearby had been as obvious to her as to anyone else who had bothered to notice. But unlike most, Mrs Smeggs knew that her loneliness was no recent circumstance. Annabel had always been alone. Even as a child, she had somehow occupied the edge of living. The little girl, barely noticed, watching the dance, but never tapping her toe except in the hidden inward mimicry of others.

Mrs Smeggs read, tears glazing her eyes. She found a few mayfly moments, jewelled with promise. They glittered briefly on the page: love, courtship, marriage and childbirth. In these rare interludes she sensed lightness and certainty in Annabel's words, until, at the turn of the page, the sinuous drag of loss and disappointment took over again.

.....DFM awarded for a lie, can't make a man what he is not, nor ever could be.

Mrs Smeggs read the line again. Whatever had been written before these words had been torn out, and no doubt destroyed by now. She felt weighed down by the awful questions this raised. Who had lied? Who was awarded the Distinguished Flying Medal because of their lying? And who had been passed over because of it? Could this be at the root of Annabel's mysterious death? Was Billy right after all? Had Annabel been about to release a time bomb - some dark secret that would bring somebody's life crashing down – a life built on lies.

Who else knew about her journals? Who could be so desperate to keep her quiet that they beat her over the head and killed her?

. . . .

CHAPTER FIVE

The sun had barely risen when Billy arrived at his grandmother's cottage the next day. He had escaped his mother's watchful eye on the pretext of taking Ruff for a walk. The wirehaired terrier didn't care why he was out so early. For him it was a thrill. Nothing beat hanging out with Billy, except of course anything remotely edible.

'Can I have some toast?' Billy demanded, barging in to his granny's cottage without greeting or courtesy.

'And a very good morning to you too, I'm sure,' Granny Smeggs replied crossly. 'Where're your manners? Why aren't you at school? Get that dog off my chair.'

'Sorry,' he mumbled. 'I've got hours yet. 'Can I – *please*?'

Mrs Smeggs was drawing up the fire with a sheet of newspaper and a coal shovel. 'I'm hardly up yet. What on earth are you doing here at this time? And you can gerrof that loaf, there's no toast. You can see the fire's not drawn. It'd taste like a sweep's cap. Go and fill the scuttle and we'll have a cuppa while it draws.'

Billy descended into the tunnel-like coal cellar beneath Granny's living room. The cellar steps smelled of cheese, apple pie, and coal. 'Have you read it?' he yelled up to the glimmer of daylight at the top of the steps.

'Come on, hurry up. I'm nithered with that door open. The draft from that cellar would blow the bill off a penguin.'

Billy quickly returned with the shiny coal scuttle. 'Miserable isn't it? I bet you blubbed. Yvonne Sparkes did, but I didn't,' he lied.

At the fireplace, the draw-paper began to scorch. Before it could catch light, granny pulled it away flooding the room with firelight and warmth. She carefully folded the paper to save for use another time,.

They made tea and drew their chairs up to the blaze. 'Did you read it all?'

44

'Of course I did.'

'I think somebody lied about sommat and gorra medal for it. The bits you need are all ripped out, but there's that bit about the DFM. And she says Tommy was in the RAF like somebody else from round here.'

'And who was that, d'you think?' Granny Smeggs asked him, tapping the exercise books with a home made cheese biscuit.

'I don't know for sure. Do you?'

'I might.'

'It could be Poshy Pearce,' Billy probed. 'You know, him at the chemists? I've heard he was a flyer, and he's gorra lot of medals.' He eyed his granny, trying to fathom her reaction, but she gave nothing away.

'How can you say that? It doesn't say that anywhere in here.'

'I didn't say it *was* him, I'm just asking,' he explained. 'There were lots of 'em in the RAF. I don't know 'em all do I? But Poshy Pearce is a clever Dick. He's always hoity-toity and tells you off for doing legs up in his shop window.'

'Legs up?'

'Yeah he always chases you off, and swears. He's a real misery.'

'Maybe, but that's not proof of anything.'

'Call it a hunch, doll,' Billy drawled, suddenly assuming an American detective voice, such as Humphrey Bogart's Sam Spade.

'Yes well, hunches might be OK in the movies, but they aren't evidence, my lad,' she scolded. 'I've known Arnold Pearce and Tommy Loveday since they were younger than you, and neither of 'em would do sommat like that.'

They bit into cheese biscuits in unison, eyeing each other warily. Silence hung over them. Mrs Smeggs spoke first, flicking crumbs off her cardigan. 'You're right though, they were together in the air-force, but Tommy especially would never have lied about anything.'

'Well somebody did. Look what she says - err - that bit at the end - the bit they didn't tear out? She says ...,' he scrabbled for the page, ' "It doesn't make a man what he is not, nor ever could be.". That's the same as saying that if you're rubbish and you tell

45

a lie to get sommat that you don't deserve, you're still rubbish when you've gorrit.'

Granny frowned, confused for a second or two, but then nodded in agreement.

'Poshy Pearce is rubbish. And no matter how many medals he's got, he's still rubbish.'

'That's only your opinion. And the best you can say about it, is that it's based on him not letting you play on his shop front. You could hardly call that evidence for anything, except perhaps his good sense. And you can't go accusing people just because you don't like them. If you're going to be a detective you have to find proper evidence, and right now you don't have any - do you?' She stared into the fire. 'And anyway, he's not the only one from round here who was in the RAF with Tommy Loveday.'

'Who else?'

'You'll have to find that out won't you? If you're a detective - do some detectivin.'

Dejected, Billy tortoised his head into his tank top. 'Well I think it's poshy Pearce,' he muttered glumly. 'He's just the sort.'

Granny Smeggs poked the fire, the reflections of flames on her spectacle lenses hiding her eyes from him. 'Mr Pearce is a hard working young man. He keeps that chemist shop beautiful. He always changes the newspaper in his scales before he weighs a baby.'

'Well I think he's the liar, and I think Tommy helped him,' Billy said, darkly. 'She even says in one bit that her Tommy was upset about sommat – sommat that had happened to their crew.'

'Yes I read that too, but we don't know what she meant,' she argued dismissively. 'It could be nothing at all, a simple competition with other crews, a bloomin darts match, or an egg and spoon race, or sommat. You can't tell from what she said. You've got to stop building things up in your mind if you're going to be a detective. You can't make things be what you want them to be. You have to find proof!' She sighed, fixing him with a steely gaze. They sipped their tea in silence, their faces lit by the fire roaring up the chimney, dragging molten light from the bubbling coals.

'Tommy was lovely. You couldn't meet a nicer lad,' she said reflectively. 'I can't understand how he got to be friends with Arnold Pearce in the first place. They were chalk and Cheddar. I expect they met up at some airfield and got together because they were both from round here. They'd been to the same school, you see, so they knew each other well enough, but they could never have been friends - chalk and Cheddar.'

'Why not? What was different about them?'

'Huh, well back then Arnold Pearce was a good time boy. He was always chasing the girls and gadding about. He wouldn't have found Tommy much fun at all. Tommy never went in for that sort of thing.' She smiled at some recollection. 'I remember when they were little ...'

'It says he died after the war,' interrupted Billy, trying to steer her back to the exercise books. 'What from?'

'He drowned.'

'Gimbals!'

'Oh yes, it was awful. It was an accident down Rivelin Valley. He was out with his dog.' She smiled sadly, as she remembered. 'Oh, him and that little dog: Molly he called it. You should've seen it - a Jack Russell. He loved it. He took it for walks by the river every day after he was demobbed. He worked at the Town Hall so he was always home bang on the dot.'

'What happened?'

'Well, they were never right sure, but they said it looked like the dog must have run into the old Walkley Bank Tilt Mill, after a cat or something. It was boarded up and fenced off with barbed wire even back then. Them old water mills are so dangerous, and the Tilt is one of the worst with all its rusty old wheels and sumps. Well he must have climbed in to fetch Molly out and fallen down one of the shafts into the leet.'

'What's that?'

'You know, the water that runs underneath where the tilt hammers and them big grinding wheels and stuff used to run. They used to make scythe blades, or shears, or I-don't-know-whats. That big water wheel on the side of the mill drove the tilt hammers and the bellows for the furnaces for forging them. Then they had men sat astride great big grinding wheels running in water troughs in the floor. It was dangerous, horrible work. My father, your great granddad, died of grinders' lung. And a lot of men got hurt with them rotten grindstones.' She gazed off into an imagined distance and dabbed her eyes on her lace handkerchief. 'Well anyway, Tommy must have fallen into one of the shafts in the floor and got washed away and drowned. Poor Annabel, she barely spoke a word after that. Not that she'd ever had much to say before.'

'But that water's hardly a foot deep. How could he drown?'

"How do you know how deep it is? Have you been scroamin about in there? You know it's dangerous. You're not supposed to be in them ruins.'

'You can look through the wire and see it,' he said, quickly cobbling together a defence. 'You don't need to go inside.'

Unconvinced, she eyed him wryly, but dropped the subject. He smothered a sigh of relief and reviewed what he had learned. He would have to tell Yvonne and get it all written into her notes, but first things first, he was going to be late for school. He would have to rush home with the dog, grab his bike and then pedal like a madman.

*

The bell had gone - assembly was over. Things looked extremely black. A painful caning was on the cards for him, even before his school day had started.

He found headmistress Sister Mary, and Sister Clare, his waspish form mistress, in the kitchen yard remonstrating with a school-milk deliveryman. The bulky dairyman wilted as the nuns berated him, wagging their fingers in his face, their great wimples fluttering like giant white butterflies.

Billy crept past unseen and slipped into school. That was the easy part. Unfortunately, his classroom was the last one in a row of several with glass partition walls overlooking the only access corridor. It would be impossible to get past all of them without being spotted by a teacher.

There was nothing else for it, he would have to bluff it out. So, marching smartly along the corridor past the teachers peering suspiciously from their windows, he smiled and nodded to them, as though he had every right to be there and nothing to hide. Each in turn sneered at him, as if discovering dog dirt in the corridor.

He found his classroom in uproar. Left unattended, his classmates were doing what they always did in such circumstances - all hell had broken out. They barely paid him a glance as he joined them. On Sister Clare's desk, the punishment cane lay unattended. Billy decided that a little extra insurance might be in order, in case his lateness had already been noted. He grabbed the cane, raising a gasp from his classmates.

At one end of the room a great gothic fireplace dominated the wall. Being past Easter there was no fire. The cold grate was trimmed with red and yellow crepe paper, intended to look like flames. Billy ran to it and stuffed the cane as far up the chimney as he could reach. His classmates' attention swung to him, starting a buzz of excited whispering and gasps of admiration.

A few seconds later Sister Clare swept into the room, rosary beads swinging from her belt, butterfly wimple fanning the air. Finding her charges so unusually quiet, she let slip a vinegary smile. Billy, proudly accepted the whispered plaudits of his classmates. It felt like a small triumph. Tomorrow would be Saturday. Sister Clare, he imagined, would spend all weekend searching for her cane, no doubt praying on her knees to Saint Anthony, patron saint of lost things.

*

With Whitsuntide approaching, Saturdays took on a new terror for Billy as his mother dragged him to the city centre for his annual kitting out with new clothes. Many of Sheffield's shops were still struggling to get back on their feet after the war, though an end to clothes rationing had been a welcome boost for trade. On the bomb damaged shopping streets, crumbling gaps, like rotten teeth, punctured the rows of shops. Some had fine Victorian and art deco facades still standing, hiding the burnt out rubble behind them. Civic buildings were pocked with shrapnel scars, several were propped up with heavy buttressing timbers.

The blitz had destroyed much of the city. More than thirty thousand bombs had fallen on shops, factories, houses, schools, and hospitals. Over one particular three-day period, at the height of the blitz, there were one hundred and thirty bomb alerts and sixteen air raids. But when it came to shopping, Billy feared the Luftwaffe much less than he feared his mother in full Whitsuntide outfitting mode.

Mrs Perks had a system for kitting out her son. It worked from the ground upwards. Shoes were always the first on her list. She would drag him around every shoe shop before ending up at the Sheffield and Ecclesall Co-op, "the Arcade", as Sheffielders called it. Billy thought it must be the biggest store in the world. Armed with her dividend card she would scour its many departments for socks, shoes, shirts and school ties. The next stop was Marks and Spencer, which, having been bombed out of its proper home, was temporarily housed in a cinema called the Lansdowne, later the Locarno. It still had its sloping cinema floor. The sales counters were levelled on wooden blocks. Young children could stand at one end of a counter and be seen over its top by the smart, lady assistant, but if they ventured to the other end would sink out of sight like the Titanic, a game many a child played to their parents' annoyance.

Mrs Perks would then drag him up Sheffield's main shopping street, The Moor, to Davy's Cafe in Fargate, for afternoon tea – no buns, too expensive, just tea. It was a rare treat in a bright, shiny place that mixed Edwardian charm with hygienic fifties glass and chrome. For some inexplicable reason, Billy preferred the soul chilling austerity of, *The British Restaurant*, housed in a dreary prefabricated building next door to the shrapnel scarred City Hall. His granny would sometimes take him there, thrilled by its gloomy ambience, as if it were the Ritz. The wartime Government had set it up to provide off ration meals for people bombed out of their houses. The portions were enormous, the food plain, salty and dreadful.

Sitting with his mother in Davy's café, wafted by the wonderful smell of roasting coffee, and serenaded by the chink of china and gentile chatter, Billy's daydream of beige sprouts and rubbery gravy ended when Arnold Pearce approached their table. He removed his trilby hat, and cleared his throat like a schoolboy summoned before the headmaster.

'Excuse me, Mrs Perks.'

'Mr Pearce …'

'I'm sorry to bother you when you're – err – taking tea with your son. I was sitting over there - and - err - I saw you. I was wondering how Billy was now after his beating. I'm sorry I couldn't catch the thug who attacked him. I chased after him, but he got away. I wish we could have identified him.'

'Oh he's fine now Mr Pearce thank you. Oh, and thanks for trying to catch the man too. It was very brave of you.'

Pearce shuffled, looking hot and pink. 'Well, I just wish I could have seen who it was.'

Billy was speechless at this, and gaped at Mr Pearce. It was such a blatant lie. He could hardly believe the man had the nerve to utter it. Of course he must know who had beaten him up. Everybody knew. It had to be Stan Sutcliffe – no other.

Pearce excused himself suddenly, and scuttled off, clutching his hat to his middle.

'That was nice of him,' cooed Billy's mother.

Billy shrugged. 'He's lying,' he snarled. 'He knows very well who it was. Why is he pretending he doesn't? What's he up to?'

'Oh for goodness sake Billy, don't start all that detective stuff again.'

....

CHAPTER SIX

It was Billy's firm opinion that the best things in pikelets are the holes. They are exactly the right size for the butter, and their rims add a touch of crustiness when toasted. Butter, air, and batter, complete the one and indivisible trinity of the pikelet. Oatcakes too, deserve similar veneration. As to which is best, that will always be a moot point. One important consideration is that it is just about possible to fit an entire hot, buttered oatcake in to your mouth at one go, whereas pikelets, once toasted, become crispy and can't easily be scrunched to the same extent.

'Pig!'

At that moment, Billy could not respond to Yvonne's opinion of him, because of the toasted oatcake in his mouth. It was not so much the oatcake she objected to, as Billy's noisy breathing as he ate it. Had he troubled to blow his nose before stuffing his mouth, she might have let it pass without comment. As it was, her expression reflected her disgust as he struggled to eat without drowning in his nasal fluids.

'Filthy pig!'

The conversation continued in this succinct and one-sided way as they entered the Ebenezer Chapel's scout hall for the annual, Spring Jumble Sale. They were not there for the bargains. As Billy had put it, they were there to *recky* the joint. He wanted to study the layout of the grey Victorian pile. Somewhere deep in its stony bowels the furniture sale would take place. The old lady's sideboard, with its secret drawer, was stored down there with lots of other old furniture waiting for the auctioneer's hammer. If Billy was going to check out the secret drawer, he must do it before that sale.

Young Doctor Hadfield spotted Yvonne, and ever anxious to hear news of her older sister, made a beeline for her. 'My word, you two look serious,' he said brightly, addressing Yvonne, before casting a sideways glance at Billy, still chewing the oatcake. After quickly assessing whether or not emergency thoracic surgery was called for, and deciding against it, the doctor went on lamely, 'What are you going to buy?'

The power of speech returned to Billy as he swallowed the last of the oatcake. Ignoring the doctor's question he put his own instead, 'Excuse me, but did you see the report in The Star about the old Star Woman? What do you think of it all?'

'Ah ha, so you two are still the detectives on the case. I've heard of your investigations. My old boss is a fan too, and obviously you're not giving up despite the coroner's report?'

'Of course not. She was murdered,' Billy said with certainty.

The young man looked shocked and cast his gaze nervously around the room. 'Shush, you need to be careful what you say,' he warned.

'I can prove it,' Billy told him.

'Let's go over there,' the doctor suggested, indicating to a quiet corner, away from the hectic bustle around stalls piled high with children's clothing, knick-knacks and shoes. 'What's your name?' he asked Billy, evidently preparing for a serious chat.

'Billy Perks, sir.'

'Well Billy Perks, it's all right saying such things to me, but some people could be very upset by them.' He looked at Billy's face, studying his reaction as if reading a map. 'The old lady fell and hurt herself,' he went on. 'It's not a mystery. Old people fall all the time. It's quite common. They fall and break bones. Old bones are brittle you see. Sometimes if a neighbour doesn't find them soon enough, they get pneumonia and …'

'She didn't have pneumonia,' Yvonne put in.

'She didn't fall either,' said Billy. 'And she wasn't all that old – about sixty or so. She just looked old and yellowish.'

'No, she was bashed on her head,' Yvonne insisted sharply.

Doctor Hadfield sighed with frustration. 'The body was seen by the police and my boss, an eminent doctor,' he argued gently. 'They saw the evidence for themselves, and didn't find cause to doubt it. If what had happened was so obvious to them, why can't you accept it?'

'Because of t'sneck nail,' growled Billy, grimly delivering his trump card.

53

The doctor gaped, as Billy told him his suspicions, and of their findings at the old lady's house. Yvonne fished under her cardigan and pulled out her notes, occasionally selecting a quote to season Billy's gabbled account.

When they had finished, Doctor Hadfield smiled and emitted a theatrical gasp of astonishment. 'Wow! I should hate to get on the wrong side of you two. You're a formidable team.' With that, he suddenly started back towards the frenzied hubbub of the main sales area. Children's coats and skirts, babies' bootees and leggings were trading briskly. The doctor stopped at one of the stalls and purchased a trilby hat for tuppence.

'Here,' he said cheerfully, returning to the pair. He plopped the hat on Billy's head and adjusted it to a jaunty tilt. 'A good detective needs a good hat. Just like Dick Barton.'

Surprised, Billy was nonetheless impressed, and nodded his trilby covered head appreciatively.

*

Outside in the silence behind the Boy Scouts' hall and the Ebenezer chapel, a narrow gap, choked with nettles and rusting old bits of church equipment, had originally provided access to a flight of stone steps down to a now redundant boiler room. It was an oppressive, forgotten canyon between towering ashlars, just wide enough for a man to pass.

Posting Yvonne on guard, Billy picked his way through the detritus to a rusting gate at the top of the steps and peered down to the boiler cellar door. Though chained and padlocked the door appeared weak with rot. He would have no problem getting through that, he told himself, and the padlocked gate would be easy to climb. All he needed was a torch and a tyre lever, and he could be inside in a jiffy. Glancing back to the chapel yard he checked on Yvonne. She waved, signalling the all clear.

The plan was to creep out of his house when his parents were sleeping, and get into the saleroom by squeezing through a heating duct that he knew led from the old boiler room to bronzed grilles in the chapel's panelled walls. He was sure there would be enough room for him to squeeze through. He'd seen the void behind one of the grilles some years earlier when he'd sat beside one at a Wolf Cubs' non-denominational harvest festival service. He was confident the grilles could be forced open from the back. There were no longer hot water pipes in the ducts, only an infamous draft carrying the squabbling calls of jackdaws and the soporific cooing of pigeons to a congregation, invariably struggling to stay awake. Once inside the chapel, he hoped it would be a simple matter to get down to the basement hall below it. All he would have to do then was find the sideboard and its secret drawer.

'Quick! Come out,' Yvonne called in a hoarse whisper. 'Somebody's coming.'

Billy adjusted the brim of his trilby hat, tugged the collar of an imaginary trench coat, and strode back to his trusty assistant.

'Well, will it be OK?' asked Yvonne, deciding not to ask why he was walking as though his shoulders had seized up.

'Sure thing doll,' said Billy, blowing invisible smoke from an invisible cigarette.

'What's up with you?'

'Nothing, Blue Eyes.'

'They're brown - Dope.'

*

In Bunny Parfitt's garden shed, Yvonne held her skirt to her legs as though avoiding demonic talons. Obscure mechanical projects, mostly unfinished, and bits of old disassembled machinery clung to the shed's creaking walls. Everything she saw seemed to be smothered in grease.

Eleven-year-old Bunny Parfitt was an eccentric mechanical genius. His reputation locally as a mad scientist almost eclipsed that of Doctor Frankenstein. Bunny had a cold, but then it seemed he always did. His nose dripped incessantly. His eyes seeped behind bottle-bottom lenses, and he sniffed with gruesome regularity.

'You deed to find adoother hair to match with this wod. It's dot evidence otherwise,' he said nasally. He peered again through his microscope at the fragment of blood stained silver, which Yvonne had carefully placed beneath the lens. 'I don't doh owt about blood, but they'll be able to tell thee what group it is.'

'What is it?' asked Billy.

'I just told thee, I don't doh.'

55

'No, what's the silver thing? Can you see what it's off of?'

'It's a bit.'

'A can see that you daft chuff, but what's it a bit of?'

'A bit,' sniggered Bunny, evidently enjoying a private joke.

'Are tha balmy or what?' cried Billy.

'He means from a horse's bridle,' Yvonne intervened uncertainly. 'Don't you?'

Disappointment flitted across Bunny's face as the prospect of teasing Billy some more evaporated with Yvonne's explanation. 'Well it's ever so small, but that's what it reminds me of. Maybe it's off a little statue of a horse,' he said. 'I'd guess at a military horse. It looks like an Army reversible bit.'

Billy shot Yvonne a disbelieving frown. 'Oh he's making it up now,' he accused. 'He's having us on. He can't tell all that from a nowty bit of silver like that.'

'Here have a look, see for thee sen,' Bunny challenged, wiping the eyepiece with his thumb and moving back a step. 'Put thee eye there and look down it.'

Billy stepped forward and spied through the brass ring down into a sparkling world of unexpected clarity and colour. 'Chuffin eck!' he breathed. 'Tha can see everything. Th'art reight an' all, it could be a horse's cheek. You can see its mouth and everything.' Yvonne and Bunny watched in silence as Billy peered excitedly into the microscopic world on the little glass slide. 'Eerrgh! Is that skin?' His head popped up from the eyepiece. 'You can see her skin on it and scabby blood and everything.'

Yvonne started giggling. Billy ignored her and returned to his inspection. 'We need to make sure we don't spoil this. It's good evidence. This really could be really, really, really important really.' His face popped into view again. 'I want it bottled up again and put away safe. When the time comes, we'll need the coppers to have a good look at it.'

They thanked Bunny Parfitt and left him in his shed, sniggering like a fool amongst his paradise of clutter and junk. He had done a good job for them, and Billy was very grateful, though annoyed by his silly giggling.

Yvonne too was still giggling helplessly as they left. Billy quickly caught her mood and joined in, thinking it was Bunny's strange behaviour that had tickled her. 'He's as barmy as a loaf,' he chuckled. 'Did you see him sniggering like a fool?'

'Take a look,' Yvonne said, giggling helplessly. She was pointing to the wing mirror on a Lipton's Tea van parked at the kerbside.

Bemused, Billy peered in the mirror. His reflection stared back at him. One eye had a thick ring of black around it. He looked like a Panda.

*

When night came, Billy struggled to stay awake. As usual, his mother had allowed him to stay up to listen to the BBC's Light Programme. It had been "Take It From Here" that night, which finished at nine-thirty. But staying awake until midnight from then, after a busy and exciting day - well ..!

*

The following night after a serious wigging from Yvonne, Billy tried again. This time he took a wet flannel to bed with him and kept washing his face with it. It worked. He heard his parents come to bed in the room below his attic bedroom, and waited for what seemed an age before counting one hundred in crocodiles. The house was silent, and beyond the little attic window the city slumbered. Still wearing his day clothes he climbed out of bed, donned his trilby hat and tip-toed silently downstairs and out of the back door.

All was black and cold. There was no moon and not a star in the sky. In the empty street his shoes clattering on the polished cobbles, he dodged from shadow to shadow, avoiding the greenish glare of the street's gently hissing gas lamps. The sound of approaching voices sent him scuttling to hide under a laurel bush in Polly Thackeray's front garden. Two policemen plodded by, so close he could have reached out and touched their capes. Their voices carried strangely on the chill night air. He waited until it was safe to move out of hiding, and then stood up slowly, but froze on hearing the sound of something bulldozing through the laurels. He dived for cover again, terrified even to breath. His mind invented all manner of monsters coming for him: a crazed grizzly bear, vampire or werewolf, teeth bared and salivating.

Round the corner of the street, out of sight from Billy, chill darkness and night noises were not new to Stan Sutcliffe. He was often out at this late hour, if not tottering home from some pub he would be loitering near the scene of his next crime. Stepping into a shop doorway to relieve himself, he luckily missed being spotted by two patrolling policemen who appeared from a side street. Keeping out of sight, he watched them as they moved away towards the tram terminus.

Barely a hundred yards away, a sigh of relief deflated Billy's chest as his wirehaired terrier, thrilled to see him, burst from the bushes. 'Ruff! Chuffin eck! You nearly scared me to death,' he whispered hoarsely. 'Whatta yer doing here? Go home.'

Telling a dog to go home is like asking the tide not to come in. Billy knew he was wasting his time, so considered his options. He could tie him up and leave him, or take him home and risk his parents hearing him, or take him with him. He thought of the commotion Ruff would cause if he left him tied to Polly Thackeray's laurel and sighed with resignation. The dog would have to come with him. Once Ruff somehow realised he was, so to speak, *on the team*, Billy could swear he assumed a slinky, foxy demeanour, as if getting into character. 'OK you stupid mutt, but be quiet.'

'Well lookee here,' Stan Sutcliffe muttered to himself, as he saw Billy Perks creep out of the same side street from which the two policemen had emerged. 'What's Perks doing out this late, and wearing that stupid hat?' He drew back into the shadows to watch him.

At the Ebenezer Chapel Billy slipped out of the gas light's glare and vanished into the blackness of the chapel yard. Stan Sutcliffe crept from hiding and followed.

Billy climbed the boiler cellar gate, and felt his way down the stone steps to the padlocked door. Ruff followed, stepping effortlessly between the gate's rusting bars. Billy shooed him gently aside at the rotting door. He daren't use the torch he'd borrowed off his mother's bicycle, in case someone saw the light. He would save it for inside the building, and for searching the secret drawer. For now, he was relying on carrots. He had eaten seven in the last two days. Enough, he thought, to warrant wearing sunglasses at midnight, if half of what people said about carrots was true.

The cellar door gave way as soon as he shouldered it. Rather too soon really and he tumbled headlong after its splintering wreckage to land sprawling on a slimy, wet stone floor. Ruff watched curiously, his head tilted to one side. The torch had gone spinning away in the darkness and vanished. Ruff sniffed it out and stood by it, waiting, as if he knew his master would need it once he stopped crawling about on his hands and knees, blindly patting the puddles on the floor.

Sweat trickled down Billy's face, yet his teeth were chattering. His clothing stuck to his body, and his hair felt glued to his forehead. Finding the torch at last, he swung its beam around the basement. Soot stained walls surrounded him in an area about the size of a garage. Half the stone-flagged floor lay submerged beneath slimy black water. From a coal shoot grating, high in one wall, a thin beam from streetlight leaned in and struck the water's surface to project eerie reflections onto the ceiling. Bits of old pipe, and a partially dismantled boiler cluttered the rest of the floor: unidentifiable rusting chunks of industrial sculpture that had not seen service in years. Ruff peed on a pressure gauge and sniffed the hinge of a furnace door.

Billy stood motionless, feeling taut and panicky. He tried to compose himself. Calm was called for. He took off his hat, hung it on a rib of dead boiler and wiped his sweating brow. What would Dick Barton do now? 'He'd get on with the job,' he told himself, struggling to mimic his hero. 'It's alright for him though, he's got Snowy and Jock to back him up. All I've got is you, mutt.' The dog thanked him for the vote of confidence with a wag of his tail, and sniffed at rat droppings.

Billy's feet were soaked. Water seeped in through the lace holes of his shoes and made strange lapping noises as he paddled about, treading on unseen objects beneath its slimy surface. His gaze followed his torch beam around the walls searching for the entrance to the heating duct. A large spider scuttled out from behind a veil of cobweb and ran along the wall. Billy shivered, and pretended he was not scared.

59

Shuffling noises from outside gave him a start. He imagined rats and monsters creeping down after him. Straightening up he stretched his shoulders, and tried to dismiss his fears. 'Come on, let's get on with it,' he told the dog, grateful now for his presence. Ruff eagerly accepted the challenge.

In the cool blackness beyond the rusting gate, Stan Sutcliffe felt around in the rubbish littering the ground and found a length of old iron pipe about the size of a cricket bat. He hefted it to his shoulder like a club and prepared to climb the gate.

In the boiler room below, Billy had found what he was looking for, a small square tunnel entrance set at about waist height in the wall. It was just big enough for him to climb inside on all fours. The spider reappeared in the faltering torch beam and scurried into the tunnel, vanishing into its unknown depths. It was as if it was inviting Billy to follow.

When Sutcliffe reached the bottom of the steps, he gently pushed open the wrecked door with his rusty metal club and peered inside.

....

CHAPTER SEVEN

Behind his bedroom curtains, Arnold Pearce shivered in his pyjamas. The bare oilcloth covering his bedroom floor offered no comfort to his chilly toes. He owned carpet slippers, but dare not move from the window to fetch them for fear he might miss something. This was the third successive night that he had spent the small hours peeking into the darkness. He was trying to catch a prowler suspected of watching his house. He would not risk leaving the window for a second, and so endured the discomfort of the cold lino and kept his prying eyes keened.

A neighbour had warned him that they had seen someone lurking in the darkness near Arnold's garden shed - nothing more than that. Arnold's imagination had filled in the rest.

Carefully sealing the chink in the curtains, he drew back from the window and lit a cigarette, shielding the flame in his hands. Annoyed with himself, he reviewed his situation. He had his job, and thanks to his war record, a whole set of new friends. His prospects were excellent. He had even been asked to stand as a city councillor at the next elections. The local Tories wanted a war hero, someone young, handsome, and respectable. Arnold was their ideal man. They claimed it was because he was a local man made good. He knew better. What they liked was that he was a war hero, highly decorated, and with just enough facial scarring from his war wounds to make him interesting to women and admired by men. The future looked good.

Even so, he felt deeply uneasy. For two weeks he'd been disturbed by the nagging sensation that someone was following him. He had not actually seen anyone. In fact, the only evidence for his suspicions was an occasional tingling at the back of his neck. However, it was enough to set his nerves on edge, but was it real or paranoia? Heaven forbid. On his worse days he had even felt that somebody had been inside his house - that his things had been moved, just a fraction. He had reported it to the police, but they had so far failed to act, pointing out coldly that he had never found anything missing, nor seen actual signs of a forced entry. According to them, no crime had been committed. Weary of his complaints, they promised to keep a special eye on the street. They did not actually accuse him of paranoia, though he suspected it. They were certainly fobbing him off, and so far he had seen little evidence of them doing anything. In fact, he had not seen a constable down the crescent for weeks, and neither had his neighbours. He knew this to be true, because he had been to their houses and asked them all.

Things would be different, he assured himself, when he became an elected councillor. He would accept no feeble excuses then.

*

Across the city on its northwest border, Yvonne Sparkes could not sleep either. Tossing and turning for what seemed hours in her tiny bedroom, eyes wide open, she lay staring at the rocking shadows of trees cast on the ceiling by the glow of the street lamps. Wild, irrational fears filled her mind as she thought of Billy and the dangers he had pledged to face that night. Tormenting questions buzzed in her brain. Would he be able to stay awake this time? Would he escape his house without waking his parents? Would he find the sideboard and its secret drawer? Had she eaten the last Minto from her bedside table? She sat up in bed and peered through her window.

Somewhere in the night out there, Billy was facing dragons, and here, in her bedroom, the Minto could not be found.

Beneath the Ebenezer Chapel, the old heating tunnel bored through the blackness. Billy squinted ahead as he crawled towards its invisible end somewhere in the chapel's walls. The tunnel was arrow straight. Going on all fours, he had just enough room to lift his face and peer ahead, though collecting cobwebs in his hair. He had ruled out using the torch, mainly because the battery was failing and he needed to conserve its power for searching the old lady's sideboard, but also, it was easier to pretend there were no spiders if he couldn't see them. But then something horrible and wet brushed his leg. 'Rats!' he squealed, bashing his head painfully on the tunnel's stone roof as shock tried to uncoil him. He was shivering with terror, and his throat tightened as if he would choke.

The wet thing moved in the blackness and licked his face. 'Ruff you idiot!' Relief swilled over him, briefly draining his tension. He ruffled the ears on the little terrier's nuzzling head. 'Thank gimbals you're here boy, but don't do that again.'

Apart from imagining spiders everywhere, crawling along the tunnel was not difficult. It had a slight upward gradient leading to the floor above. It was dry and gritty, and though it hurt his knees a bit, it was easy going. Several yards in, he sensed the wall to his right veering away into a black void. It was disorienting, and made him feel the need to get his bearings again, so he risked using the torch.

He was astonished to find himself beside a deep alcove, big enough for a grown man to lay out comfortably. That was precisely what someone had been doing. There was a bed of newspapers and cardboard, with a couple of neatly folded army blankets on top. Beside the bed was a cardboard box. He peeped inside and found a strange assortment of items. There was a pair of scissors, a table fork, a soup dish, a can opener, and a Dandelion and Burdock bottle. But the thing that trapped his attention was a blue, leather covered jewellery case. It had gold coloured hinges and a flip catch. Embossed in gold on its lid was a military insignia. Billy flipped the catch with his thumbnail and carefully popped the lid. Inside, on a bed of blue velvet, five military medals lay neatly displayed in a row. The silk lined vault of the lid held a crumpled photograph. His fingers gently slid over the shining medals. The ribbons were as bright as new. The photograph showed a group of young men sitting on boxes and jerrycans. They were playing cards. An ammunition box served as their card table. The location was a military airfield. RAF Wellington bombers lined up in a sunny haze behind the men.

The torchlight flickered and dimmed making him feel panicky. He quickly raked through the remaining items in the box. There were a couple of empty beer bottles, some candle ends, and a dog-eared clipping from a newspaper. Billy had no need to read it. He recognised it as one of the articles The

Sheffield Telegraph had printed a few weeks earlier about the Star Woman's death. He left it in the box, certain there was nothing else there to attract his interest and switched off the precious torchlight to conserve its battery.

In blackness again, he felt cold and isolated. The little alcove had seemed almost homely with its bed and personal possessions. He had found it strangely comforting. Now he was blundering onwards again, his face tormented by unseen spiders' webs. Sharp grains of grit abraded his bare knees and knuckles.

The tunnel was longer than he had expected. When he'd briefly flashed his torch beam up it before setting off, the end had not looked so far away. Even the boiler room's slimy, flooded floor, was beginning to seem inviting, compared to his endless crawl in black, airless confinement. He felt trapped and squashed, as if the walls were closing in. He began having doubts about where it would lead him.

'Poncy Perks! Where's tha think th'art going?' Stan Sutcliffe's sneering voice called from the blackness behind him.

Billy's heart pounded. How did he get here? Had he been following him all the time? He scuttled faster to get as far away as his painful knees would carry him. He knew that if Stan came after him, he would be stuck and helpless, unable to turn round to defend himself. As it was, escape looked impossible unless he could get out at the top end of the tunnel. For a second he considered retreating to the alcove. At least there was room in there to turn round. He might even find a weapon of some sort for defence. The trouble was Stan already sounded very close. Going back to the alcove would just make him closer. He might not make it before Stan grabbed him.

A few more knee skinning yards and he at last reached the first of the heating grilles. Peering through its decorative piercing he could just make out the faint glow of street lamps illuminating the chapel's opaque leaded windows. He had no idea which grille it was. It could be one up near the organ, or down under the lectern, he could not tell. He didn't care either. All he wanted was to escape from Stan Sutcliffe.

In the gloom, he could just make out the tunnel's route on to other grilles and the faint light that seeped in from them, but was alarmed to see the walls converging. The tunnel became progressively narrower before coming to its end. It was useless trying to go further. He would be stuck. Desperation drove him. He pushed at the heating grille with all his strength, but it did not budge. He reversed the force and heaved at it with painful, grasping fingers. It was fixed solid. Again, he pushed, then pulled, trying to free it with a rhythmic rocking motion. It did not move and the bronze-coated metal was soon slick with blood, his blood. He pushed again, but his grip was weakening, his hands and knees ever more painful. Sweat and sooty tears stung his eyes. It seemed hopeless. There was no escape.

'You're stuck, Perks. You can't get away. I've got thee cornered like a rat. And guess what? I'm going to roast thee alive.' Stan struck a match; its brilliant flare illuminated his vicious grin.

Terrified, Billy gaped back down the tunnel. Stan was pulling sheets of newspaper from the bedding in the alcove. When he had gathered a sheaf he started to back towards the tunnel entrance, laughing evilly. Billy was mesmerised. Stan seemed crazed. Was he really mad enough to do it? Surely even he wasn't stupid enough to set a fire beneath the chapel? He couldn't mean it. And hadn't he already had his revenge behind the rabbit hutches? Was he really going to burn the chapel down, didn't he realise … Billy shook the heating grille with all his might, but it wouldn't budge.

At the tunnel's mouth Stan eased himself down to the boiler room floor. Horrified, Billy watched him roll up the newspaper to make a torch and put a match to it. Luckily the flame didn't catch. Ruff whimpered and burrowed in behind his master. Stan struck another match, laughing wickedly. A faint blue flame glimmered and sparkled weakly before suddenly flaring up, flooding the tunnel with its hot brilliance. Sutcliffe gazed at it, a look of evil fascination on his face.

Acrid smoke began to reach Billy, stinging his eyes and nostrils. He pulled his dog close fearing for him as much as for himself. Blinking and coughing, he rubbed his eyes on his sleeve. When he looked again, Stan was no longer in the mouth of the tunnel. The flaming torch was not there either, though it was still burning. Its unseen flames illuminated the old boiler room walls, picking out every sooty detail of them.

Listening with all his concentration, Billy heard the sounds of movement, then a deep muffled voice. Whose it was, or what was said, he could not tell. Perhaps whoever owned the bed and the medals had come back and found Stan invading his home? Or, he hoped, it could be the police. He knew there were two constables patrolling the area. Perhaps they had heard Stan and come to investigate. He prayed it was the police. Having to explain his presence under the chapel would certainly get him into all sorts of trouble, but it was better than roasting alive.

Again, he heard a man's voice. It was a soft low mumbling sound, too faint to form into words. Stan's voice however, was distinct and fearful. 'You!' he cried. 'I told you I won't tell nobody, I swear. You don't have to worry about me.'

Billy wished he could see what was going on. Apart from the now fading glow of Stan's burning newspaper on the cellar walls he could see nothing, not even shadows. Suddenly there was a loud crack. The sound punched painfully into Billy's eardrums. Stan Sutcliffe yelped like a puppy dog - then silence.

Breathless, deathly silence fell on the darkness. Billy felt as if his ears were stuffed with cotton wool. He grabbed his trembling dog and hugged him. Was it a gun shot? What was going on? It sounded like gunfire, but how would he know?

Ruff snuggled up to Billy's chest, whimpering. Billy tried to comfort him, feeling he needed the dog's quick warmth and company every bit as much as the poor creature needed him. He had no idea what had happened, but expected somebody very dangerous to come poking into the tunnel at any moment. If someone had shot Stan, it could be his turn next. Grasping his dog under one arm, he scurried backwards down the tunnel to the alcove, as fast as his bloodied knees would carry him. Pressing himself deep inside the alcove, he pulled the army blankets and remaining old newspapers over him and placed a hand on Ruff's muzzle, praying he could keep him quiet.

Through a tiny gap in his camouflage, he saw the light of a powerful torch beam flash along the tunnel walls. There was the sound of wheezy breathing, as if someone was struggling to

66

climb inside. Then silence. Billy waited, hardly daring to breath. His body ached. He desperately needed to stretch his limbs, but dare not move. Concentrating on the slightest sounds, he waited, passing the time in terror.

How long he waited, he had no idea. The memory of Stan's short and terrifying scream still played in his head. What had happened? What would he find if ever he managed to escape his stone tomb?

At length he plucked up courage to push his head a little way out of the imagined security of his cocoon of newspapers and blankets. He peered down towards the boiler room. All was silent and dark. Stan's firebrand had fizzled out. Nothing moved. There had not been a sound since the wheezy intruder, yet still Billy waited, breathing silently, his senses straining the air for clues of anything that would help him to build a picture of what might await him.

The faintest glow, a mere grain above darkness, began to outline the tunnel's entrance. Billy studied it, trying to confirm that it was real light and not merely a fading impression on his retina, but no, it was light, he told himself. Dawn was at last seeping down, even into the hidden corners of the old boiler room. Night was ending, and somehow he had survived it so far. He thanked heaven for that, though his relief was short lived. For he quickly realised that dawn would bring him more trouble. Somehow, he had to get away and creep back into his bed before his mother went into his room to wake him. How would he explain his filthy clothes and scratched hands and knees? He sagged gloomily, wishing he had never fetched that ball from the Star Woman's back yard.

With weary caution, he crawled towards the tunnel entrance, stopping frequently to listen for any sounds. At last, he stuck his head out into the boiler room. There was Stan's body, stretched out on the floor, face down. Sooty water hid one eye. The other, wide open, stared at the boiler room's shattered door. It was as if Stan had watched his killer leave as he breathed his dying gasp.

Billy climbed down to the filthy floor and stretched his painful limbs. He stood over Stan's corpse trying to work out what might have happened. The sound of the day's first trams, rattling past, intruded. They seemed bold and loud now that dawn was brushing even the darkest alcoves of the new day.

There was no doubt about it - Stan was dead. This time there was no need to poke around taking pulses. His mouth was mostly under water. If he had been alive, he would have been blowing bubbles. He could see no blood. The wound must be underneath him, on his front. Billy tiptoed past the corpse and made a dash for the door, almost tripping over the dog who was every bit as anxious to get away.

Outside in the chilled air, dawn was brightening the eastern sky. Brash, fluting trams pounded their silver rails, scooping up clutches of cigarette smoking steel workers to take them to their six-o-clock shifts. The day was starting with no mind to the horrors of the night. Sparrows clamoured about the chapel yard. Cats stalked, dogs barked from yards and gardens. Heavy boots ground on cobbles, beating out their random rhythms, and a young man lay dead in a pool of sooty slime.

Not all detective work would be fun; Billy had expected that. But now, he reminded himself, in just a matter of a few weeks he had seen two corpses, both brutally murdered. The terrifying realisation that someone was out there, killing people, and for reasons that still eluded him, impressed itself chillingly. He'd put Yvonne at risk too. How could he protect her? He had blubbed like a baby when he thought that Stan was going to burn him. What sort of protector did that make him?

What had he started? What could he possibly do against people with secrets and guns; people who coldly killed for their own unknowable reasons. He was facing grown ups, free to go wherever they like, and do whatever they wanted. What could he do against that? And if, by some lucky accident, he did manage to get close to the killer, he too would most likely end up drinking sooty slime like poor Stan Sutcliffe. He and Yvonne were going to have to face facts - make some grown up decisions. But for now, that would have to wait. The great detective had to somehow sneak home before his mother found him missing.

The back-naks offered the safest route, he decided. If he went onto the streets at this time of day he was certain to meet his dad, or if not him many a man who could tell his dad that they'd seen him. Back-nacking, scroamin through people's back yards, would keep him out of sight. The last thing he wanted was another confrontation with his father.

From a thick stand of lilac in the chapel yard, he waited, watching the men chatting at the tram stop opposite, cigarette smoke hazing the bubble of banter around them. The chill dawn carried their voices, low and friendly, and rippled with laughter. Their faces looked pink and scrubbed beneath flat caps, their white cotton sweat towels tied about their throats. A tram slid up to the stop and scooped them away. The street was quiet again, and he could set off on his secret way home. Ruff would follow or fend for himself.

Unseen, another watched that morning. He saw Billy climb the first wall into the back gardens of the houses beside the chapel. He would have to quickly fetch his few belongings before the boiler room filled with police. They were sure to be around soon.

*

Battered, dazed and feeling so far out of his depth that nothing made sense, or offered the least bit of comfort, Billy lay on his bed staring blankly at the hairline cracks in his bedroom ceiling. Images of all he had seen in the last few weeks formed and reformed in the chaotic patterns of crazed whitewash: corpses staring, gaping and cackling, gun-fire in his head, blood squirting from the old lady's toasting fork rack and sliming itself into words on paper, words with voices and ghostly weeping.

Annabel's tragic death was twisting everything out of shape. Death brought life sharply into focus. The detective game, however well intentioned, had become real and dangerous beyond all expectation. It seemed as if corpses were cropping up at every turn. Mysteries were weaving themselves around objects and stray events like ivy up a tree. They sprouted and spread, rapidly enveloping everything, veiling and distorting the truth.

. . . .

CHAPTER EIGHT

Waiting for the police to find Stan's body had Billy on tenterhooks, driving him into sullen isolation in his room. At any moment, he expected his world to come crashing down. Two days had passed since Stan's brutal murder: two days on which Yvonne had knocked at his door several times to ask his mother if he could come out and play. Mrs Perks had explained that her son was not well. She said he had fallen, badly skinning his hands and knees, and was sick and off his food.

'If he doesn't buck up today, I'm getting the doctor.'

Finally, Billy could stand the waiting no longer. As soon as his mother left for work, he dressed, swilled his face at the kitchen sink, flattened his hair with a slick of soap bubbles, and ran out of his house to go to the telephone box. He would make an anonymous call to the police, but would disguise his voice, and be sure he was off the phone quickly, before they had any chance to trace the call to him.

He planned to disguise his voice by mimicking an Irish priest he knew, but first he needed two pennies for the phone box. It would be safer to make a call directly to the police station, rather than to risk making a free nine-nine-nine call. He remembered that when they had telephoned to report the old lady's death, the emergency operator had made them repeat everything. It had taken ages. This time, he was determined his call would be short and impossible to trace. He would tell them where to find Stan, and then put the phone down. He would not be caught out by their questions, or be tricked into hanging on.

He searched, but there were no coins lying around the house. The old tea caddy in the kitchen contained a ten-shilling note. He might as well commit suicide as take that. Granny Smeggs would certainly give him the money, but only if he told her what it was for. That would mean lying to her. He didn't want to do that – though only because she always tricked him and found him out. Anyway, he told himself, it didn't matter. Getting a few

70

coppers would be easy, but it would involve a shameful deception; one he vowed to undo at the first opportunity.

Old Pop Meaks kept a corner shop. It was scruffy and stank of cats. At least six of the evil brutes gazed imperiously from the tops of glass lidded biscuit tins and boiled sweets' jars on old Pop's counter top. In the yard behind the shop, wooden crates of Tizer, Dandelion and Burdock, and lemonade bottles were stacked for collection by the distributor. Like the shameful thief he had become, Billy stole into the yard, and soundlessly removed an empty Tizer bottle. After a moment to compose himself, he calmly strolled into Pop Meak's shop and placed the bottle on the counter. The old man smiled warmly and dutifully paid him two pennies.

With coins in his pocket, and feeling that everyone in the street was looking at him, accusing him of being a heartless thief who would take the very milk out of a blind man's tea, he ran to make his call. Near the telephone box at the end of the street the butcher was hanging rabbits on his window rail. Billy felt he glared at him accusingly, as if warning him never to place his thieving feet inside his shop.

He found Mr Wragg in the telephone box, a clipboard of printed forms in his hand. Billy groaned, but not because he expected the call to be a long one, but because Mr Wragg was the fishmonger and would leave the phone box stinking of fish.

Billy liked Mr Wragg. He was a joker and a bit of a card. When children were in his shop, he would skilfully throw his voice so that fish suddenly spoke to them. Younger children either howled pitifully and clung to their mothers, or happily conversed with cod and haddock without batting an eyelid. Kippers had Scottish accents, cod sounded German, and skate were cockneys. Hearing from a sad eyed conga eel that you shouldn't fiddle with the parsley leaves edging the icy display, was a bit of a shock at any age, and brought squeals of laughter from young and old alike.

At last, the fishmonger finished his call. He scribbled on an invoice with a pencil from behind his ear and eased himself out of the phone box. He ruffled Billy's hair as he passed him. 'Ayup, Billy. Tell thee mam I've got crabs.'

71

Billy nodded and forced a smile. He hesitated at the telephone box door for a moment to make sure the fishmonger was not going to hang around, then slipped inside. He began leafing through the telephone book and took a moment to rehearse his Irish accent one last time.

He dialled the number.

'Hello Police, Hammerton Road.'

Billy gagged with horror, dumbstruck by the sound of Sergeant Burke's voice on the telephone. His was the last voice he had expected. It threw him into panic.

'Hello who's there? Come on, speak up, don't be shy.'

'Stan Sutcliffe's dead,' he croaked. 'He's under the Ebenezer.'

'Who's that? I know you don't I? I recognise that voice. What do you say about Sutcliffe?'

Slamming the phone down Billy ran outside. It had all gone terribly wrong. He had panicked and forgotten to disguise his voice. Sergeant Burke now knew it was him. Sooner, or later he'd have to explain how he knew where Stan was. Everything had gone wrong. His mother would cry, his father would give him that awful, sneering look of disappointment and never speak to him again. He might even be sent to jail for the rest of his life.

. . . .

CHAPTER NINE

The damage was extensive. It ran from the glossy flare of the black Rover Six's front nearside wing and along its running board. Deeply gouged grooves, stained with the green paint of the coach-house door marked the polished coachwork. Billy stopped his bike at the gate and watched bewildered as the old doctor, furiously denied the evidence of his eyes and his car's screaming protests, and kept on driving forward, stripping even more paint off his car and the coach house door.

Greenhow eventually stopped revving the engine and erupted from the car in a burst of fury, arms waving, and curses flying. Stepping back, he slammed the car door, and shaking with fury gaped at the damage. He raged at the vehicle, kicking its coachwork and wheels. Purple faced and spluttering, he cast round for something to hurl at it. When he saw Billy, he froze. 'What do you want?' he screamed. 'Get off my drive. Get away from here.'

Billy pedalled away as fast as he could. It was well known the Doctor had a temper, but Billy was astonished to see him behave so irrationally. Pedalling blindly in his haste to get away he steered himself into a quiet street that ran at the back of a row of large Victorian villas. It was unfamiliar territory, and he slowed down to look around. It was a forgotten backwater, which he supposed had been a service lane for the grand houses, such as the doctor's, that fronted the main tree-lined street.

Suddenly his bike stalled. It hung motionless, locked by brute force. The brute was old man Sutcliffe, poor Stan's father. He seemed to have leapt out of nowhere and grabbed the bike's handlebars, his hard hands covering Billy's, crushing them against the metal. He had a grip like steel. 'Who was it?' the old man demanded.

His meaning was obvious. 'I never saw anything,' Billy wailed, trying to wrench free.

'You liar!' Sutcliffe spat, swinging his fist into Billy's temple. The bike lurched as he released his grip on it, tipping Billy onto mossy cobbles. Sutcliffe pushed the bike down hard on top of him, and leaned his weight on it, trapping him beneath it. One of the pedals ground into Billy's shin, the saddle pressed against his throat, choking him.

'They're saying you was in there. Don't deny it. Somebody saw you climbing over a back yard wall next to the chapel. Everybody knows you were there. You saw my Stan get shot. Who did it?'

Blood oozed from Billy's shin as the bicycle pedal ground into him. He could not move. Sutcliffe had him helpless, clamped to the ground like a mouse in a spring trap. He twisted and fought, gazing around for help and inspiration; there had to be some way out. The lane was deserted, its Victorian back gardens screened by mature trees and shrubs. It was more like a cobbled pavement winding through a forest, than a suburban street. A few minutes earlier he had been rattling a dolphin shaped knocker on the door of the little hexagonal gate house that Doctor Hadfield rented from the owners of one of the great villas. He'd not found him at home. Now he desperately wished the young doctor would appear in his ancient Austin Ruby saloon and deliver him from Sutcliffe's madness.

'Who shot my boy?'

'I wish I knew. I just heard voices.'

'So you were in there? I knew it. Who did it?'

'All I know is, it was a man, but I don't know who. If I knew I'd tell you. Crikey, I'd tell the police, I promise you. Stan didn't deserve killing.'

'No he didn't,' sobbed Sutcliffe, great tears welling in his wild eyes and running down his stubbly face. 'He wasn't never going to kill nobody. He might scuff people up a bit, but he was never no killer. He was a good boy my Stan.'

Recalling Stan's last words to him, something about roasting him alive, Billy decided only a lunatic would debate the point with a lunatic's father.

'He had fifty quid on him.'

'I didn't take it,' cried Billy.

'I know, the coppers showed me it. They found it on him.'

Some point was being made that Billy was missing, and he frowned stupidly at Sutcliffe. The old man failed to offer further explanation. He released Billy and pulled a piece of crumpled newspaper from a trouser pocket. He smoothed it out on his stomach and read from it, "containing ten five pound notes." He gazed around despairingly, shaking his head.

Was it the money, or the fact that he had it? Billy wondered, scrambling out from under his bike.

'He never had no fifty quid in all his life,' Sutcliffe said sadly. 'Then when he's dead, he makes the big time. They found it in his pocket, all fresh new fivers, like they was straight from a bank. How'd he get 'em? I know everything he was doing. We was partners – family. He never had no fifty quid as I never knew about. So where did it come from - eh? Then somebody kills him.'

'Honest Mr Sutcliffe, I didn't see anybody.'

Suddenly the old man glanced around suspiciously, his body tense and crouching. 'Did you hear sommat? Somebody's coming.' He whacked Billy across the face and started backing away. 'I'll get you some other time Perks. You better have some answers for me next time.' Suddenly he was gone, vanished into the tangled greenery and Billy was alone again.

Gingerly rubbing his stinging cheek, he looked around nervously, but couldn't see anyone. The lane was silent, its large stone villas impassive.

*

Later that evening Yvonne looked for Billy. She was annoyed, and the eerie sensation that unseen eyes were watching, unnerved her as she crept into their secret meeting place. This was a large disused greenhouse behind a screen of advertising hoardings. It was a good spot, out of sight of the road, and surrounded on three sides by the rickety fences and unkempt shrubberies of adjoining back gardens. Secret runs and get-aways were plentiful through hidden tunnels of privet and rhododendron. They could move unseen along the stuttering winds of no-man's land, the hidden highways of foxes and cats, where old buckets went to die like elephants.

The neglected greenhouse and the land around it, were wildly overgrown, but the building was dry. Almost all its window frames were intact, and glazed with whitewashed glass. Billy's whispered message had seemed vitally urgent, yet she found herself waiting alone, angry and nervous. And, certain she was being spied on.

It would be their first meeting for almost a week. She had been to the Perks' back door several times to ask if he would come out to play, but his mother had said he was sick and could not see visitors. Even so, she was not prepared for just how sick and care worn he appeared when he eventually arrived.

'You're late,' she complained. 'This place is really spooky when you're on your own.'

'Sorry, I was trying to see Doctor Hadfield, and …'

'Why didn't you let me see you?' she interrupted, her displeasure thawing as she saw his pale face and the Elastoplasts on his knuckles and knees. 'You look awful.'

'I'm sorry. I didn't know what to say to you. I've been all mixed up. I told my mam I was sick. I chuffin well am an' all.'

They sat facing each other in a couple of creaking deck chairs between ghostly rows of desiccated tomato plants.

'What's up with thee hands?' she asked.

'I cut 'em in the tunnel. They're a lot better now, but I couldn't do up my shirt at first. Then old Sutcliffe crushed 'em.'

'Crickey!' Yvonne gazed at him, listening intently as he told her of his ordeal. Her eyes almost popped out of her head when she heard of Stan's shooting.

'Crikey! I'd have been scared out of my wits,' she gasped.

'Well I was,' he admitted, without the slightest hint of his usual bravado. 'I've never been so scared, and I still am. That's why I went looking for Doctor Hadfield, because he bought me the hat. I was going to tell him that I wasn't going to be a detective any more, but he wasn't in. All I got instead was a load of earache from old man Sutcliffe. He hurt my shin and bashed my face, and scrunched my fingers on the handlebars.' He sagged forlornly in his creaking chair. 'I've had enough. I'm just beginning to realise a few things about this detective lark.'

'Such as?'

'Well, I guess somebody killed Stan because he knew sommat. I think it was sommat he got paid fifty quid for. I heard him begging for his life. He pleaded and promised he wouldn't say owt. So that proves he knew sommat. Whatever it was, he got fifty quid – but it cost him his life. That proves it's sommat really important that they want to hide.'

'Who does? What could he have known?' Yvonne asked. 'They said about the fifty pounds in the paper, but he could have got that anywhere, you know what he was like.'

'No, his dad didn't even know about it. They were like twins them two. He would have known. They never did nowt without each other.' He scratched tentatively at the sticking plaster on his scarred knees, marshalling his thoughts. 'No, this must have been special; a really big secret he even kept from his dad.'

'Humm, well you know what they say about thieves and loyalty?' Yvonne said, shaking her head.

Billy didn't, but felt he'd had enough of looking stupid for one day, so nodded, pretending he did.

'Do you think Stan knew who killed Annabel? Could it be her killer who did him because of it?'

'I don't know,' answered Billy wearily. 'I haven't a clue, and the more I find out the less I seem to know. But if they're watching us, which they probably are …'

'Oh they are,' she interjected. 'I can feel it all the time.'

Looking scared, Billy peered suspiciously through the whitened window glass. 'If they think we've found out sommat about 'em - it's curtains. They killed Stan to shut him up. Why should they stop there?'

'But we haven't found out anything.'

'Yeah, I know that - you know that - but they don't know it.' He blew a despairing sigh, and gazed miserably at the crumpled sticking plasters on his hands. For a while they sat in silence, each raking over their thoughts.

Billy spoke first, startling Yvonne. 'And another thing, they shot him with a gun! That's like a proper killer would do, you know like a gangster, or somebody. I mean, it's not just somebody bashing him on the head like they did to old Annabel.'

'You really do want us to give up don't you?'

'Well of course I do. I mean, Gimbals, who has guns and is ready to use 'em - nobody but gangsters and posh mister bigs.'

'Mr Biggs?'

'Yeah, like George Sanders in the movies: rich blokes who talk posh and hire crooks to do their dirty work for 'em.'

'Do you think Stan was hired by a mister big?'

'I don't know. All I know is we could get shot. I'm scared, Wy, and not just for me. I've put you in danger. This's all got too big for us. It's changing everything. I've lost my best friend, not you, my other best friend. I stole tuppenz from Pop Meaks, I've lied to my Mam, my dad hates me, and now Sergeant Burke knows it's me who rang up about Stan. And on top of it all, I nearly caused the chuffin chapel to get burnt down.'

'But we made a promise to Annabel,' Yvonne reminded him. 'We knew it could be dangerous. We expected it. It was obvious from the start. If you investigate a murder you can be sure that at least one person will get cross about it.'

'Who?' Billy asked dumbly.

'The murderer, dummy!'

He sagged back in his deck chair, his head turtling into his green corduroy jerkin. In his mind's eye all he could see ahead was prison, pain and death. If the killer didn't get him, Sergeant Burke would. He'd spend the rest of his life in jail doing hard labour. He would be exactly what his father said he was, a useless waste of space.

The greenhouse door burst open and Kick Morley exploded into their midst with all the theatrical suddenness of a pantomime demon. 'They've found Stan Sutcliffe riddled with bullets at the back of the chapel. Dead as Dodo shit.'

'Kick! It's you.'

'Yeah. Who d'yer think - Popeye's granny?'

Billy was shocked, especially after their last, acrimonious meeting. 'It's good to see you. I thought we - err - I thought ...'

'We need a proper plan,' Kick interrupted, animated with enthusiasm. 'I've been reading about it; 'It's called MOM. That's what we need.'

Yvonne looked at Billy, a frown betraying her misgivings. She shrugged and retook her seat. 'MOM?' she asked.

'Opportunity, means and motive,' Kick announced proudly.

'That's OMM,' Yvonne said.

'Motive, means and opportunity,' said Kick, trying again.

'That's MMO,' said Billy.

'Yeah, now we only need Larry and Curly for all the Three Stooges,' Yvonne quipped.

Kick looked bereft for a full quarter of a second, and then dashed to the far end of the greenhouse. The pair watched him bemused. Neither had the slightest notion what he intended. Even when he returned with a plywood board about the size of a large tea tray, its potential in his unpredictable hands remained a mystery. Kick grinned at them, inviting them to share his enthusiasm. He leaned the board against a stack of terracotta plant pots and stood back to admire his handiwork. The board's bleached grey surface was stained with little round watermarks, evidence of a past life on a potting bench. Its future use however, as Kick proudly scanned their faces, remained infinitely unknowable.

From a pocket he produced a stub of chalk and drew two vertical lines on the board to create three columns of equal width. At the top of the first column he wrote MEENS.

Yvonne resisted the urge to correct his spelling. In the next column he wrote OPP and in the last MOT.

'What we do is we write in these columns everybody who could have done it, if they had wanted to, and had something to do it with.'

Yvonne could not conceal her surprise. 'That's a very good idea,' she gasped.

'But it's dangerous,' argued Billy. 'I've just been saying we should leave it up to the police.'

Yvonne stood up and put a consoling hand on Kick's shoulder. 'You'd better sit down,' she told him. 'I think you need to hear this.'

Again Billy recounted his story and explained his concerns. Kick appeared unmoved, though expressed some disappointment that Billy had not actually seen Stan shot.

'Well we knew it'd be tough,' he said finally. 'I mean, we did, didn't we?'

'You don't understand,' Billy cried, 'We could all get done in. There's a nutcase out there killing people and we could be next.'

'Yeah, but you'll be all right won't you?' Kick assured him. 'You'll be safely in jail once old Burke gets hold of you.'

Yvonne groaned despairingly. 'You know what?' she said. 'I don't think that helps him much.' Then raising her palms she signalled her call for calm and attention. 'Right! That's it. Now let's stop all this. We know it's dangerous. We know it's tough, but we've already started. This beehive has already toppled. It's too late to back out. We're probably on somebody's hit list already.' The boys stared at her in silence. 'Gimme the chalk. Let's gerron with it. The sooner we get this killer behind bars the sooner we'll be safe.' She glared at them, demanding their agreement.

Kick leaned close to Billy. 'What's she mean about beehives?' he whispered.

'Oh, it was on Dick Barton the other night.'

'Fair enough.'

Yvonne glared at them from the board. 'Right, whose's the first name on the means column?' she snapped.

'Err, I think I got it wrong,' said Kick.

'Shurrup!' yelled Yvonne, sticking her face close to his. 'You did, there's an A in means.'

'No, I mean I think motive is first.'

'Shurrup, it's staying like that.'

Nobody moved for what seemed a long time. Then Yvonne straightened up and began to write her father's name in the first column. 'He had the means because he was on the street at five. He goes right past Annabel's door on his way to work.'

'At the tram sheds,' Kick said unnecessarily.

'Yes, at School Road,' growled Yvonne, her patience ragged. Calming herself, she stretched her spine and stood ready to write on the board again. 'Now we think she was killed early in the morning, probably around five, because of the ashes in the grate, remember?'

Billy nodded, beginning to get the idea. 'But we all know that your dad didn't want to kill her, so that's a zero in the MO column,' he suggested.

80

'How do we know?' queried Kick.

'Because he's my dad, you wassock!' Yvonne yelled indignantly.

'Oh yeah, I gerrit,' Kick said, flinching as Yvonne swung a false punch at him.

'But he might have seen others out on the street,' said Billy. 'We could interrogate him. He could have some valuable leads.'

*

Sergeant Burke filled the armchair, his bulk seeming to darken the room. From the kitchen door, Mrs Perks cast another worried glance in his direction. 'Are you sure you won't have a cup of tea, Sergeant?'

'You're very kind, Mrs Perks, but I think *not* is best. '

"He thinks not is best." Marian Perks mulled the phrase over in her head. No matter how many times she repeated it, or how she shifted the emphasis, it felt deeply doom laden. She glanced at the mantel clock. It was almost six. Her husband would come through the door at any minute. He'd be hungry and exhausted after a long day on the furnace stage. He was on "Hot Money" all week, lining the furnaces with firebricks. It was good to get the extra pay, but it made him irritable, tired and dehydrated. Certainly in no mood to hear a policeman report his son's latest mischief, or worse. And, where pray, she wondered, is the star of this drama? As usual, he was late for his tea. It was oxtail with dumplings and the potatoes were ready to fall.

First through the door was Billy, bright with anticipation, and eager to see her. The greenhouse meeting had raised his spirits. Kick's enthusiasm and Yvonne's assiduous management, had eased his apprehension and feelings of guilt. Now they had a plan, and the future seemed less threatening.

Discovering Sergeant Burke wedged into a Perks' armchair, soaking up the light like Satan in a coal cellar, changed everything in a flash. He was about to tell his mother that he had spotted his dad at the bottom of the street. He was about to ruffle the head of the dog that was bouncing around his legs. He was about to tune the wireless to the Light Programme, ready for Dick Barton at six forty-five. Instead, gloom fell on him like a sack of soot. Whatever was to happen next would not be good.

81

Jail, hard labour, tears and his father's further disappointment; all were just seconds away.

'There's somebody to see you,' his mother said flatly.

Billy tried to calm Ruff, for whom the best thing in the world had just happened. It was not easy. Eventually the little terrier got the message and slunk under the table, unsure what he had done to deserve such rejection.

'We'll wait for the Mester,' said the policeman. 'I think that'll be best.'

"He thinks that'll be best." Marian Perks repeated inside her head. Huh, best for what?

Billy sat at the dining table, refusing to react to the little dog, head butting his shins. When Frank Perks pushed through the door Ruff bounced out for another session of, *welcome home dear plaything*, only to be inexplicably rejected once more.

'I'm sorry to spoil your teatime, Frank, but I've got to ask the lad some questions. Now I don't want you to worry. I'm sure it'll all make sense when we've talked for a minute or two.'

Eyeing the policeman suspiciously, Frank Perks removed his donkey jacket and cap and hung them on a hook behind the door. 'The lad's been sick,' he said. 'He hasn't been out of the house for a week. He's not involved in owt.'

'Well that's exactly what I'm expecting to find, Frank. I'm not here to blame him for anything. As a matter fact, I think he might be able to help us a great deal.'

'Help you, how?'

'Aye well, he could be very important to our enquiries, a key witness.' The sergeant sat forward in the armchair as Frank Perks seated himself on the settee opposite him.

'Now this visit is not official you understand,' said the policeman. 'Do you mind if I ask him some questions?'

'Billy, come and tell the sergeant what you know. He says you're not in trouble.'

If only that were true, thought Billy.

Eager to bring an end to his mysterious ostracism, the dog jumped up beside Billy as he joined his father on the settee.

'I know where you were the other night, son,' Sergeant Burke said softly. 'So before you answer any questions - think on.

You're not in trouble with me, and your mam and dad'll want you to keep it that way. So you know what I want, don't you?'

Billy nodded, and tried to swallow the lump in his throat. Frank Perks cast a puzzled glance at his wife.

'And what is it that I want, Billy?' the sergeant persisted gently.

'The truth,' mumbled Billy.

'Aye, that's it, lad - the truth.'

'What's this all about?' Mrs Perks asked sharply, concern for her son driving her impatience.

The sergeant did not respond. He was concentrating on Billy, determined to hold eye contact with him. 'You left your hat behind. It's evidence in a murder enquiry now. You can have it back when we close the case.'

'Murder!' gasped Frank Perks. 'What're you saying?'

The sergeant turned to him. 'You heard about Stan Sutcliffe? Well I think your lad here saw it happen? Didn't you, son?' He turned to Billy. 'I think you saw it all, and I think you're frightened now, as anybody would be who's witnessed a killing like that. But now I'm sure you're ready to tell us all about it.'

*

Scout camp at Hesley Wood, the football match at Hillsborough, pocket money, use of bike, but not the cleaning and oiling thereof, Vimto lollies, playing out with his pals, Dick Barton on the radio, and going to the Festival of Britain on the steelworks' trip; Billy's list of *forbidden pleasures* was growing daily. It seemed that everything he enjoyed, or hoped for, was now under a prohibition order. He was grounded until Whitsuntide - four whole weeks. His days withered to simply attending school and then sitting at home, forced to join in rug pegging with his parents as they listened to the wireless. He was tasked with cleaning every noxious and unpleasant place, such as the hen house, the coal cellar, the filthy old air raid shelter, and his bedroom. Visits to his grandmother Smeggs were timed with the egg timer. His mother demonstrated that three flips allowed him just enough time to run to her cottage, fill the coalscuttle, and run back before the sand ran out.

After a week of cold silences and prohibitions, relations took a further dive when a young constable called at the Perks' house. Reciting from his notebook, the pimply officer delivered what he claimed was an invitation from Sergeant Burke. Billy was to be at the Police Station after school the following day. This time it was official, and a parent or guardian must be with him. Mrs Perks loudly informed the constable, in the presence of her son, that he would be there, and that she would lose pay and finish work early to accompany him.

Things really could not be worse, he thought - though he had overlooked the capacity of a mother's love for making them even more complicated.

'Well, if I'm going to lose pay,' she told him, in an accusatory tone, 'I might as well take the whole afternoon off so I can get you to the doctor's. I don't like the look of you.'

The following afternoon his mother met him outside school. She led him away, as he resolutely endured his mates' jeers. They, of course, thought the whole thing was a hoot.

The police station, a solid looking low brick building, dominated the street corner in a residential area. Iron railings on a stone perimeter wall shepherded visitors to steps up to its front door in an uninspiring facade. Sergeant Burke had been stationed there since it was built in the thirties. He was as much a part of the place as the blue lamp hanging over its door.

Inside, the air was full of the clatter of typewriters and the jangle of telephones. Desks were piled with papers and bulging manila folders. Police officers worked on their files, milling about, grouping at desks, dispersing, and regrouping.

'Ah, so you're Billy Perks,' said the desk sergeant, somewhat scornfully.

Silence fell on the room and hung there for several seconds as everyone looked up to see who was Billy Perks.

'Have you any idea how much paperwork you account for in this building, my lad? Of course you don't. Well I do, young man, because most of it has to come across my desk.'

'I'm sorry, sir,' mumbled Billy.

'I should hope so too.' He pulled Billy away from his mother and whispered in his ear. 'Mark my words, Billy Perks, your description has been given to Interpol, the FBI, the Kremlin and every copper in the empire. You put a toe wrong, my lad, and you'll spend your life in the worst nick in Arabia, eating rats and drinking camel pee.'

The office racket had started up again as a side office door opened and Sergeant Burke leaned out from it. 'That'll do, Tom,' he called. 'Master Perks is my special witness. He's helping our enquiries. And if you weren't doing *his* paperwork, you'd be doing somebody else's, so what's the difference?'

Billy's mother fired a hostile glare at the desk sergeant and ushered her son towards Sergeant Burke. Inside his cramped office, they were waved to brown, bent-wood chairs. The sergeant sat down opposite them, beneath a wall displaying numerous framed photographs of himself and two other men, showing off large salmon and trout they had caught at various rivers and lochs. Billy thought how out of place the neat gallery of smiling faces seemed in such a dreary room.

'The trolley will be round in a bit. We can have a biscuit and a mash up,' said the sergeant amiably.

'What's this all about?' Mrs Perks asked. 'He told you everything the other day.'

'I'm sorry, but there are a few things that don't add up. I'm afraid I've had to make it official this time. That's why you've had to come here with him. I expect you've had to take time off?'

She nodded sourly.

'Aye, I thought so. This is why it's important he tells us everything.' He turned to Billy and leaned towards him across his cluttered desk. 'You know lad, what you said about old Mrs Loveday, set me thinking. I've been looking into a few things myself. If I tell you something, will you keep it to yourself?'

Billy began to feel less threatened. The policeman was talking to him almost like a fellow detective. 'Yes sir,' he said, shuffling forward on his chair.

The sergeant leaned closer. 'The sneck nail clue,' he whispered. 'It took intelligence to spot that. It's had me thinking ever since, but I don't make the connection with old Annabel and you being in the boiler room at the chapel. You didn't explain why you were there?'

Billy remained silent, gripping the seat. The policeman was leafing through his notebook. 'Here it is. This is what you told me. I wrote it all down. You said your dog was in there and you followed him. You saw Stan lying dead on the boiler room floor. You didn't see anybody else and you ran home and went to bed. Then you said you were too scared to tell anybody and you didn't want your mother to know you'd been down in that boiler room at night. But then your Mam found you trying to get your mucky clothes into the wash tub without her seeing them, so you had to tell her. Is that what you said?'

Billy felt his economy with the truth had covered all that he had needed to volunteer. He felt he had not lied – exactly. And nothing he could have added would change anything about Stan's murder. He did not know who had killed him, nor had he seen anything. What useful purpose would he serve by volunteering more? 'Yes that's it,' he said.

'You were in the boiler room weren't you?'

'I could see Stan from the door. The door was all busted.'

'There you go again, Billy. You're not answering my questions. He should be a politician, you know,' he chuckled, smiling at Billy's mother, anxious to keep their meeting as stress free as possible. 'Now lets try again, Billy, I didn't ask if you were in the doorway. I said, you were in the boiler room, weren't you?'

'I've told you what I saw,' cried Billy, ready to burst into tears. 'He was dead on the floor. I don't know who killed him. I didn't see anybody kill him. That's the truth.'

It was the truth. He was not lying, but the sergeant looked far from ready to accept it.

'Billy son, there's no call to be frightened of me. I think you're a bright boy, and I don't think you're telling lies. The thing is, Billy, I know that you're not telling me everything. Your hat was in the cellar. That shows you're holding things back. You might not think they're important, but they could be. They might even be crucial. While ever you keep things back from us we can't get to the bottom of it all.' He turned to Billy's mother. 'Look Marian,' he said, his tone softened by friendly concern. 'I have to know it all, and I know he's holding out on me. He's going to get himself in even deeper bother if he doesn't tell us everything.'

'Are you Billy? Is there something more?' she asked him.

Nothing that will make any difference to who killed Stan, Billy was thinking.

The policeman leaned back in his chair. 'Aarh, I hear Mrs Taylor coming with the tea trolley,' he said, his mood lifting. 'I think we deserve a biscuit and a cuppa, don't we? We always have a mash about this time. I might be able to find you some Tizer, or sommat, Billy, if you want, or will you have tea? Do you like your tea sweet? I do, I like it very sweet. Do you take milk? We have nice biscuits too. Do you like Ginger Nuts? What did the tramp do?'

'He weren't there,' Billy blurted. Then his heart sank. He realised he had been caught and kippered by an expert, just like the salmon in the sergeant's dusty photographs. He looked at his mother and saw her disappointment. He knew he had let her down - it was written all over her face.

The sergeant leaned back and stared at him with unblinking eyes. 'Are we going to get down to business now, Billy?'

The office door swung open and a tea trolley rattled in, pushed by a delicate, prim woman, wearing a brightly coloured floral smock. She struck Billy as being quite out of place in the dark brown office with its fishy black and white photographs and shelves of dull cardboard files. The tea-lady smiled at everyone, and quickly assessed from the sergeant's demeanour that tea all round would be in order. Her head flicked, as if dismissing a wasp or wayward curl from her eyes, as she began pouring. The first cup went to Billy's mother. Billy accepted the next. He was astonished to see the tea lady wink at him. He watched her pour the sergeant's tea, flick her head and wink at him too, though he appeared not to notice. Biscuits were handed round, each accompanied by a wink or a flick of invisible wasp avoidance. The biscuits were not Ginger Nuts.

'This is the little boy that was beaten up on Orchard Road isn't it?' enquired the tea-lady, smiling sweetly at Billy. 'I'm glad to see you're all right now. I saw the man from the chemist's chasing that young hooligan - you know - him who was shot.

87

Well it's too late to do anything now isn't it, God rest his soul. It's the mothers I feel sorry for. They bring them into this world and then they have to watch them turn out wrong and get shot.' She turned to Billy, tilting her head. 'Anyway I can see you're not like that.'

Sergeant Burke had been on the verge of ending Mrs Taylor's interruption, when something she said caught his attention. 'Just a minute Mrs Taylor, are you quite sure it was Stan Sutcliffe you saw Mr Pearce chasing?'

Mrs Taylor frowned indignantly. 'Of course I am. I always get my – err – what's it – facts right. I saw Mr Pearce from the chemist's chasing young – err – Sutcliffe along Camm Street where I live. They were shouting. It was before he was killed. Well I mean it was when he'd bashed nice young Billy there.'

'Are you sure, because Mr Pearce said he could not identify the person?'

'Well I don't know why not, they were as close as I am to you. I was cleaning my transom. I was on the inside. I'd already done the outside because of the pigeons. They're filthy those birds. I have to clean that window twice a week no matter what. They don't bother with the others, but they get my transom every time and it's hard work getting up there with my legs ...'

'Thank you, Mrs Taylor,' said the sergeant, standing suddenly. He ushered her back towards the door. The tea lady's head flicked and she winked and backed her chinking trolley out of the office.

'I expect it's no surprise to hear that it was Stan who attacked you?'

Billy was not surprised, but was still thinking of what Mrs Taylor had said; Pearce and Stan arguing like that. It struck him as distinctly odd and he decided he would have to pay her a visit to learn more.

'I shouldn't say so, but the Sutcliffes have been on our books for years,' the sergeant was saying as Billy's thoughts surged through growing questions. He had always suspected Stan. He recalled finding the small crow bar at his feet. He had assumed then that Stan had been using it to break into the old woman's house. Perhaps it was him who had dislodged the police notice

88

from the door and left it to fly around the skittle yard? Maybe he had been paid the fifty quid to break in, or was it something he wanted for himself, like the mythical gold coins? Billy had to find out. And also, why had Pearce pretended not to recognise Stan. Were these two things connected? Mrs Taylor, he thought, might be able to shine light on these mysteries.

The sergeant shuffled noisily in his chair. 'Now Billy, you were telling us about the tramp. You said he wasn't there.'

Misery swilled over Billy. He had hoped his slip had passed unnoticed, but the sergeant's unblinking gaze burned into him across his steaming teacup.

'I think you've got some explaining to do, Billy,' he said. 'So! Let's begin with the tramp. Not there eh? How do you know about the tramp? You can't possibly know unless you've been up the conduit in that old boiler cellar. Come on, let's have the full story this time.'

Billy looked at his mother. A large tear rolled down her face and plopped into her teacup, but she didn't move a muscle.

'You were up there weren't you?' persisted Sergeant Burke. 'Were you there when Stan was shot? Did you see who did it?'

'I was hiding. I heard them. The only voice I heard was Stan's. I heard him promise not to tell anybody. Then I heard the shot. It was massive. I was deaf, and I never saw anybody - I swear. After the shot, I hid and waited. My ears were ringing. I couldn't tell what was going on. I waited until it was safe, then I came out. That's when I saw him dead on the floor. I ran home.'

'What time was this?'

This was the dreaded question. When he answered it, he knew that he would never see another Sheffield Wednesday match as long as he lived. He'd be grounded for life.

'It must have been at night,' said the sergeant, 'because we know about that tramp. We know him very well. He's a bit sensitive about the scars on his face and hands. He likes to keep out of folks' way. He usually hides and sleeps all day. He's not often seen out in daylight. Our night patrols often see him wandering round the streets. He's harmless, but even so you'd never have got up that conduit in the day time, because he would have been there. He'd have chased you out.'

'It was after midnight ...'

'Don't be silly! You've not been out after midnight,' his mother scolded.

'It's true Mam. I'm sorry,' he admitted tearfully. 'I waited until you were asleep, then I went out. I had to see inside the secret drawer. I thought I could get into the sale room through the heating duct.'

....

CHAPTER TEN

'I suppose it was that silly mother of mine who told you about the secret drawer,' snorted Mrs Perks bitterly.

Thank gimbals, thought Billy, his sense of relief enough to ripple a string vest. At last, she was speaking to him again. In oppressive silence, they had climbed the steep mile or so from the police station to Doctor Greenhow's surgery.

'She's no right filling your head with nonsense. I swear she gets barmier the older she gets.'

'She told me it was at the back of a drawer,' he argued feebly, eyes firmly focussed on the ground. 'I wanted to see if it had clues in it, but old Leaper took it to the saleroom and ...'

'And you thought it'd be all right to break into a chapel,' she interrupted, adding sanctimoniously, 'a house of God. You should be ashamed.' She sniffed and sighed. 'You might have been killed.'

'I'm sorry, Mam.'

'There's nothing in it, you silly boy,' she went on. 'She kept her rent book in it, that's all, and your grandmother knew that very well. She could have told you.'

Billy was astonished that she knew anything about it. 'How did you know?'

'Everybody knew about it. There was nothing in it. She was old and poor. She hadn't anything, certainly not gold coins, like they're all saying.'

'I wasn't looking for gold coins. I never believed that. I thought – maybe some letters, or photographs or something?'

'Her rent book and her gas bill in her Tommy's tatty old folder. That's all.'

'A folder?'

'Yes, she hadn't anything worth a farthing in that whole house, the poor old thing.'

'What about the folder?'

91

'The folder?' she hooted. 'That's worth nothing; a scruffy old folder Tommy made at school. She loved it. Talking about that damn folder was the only time I ever heard her string more than half a dozen words together.' She glared at him, disappointment dulling her eyes. 'Some mothers have sons they can be proud of. Sons that make them folders, instead of making them have to take time off work to go to police stations.'

Billy flinched, but felt he must plough onwards. He was now in so much trouble it could hardly get worse. 'What did it look like?'

'It was just cardboard, but it was nice. He was very good at drawing, was Tommy Loveday. He was good at anything to do with art and carving and that. He made some nice things.'

'What was it a picture of?'

'I don't know, sort of Egyptian. A bird, I think.'

'And a lion?' Billy asked, staring at his mother, this font of knowledge he had overlooked.

'You see, I sometimes took her bill in to the gas board in town when I went to pay ours,' she explained. 'They'd all made folders at school, something to do with history. They all made them. Not me though, I wasn't in the same class.'

Another bombshell of amazement exploded in his head. 'You knew Tommy Loveday at school?' he spluttered. 'That's unbelievable.'

'Of course I did,' she piped. 'I went to school, didn't I? I didn't just spring from the ground, ready formed as your mother you know. I was a child too once, though not as stupid and disobedient as you.' She glared at him as if doubting he could possibly be her son. 'Tommy was younger than me,' she went on. 'We never had anything to do with each other. All I remember is they made fun of him because he was quiet like - you know - a bit shy.'

They had reached the Doctor's surgery. Mrs Perks put her shoulder to the ornate cast-iron gate at the garden entrance and pushed on through. Billy followed up a stone-flagged path. He could see the doctor's Rover parked in front of the coach house doors, one of which now leaned on its recently broken hinge.

The doctor's house stood on a gentle rise, overlooking extensive gardens. It was an imposing stone villa, the sort of house successful cutlers built to impress their friends in the eighteen eighties. A border of copper beech, and chestnut trees assured its tranquillity. A monkey-puzzle tree dominated the perfect lawn.

A dimly lit white glass sphere, about the size of a soccer ball, hung from a lamp bracket over a side door. On it, black lettering spelled the word SURGE. Halting beneath it, Mrs Perks pressed a bell push. After a worrying delay, an old woman admitted them, scrutinising them closely. She ushered them to one of two battered pine benches in a joyless entrance hall, which served as the doctor's waiting room. Its green and cream painted walls were in urgent need of refreshing.

'It's Perks, isn't it? You're lucky you are. The *Doctor* wants to see you himself,' said the woman, enunciating the word doctor, with all the reverence and awe that one might reserve for the King, or Sir Len Hutton. 'When I showed him the list this morning he said as how I was to make sure he sees Perks himself. "Don't let young Hadfield see him," he told me. Oh yes, you're very lucky you are.'

At that moment, Greenhow opened his consulting room door. A middle-aged woman, wrapped in furs, beneath a large veiled hat, sallied forth like a galleon. Bidding her an effusive farewell, Greenhow mimed frantic instructions to his receptionist to open the outer door for the woman's stately egress. Squashing themselves back against the wall to make room, Mrs Perks and Billy watched anxiously as the woman hissed sedately by. Billy felt enveloped in her aura of powder and perfume. He gaped, transfixed by the glass eyes of several dead animals gazing forlornly from her coat collar.

'This is Perks,' the receptionist told the doctor, indicating to Billy.

Old Greenhow's eyes remained fixed on the rear end of his departing patient as it disappeared regally behind the closing door. Finally, he turned to Billy, and then glanced sourly around his crowded waiting room. 'I'll see Perks now,' he barked to his receptionist, as if she alone could hear him. 'Send the rest of them home. Tell them Hadfield's had to go out on a call, or some such thing.'

'Aye but Doctor, I'm reight badly tha knows,' one woman cried angrily. 'I've been waiting for thee for over an hour.'

'Ayup, I wer eer before thee,' another cried. 'And th'art not as badly as me.'

'I am badly tha knows. I were across our yard last neet more times than a weshin line.'

'We can wait,' Mrs Perks offered, anxious to avoid trouble.

'This way boy, don't waste my time,' said the doctor. 'Is this your mother?' Flustered, Billy nodded as the doctor gave him a patronising swat on the head with an ink spattered, brown paper file, and ushered him into his consulting room. Mrs Perks followed, only to be cut off as the doctor closed the door on her.

'I'm sure we don't need your *mummy*. You're a big enough fellow to look after yourself - eh?'

Silent and rigid, Billy eyed him nervously. The memory of him kicking his car was still fresh in his mind. Greenhow washed his hands, studying Billy through a mirror fixed over a small sink. 'You're a bit of an adventurer I hear?'

Billy returned a puzzled glance, and shuffled his feet, nervously wondering if he should sit down or not. He let his gaze wander around the room, taking in the clutter of medical wall charts, faded prints of stags bellowing over misty waters, and a photograph of young naval officers lined up like a silver buttoned football team. The face of a younger, happier version of the old doctor, smiled out proudly from the carefree ranks.

'Hum, I was in the Atlantic most of the great war. Ship's surgeon,' Greenhow said, mistaking Billy's casual glance at the photograph for actual interest. 'I finally got out Christmas nineteen-nineteen. It wasn't a moment too soon. Those were hairy days my boy, four years on the knife edge. You never knew when it might suddenly all be over. Boom!' He shook his head ruefully, as he towelled his hands. Then, eyeing Billy diffidently, he wafted a hand in the direction of a visitor chair at the end of his cluttered desk. 'Sit boy, sit. You make the place untidy.'

Billy smelled Christmas pudding as they manoeuvred passed each other to take their seats. It must be alcohol, he guessed. Christmas was but a faint memory, and even he had heard of the doctor's fondness for brandy. It was even rumoured a child had died because of it.

'So now then, Old Stick, what's the matter?'

'I'm not badly anymore,' replied Billy flatly, partly because it was true, but mostly because he disliked the doctor, and wanted to leave as soon as possible.

'You've had a few adventures lately,' Greenhow said. 'I believe you found the body of that unfortunate rascal, young Sutcliffe?' Billy dropped his gaze and made no reply. 'I expect you've told the police all about it by now? I bet they were very pleased with you. They like boys who're brave and truthful.' The doctor leaned over and patted Billy's elbow. 'Me too. I like honesty and courage in a chap.'

Choosing a stethoscope from a tangle of miscellaneous equipment on his desk, he placed it around his neck. 'Take off your jacket, Old Stick.' He reached and grabbed Billy's wrist firmly and held it for a while between his finger and thumb. 'What did you tell them? - Pulse is fine. - What did they say? - These fingers seem to be scabbing over nicely. Mouth open, let's see inside the old cake hole. Stick out your tongue – errggh – put it away again. All's fine in there. Were they pleased? Any pains in the old breadbasket? Let's see shall we? Stand up, Old Stick.'

After a few moments more of prodding and poking, the doctor sat Billy down again. He began scratching words on to a dog-eared record card with a pen he dipped frequently into an ink well, spattering ink spots over his desk and papers. When he had finished he tossed the pen aside, and leaned back in his chair to study Billy's face. 'Did you see the gun fired?' he asked.

'No.'

'But you heard them talking?'

'No.'

'But you *were* there when the shot was fired?'

'I told the police everything I know. I was hiding. I didn't see anything.'

'I hear you're a bit of a detective. Young Hadfield tells me you're a bright boy. Is that true? He says you've unearthed clues the police had missed. Did you really?'

'I'm not doing it anymore. I've stopped being a detective.'

'Why?'

'I don't know; I just stopped. I couldn't find out owt, so I've given it up.'

'Did you know she was writing her life story?' the doctor asked him. 'What a waste. Who'd care? I'm told that old fool the vicar was encouraging her. Do you know Reverend Hinchcliffe? He was her editor. Damn foolishness!'

Billy did not know what an editor was, but resolved to visit the vicar to find out. 'I think it could be an interesting story,' he replied, happy to disagree with him. The doctor's lack of reaction to this was disappointing, so Billy tried again. 'My granny told me that Mrs Loveday had many secrets. For instance, she knew that somebody was given a medal in the war that should never have been theirs. The old lady's son was involved somehow. Maybe she would spill the beans in her life story?'

Again, the doctor was utterly indifferent and merely sniffed with mild disapproval. 'Well whatever she was going to say, we'll never know now – eh? They couldn't find any papers, or her manuscript, so that's the end of that.' He rose from his chair and patted Billy on the shoulder.

'I didn't know they were looking for any papers or manuscripts?' said Billy, his curiosity alerted. 'I mean to say, if they are so sure she wasn't murdered, why would they bother to look for anything? Surely they'd just close up the house and that'd be that.'

Greenhow peered at him thoughtfully, then shrugged. 'Hum, bright boy, bright boy. I expect you're right, but I don't know, and I've other things to worry about. Luckily it's not our business, is it?'

'No it isn't, and I especially don't care, now that I'm not a detective anymore,' said Billy. 'I hope I never hear about it again.'

The doctor was inspecting him minutely. It made him feel very self-conscious. Heat flowed into his cheeks. Suddenly the old man sat down again and scribbled an afterthought on the record card, spattering ink across his stethoscope and papers.

'What are you writing, sir?' asked Billy, wondering what he had said that was worth such effort.

'Notes, my boy,' replied the old man, peering fiercely over his spectacles.

He held up the card and read his addition to himself. 'You can't overstate the case for good note taking - as I am forever telling my young colleague Doctor Hadfield. Take my word for it, Billy, write it down and it'll stick - always there for reference and reassurance.' He dropped his pen into the cluttered inkstand with an air of finality and rising from his seat, moved quickly around his desk. 'So, no more sleuthing – eh? Quite right too; let the police do what they're paid for. You need to concentrate on your schoolwork.'

He opened his consulting room door. In the waiting room the same people were still in their seats, resolutely hanging on to their places in the queue. As a body they rose to face the doctor, their expressions set in grim determination. Greenhow ignored them and turned suddenly to Billy. 'Did you know that chap Sutcliffe?' he asked softly. 'Or his father? Did you turn up any evidence to connect them with Mrs Loveday's death?'

'No – you don't mean gold coins do you?' Billy asked, intrigued by the afterthought.

Greenhow pulled him back into the consulting room and closed the door. 'Gold coins? What gold coins?'

'Oh it's just a stupid rumour. She was supposed to have some sovereigns in a sock, in a secret drawer. Everybody thought Stan might have believed it.'

The doctor was impassive. 'So you think young Sutcliffe knew this? And his father too, I suppose? Do you think they knew about the – err – secret drawer thing?'

'Everybody knew,' Billy said. 'There was nowt in it but her rent book.'

Greenhow opened the door again and gently eased Billy through into the waiting room. 'I thought I told you to send them all home,' he barked at his receptionist. 'Why the blazes are they still here? Get them out! Surgery is over. Go on get out. Why the blazes can't you people do as you're told? I knew this damn National Health scheme would be a disaster Get out of here! Come back tomorrow if you're not malingering.'

*

At the old greenhouse, Yvonne, Kick and Billy found the name *Arnold Pearce* chalked on their Motive-Opportunity-MEENS board. The figures 5.30 were chalked against it.

'Did thar write it?' Kick asked Billy.

'No!'

'And it weren't me neither,' Yvonne cried, as their accusing eyes turned to her.

'I told my gran about the MOM board,' Billy said. 'I asked her who was around early on that morning when the old lady was killed. She's always up at first crack of sparrow fart. She'd know if anybody else was up too.' He fixed Yvonne with a steely stare.

'What?' she demanded huffily.

'The only person she saw was your Dad.'

Yvonne was unmoved. 'Well you know he's up early. I already told you. It was me who wrote him on the board.'

'Did you ask him if he'd seen anybody else - like you said you would?'

'Of course I did. I said I would, didn't I? So I did.'

Kick armed himself with chalk and stood poised by the board. 'Well go on then.'

'The milkman…'

'Old, or young?' Kick demanded efficiently.

'Old. I was just going to say,' she answered crossly.

'Gerron with it,' Billy snapped.

'My Dad of course and the doctor ...'

'Old or young?' demanded Kick, unrepentant.

'I was just going to say,' Yvonne cried, her face turning pink. 'The old one.'

Billy looked gloomy. 'Is that the lot? Huh, nothing fishy there. You'd expect to see any of them - it's their jobs.'

'But what about Arnold Pearce though? It's not his job, and somebody thinks he should be on the list.' Kick vigorously underlined the name on the board.

98

'Yeah, but Yvonne's dad didn't see him did he?' Billy argued, his confidence in the MOM board beginning to wane.

'Well neither did your grandma,' Yvonne retaliated.

'I'll ask her again,' Billy promised. 'You ask your dad again too. We'll leave it on the board for now, but if they didn't see him we'll have to rub him out.'

*

Later that afternoon, over apple cake and tea, Billy confronted his granny.

'Don't talk with your mouth full,' she told him.

'You just did.'

'Yes, but only because I had to tell you not to - you bad boy. Go and fetch the coal up. It's cold enough to freeze a duck's quack.'

Billy dashed into the cellar and filled the coalscuttle in record time, eager to get back to interrogate his granny. A noisy swig of tea, a swallow of cake and he was ready to try again.

'Why don't the old doctor and Sergeant Burke like each other?'

'Who says they don't?'

'I do.'

'I don't know what you're talking about. I mean, I wouldn't say they were best friends, but I think they get on well enough. It was Doctor Greenhow who tried to save his little girl.'

'Sergeant Burke's? I didn't know he had a daughter.'

'No, she died, bless the little mite. She was only four. The poor sergeant was heart broken.'

Billy shuffled in his seat, recalling the coldness he had seen between the two men, outside Annabel's cottage, but his mind was moving on like a bee in lavender. 'You said you only saw Yvonne Sparkes' dad, but somebody else told us they saw poshy Pearce. They've written it on our MOM board. Why didn't you tell me he was around – you must have seen him?'

Granny Perks chuckled and raised a finger whilst chewing urbanely. Billy knew she was deliberately keeping him waiting, but refused to rise to her baiting. At length she put her bony finger to her lips and spoke softly, 'Shush. Keep it down. I did see him, but I ...' Her eyebrows hovered above her spectacles as

99

her face took on a censorious expression. 'I didn't want to say anything for the sake of a certain lady's reputation.' She gave Billy a wry smile, for what reason he had not the faintest idea. Then, springing forward in her seat, she wagged a finger at him. 'And you mustn't say anything, young man. It's not our business.'

'What's not? I don't know anything. What lady - whose reputation? What are you going on about?'

'I saw him leaving a certain lady's house at five thirty in the morning.'

'Whose?'

'If you can't guess, I can't say. So just think on.'

That was all she would say. Billy was baffled. And why, he thought, did they always say, "Just think on." What was that supposed to mean?

An hour later, he met with Yvonne. Even she was unable to fill in many of the gaps for him. Granny's enigmatic nods and knowing winks remained mysterious. 'It could be Miss Burkinshaw at the library I suppose,' Yvonne speculated. 'She always blushes when he goes in there for some books. He reads a lot of books I think.'

Before his curfew, oblivious to the embarrassment he was about to heap on the poor woman, Billy was knocking on Emily Burkinshaw's door, ready to ask her if she could confirm that Arnold Pearce had been leaving her house at five in the morning. The wail she let out when questioned, startled sparrows in her yard and set dogs to barking. Billy backed away astonished as she burst into tears and slammed the door in his face.

'I guess that's a yes then,' he told himself.

Turning from Emily Burkinshaw's door, he was surprised to see that dusk had crept up on him unnoticed. The incandescent mantels in the street's gas lamps were gently popping and hissing as they warmed up for the long night. Folk were calling home their wandering dogs, and drawing curtains at their windows.

Soon it would be dark enough, thought Billy, to slip into the Ebenezer Chapel yard for another look at the boiler room. He wanted to find the medals and the photograph. He had decided that leaving them behind, had been a big mistake. He hoped a quick scamper up the tunnel would put that right.

His mother had set his curfew at seven-o-clock, and then up to bed as soon as Dick Barton finished, punishment for his brush with the law. These days, the slightest deviation from any of her rules brought the roof down on him. He was already past his curfew; another ten minutes would not make the situation any worse. Setting off at a trot he made his way to the chapel as thick smog began rolling in like brown ghosts, gathering in the gas lamps' glare

The gate to the flight of steps down to the boiler room had a new chain and padlock. He quickly climbed over it and picked his way down the stone steps to find a sturdy new door in place, heavily bolted and padlocked.

Turning away miserably, he headed for home. Whoever had been sleeping in the tunnel would have moved away long before they put the door up, he reasoned. It was idiotic not to have realised. He decided not to tell Yvonne.

He ran along the foggy street, pushed through the cinema queue snaking around the front of the Walkley Palladium and clambered breathlessly up the steep hill to his home. At his gate, Constable Handley loomed out of the brown smog and grabbed his collar. 'Where're you off to in such a hurry?'

'Nowhere, I live here. I'm late. I'll get killed if you don't let me go in. I'm supposed to be in by seven.'

'Huh, well in that case, we'll all be going to your funeral then; it's a quarter past already. Where've you been until now?'

'Just round and about - playing.'

'We've had a complaint.'

'It weren't me.'

'Well of course not. I bet you're little Mr Innocent.'

'The Sergeant's been here already, asking me questions.'

'Yes well he's off in Ireland today with his big shot fishing friends, so you've only got me this time,' the constable said testily. 'Some medals have been nicked. Have you seen 'em?'

Billy gulped. Did he mean the ones he'd seen in the tunnel? Or were there some others? 'Where were they nicked from?' he asked, trying to buy time to think.

'It was a burglary - a private house,' the constable told him. 'People saw somebody hanging around on the day it was done

101

over. It's a queer business because only the medals were taken. There was plenty of other stuff they could have nicked, but they didn't. That's why I think it's kids – like you.' Handley stared accusingly at Billy as if trying to read his mind. 'Anyway keep your eyes open, *Detective*. They're in a blue leather case about as big as a library book. If you see anything, or hear of anybody selling owt like it, let me know.'

The last few words had passed over Billy as he spotted his mother rapidly approaching him from the house. He faced her feeling distinctly queasy. Life, as he knew it was about to take yet another unpleasant turn. Mrs Perks' face wore an expression of icy fury. Not only was her son out late, despite warnings of the direst consequences, but he was, yet again, in the presence of a police officer. It could not be worse.

As his life flashed before his eyes, Billy heard Constable Handley cheerfully greet his mother. 'I'm sorry the lad is late, Mrs Perks,' he sang pleasantly. 'It was my fault. He's been helpful to me on a very important matter. He's a good lad. I hope you'll not punish him because of me.'

Billy's opinion of the constable soared. His mother smiled and sighed happily.

*

Saturday mornings presented Billy with opportunities to rebuild his damaged reputation with his mother. He would rise early, get himself ready, and carefully review the tasks he could volunteer to perform for her. If there was nothing too tedious, or strenuous on the horizon, such as cleaning out the hen house, or bathing the dog, he would suggest chores. Jobs like whitewashing the cellar steps, or the outside toilet were his favourites, but as he had recently done both, volunteering was becoming a risky strategy, the best jobs having all gone.

'Do you want any shopping, Mam?' he asked desperately.

'Oooh yes, love. I need some things from the Co-op, but first you can get your granny's prescription from the chemist's. That'll be a big help. Thank you, love,' she said, and started a shopping list on the envelope containing granny's prescription.

Billy congratulated himself. He didn't like the chemist's shop, but the Co-op was fun. He enjoyed shopping there.

At the chemist's, Arnold Pearce glared at him sourly as Billy took his Granny's prescription from its ink spattered envelope and handed it over to him. Pearce snatched it without a word and stalked off to his pharmacy at the back. A few minutes later Billy left the shop with Granny's tablets, and a strong feeling that Pearce wanted to speak to him for some mysterious reason.

After dropping off granny's pills, he ran to the Co-op. Yvonne's sister, Marlene, was the store's cashier, elevated in a glass kiosk high above the sales floor. Whenever he went there he would wave to Marlene, and wonder what it was like to sit up there above the counters, able to see every transaction. Along with tram driver, it was a job he aspired to. It had celebrity, position and trust; in every respect, an elevated office.

From each of the Co-op's several service counters were strung steel cables, like tightropes, across the ceiling to the cashier's kiosk. Trolleys, with little brass cups hanging beneath them, whirred and clanked to and fro, carrying sales slips and cash from the counter assistants to the cashier. The cashier's job was to unscrew the cup from its trolley, check the sales slip and the payment tendered, and issue the appropriate change. She would put the change in the cup and pull a lever whizzing it back to the sales counter. By this means, customers got the correct change, and a hand written receipt. The cashier's most important task however, was to enter the *Divi,* in a great ledger held in guarded splendour in the glass kiosk. Every customer had a Co-op Dividend number. Every purchase was recorded and the due dividend calculated and entered. When they had saved enough, customers could cash in their Divi and spend it.

Doctor Hadfield was in the Co-op when Billy arrived. Bunty Griffiths, the sales assistant was serving. Billy saw the doctor fold a small piece of paper inside the ten-shilling note he tendered. Bunty blushed, giggling and pretended not to have seen it as she put the ten bob note into the brass cup and fired it off to the cashier's kiosk. Billy watched, and saw Marlene laugh in her elevated office as she read the little love note.

'Where's your hat?' the doctor asked, turning to Billy.

'The cops arrested it,' he replied.

'Arrested it?' queried the doctor.

'Yeah, it's evidence,' he explained.

'Hard luck, old boy. A detective needs a hat.'

'I'm not a detective any more. I've gen it up.'

'Oh, and why have you given it up? I thought you seemed very good at it.'

'We weren't finding enough out, and the police were telling me Mam and Dad, so we've gen it up. And anyway we can't do a lot because they won't tell you anything if you're a kid.'

'What things?' asked Doctor Hadfield.

'Well about the ortosky and stuff,' said Billy.

'The what?'

'The ortosky,' Billy cried. 'I mean, if she was bashed with something instead of falling down like they said. I need to see the ortosky. I've seen it in the movies. It tells you how they were killed, so you can work out how to prove it.'

'That's autopsy,' explained the doctor, smothering a chuckle. 'You mean autopsy - a post mortem examination. I don't even know if there was one.'

'No, but if there was, I'm not allowed to read it cos I'm only eleven.'

The doctor sucked his cheek. 'Yes, hard luck, old bean. I see what you mean.'

'Now an old man like you,' said Billy smiling coyly. 'If you were a detective and not just an assistant doctor, they'd let you see it and all the photos – they take photos at autopsies, to see if there are any bits of silver in the wounds.'

'Bits of silver?' Hadfield queried, his pride more hurt at being thought an "old man" than merely "an assistant doctor".

'Yes bits of clues of what she were bashed with.' Billy was disappointed that the doctor seemed so dim and felt compelled to explain to him. 'If you get bashed with a cricket bat, or a house brick, they can examine your wound under a microscope and see bits of cricket bat. That's how they can tell. It's called forensic.'

'Or even house brick,' volunteered the doctor.

Billy nodded, unsure whether he was mocking him, or not. 'Did they check that with Mrs Loveday?' he asked rhetorically. 'Of course not. They all jumped to the same conclusion as Doctor Greenhow, because he's a big important doctor and they're all scared to argue with him.' He stared up at Hadfield trying to assess any impact his words might be having. 'So, there could be clues in the wound that nobody has seen, or worse still, not even looked for.'

Doctor Hadfield's eyebrows arched up his forehead. 'Wow! You've really thought about this haven't you? I'll tell you what, I'll enquire. I promise you. And if there was an autopsy or any photographs of the wound, I'll take a very close look at them. Oh, and by the way, don't worry, I won't tell anyone you haven't really given up being a detective.'

. . . .

CHAPTER ELEVEN

Kick was at the greenhouse when Billy arrived. Mud caked a vibrant new bruise on his cheek. It made his right eye look drawn on his face with crayons. Football boots, strung on their laces, hung about his neck, smearing mud on to his white school shirt with every move. Billy found himself imagining the howl of dismay from Kick's mother when she saw his damaged face and muddied shirt.

Reading Billy's curious expression, Kick explained that he'd been hit in the face by a ball.

'Hum, football's a tough game,' said Billy.

'This weren't football. It were a dog called Mark,' he said, enigmatically. 'It's old Ma Simpson's dog. Somebody threw a ball for it and it hit me smack in the eye.'

'Ma Simpson?'

'Aye, and d'yer know what? She were a skoyl-teacher in the olden days. She taught Tommy Loveday when he were at skoyl.'

'Gimbals! I thought she was dead.'

'No, she's not dead. Her son is our coach, and he sometimes brings her in his motorbike and sidecar so she can let her dog crap in the goal mouth.'

'Lovely.'

'Once I heard she was Tommy's old skoyl-teacher I asked her about him,. She said he were a wonderful boy.' Kick's eyes rolled mockingly. 'He sounds a right Nancy-boy if you ask me. She started going on about him: never in trouble, never late, never in fights, never naughty, a real little goody-goody, and of course he were brilliant at everything, especially art.'

'Did you ask her about the folder?'

'Of course I did, and that were mistake an' all,' he groaned. 'She went raving on about it. I thought she'd never shurrup. She said all her class had to make 'em, but little goody-goody Tommy Loveday's was perfect, of course.'

'What'd it look like?' Billy asked, eagerly. 'Did it have a bird and lion on it?'

'I don't know about lions and birds. She just said they all made folders about Alexander the Great and his were the best.'

Billy's disappointment was brushed aside by Yvonne's sudden arrival. Breathless and agitated, she burst into the greenhouse. 'Did you see him?' she cried. 'Look, him over there.' She pointed to a thick stand of bushes at the far end of the tangled neglect that had once been a vegetable garden. 'He's gone now, but he was there, I swear it - a man spying on us.'

'Well there's nobody there now.' Billy's gaze swept the rampant dereliction. 'I didn't see him, but I'm sure somebody's been following me around an' all. I sort of feel them watching me all the time, but I never see anybody.'

'Who is? D'yer mean the tramp?' Kick asked. 'He's always hanging around. I bet it's him who was living in that tunnel. And don't forget, it was a tramp who told thee mam when you got bushwhacked,' he reminded Billy.

'So, that means he must be on our side,' Yvonne said, her tone faltering between optimism and uncertainty. 'I mean he's not a hit man in the pay of the killer?'

'No, but he might be the killer,' teased Kick, chuckling evilly.

'Next time I see him I'm going to follow him,' said Billy. 'If it was him who had the medals, I want to talk to him.'

'Just be careful,' warned Yvonne.

'I've got to go,' said Billy. 'I have to be in by seven, or get murdered by my mam again.' Curfew was looming and he was determined not to break it. Relations with his mother had been steadily improving, though his father still ignored him.

*

The following Saturday brought word that the police had removed the notices from the Star woman's cottage. Her furniture could now be sold. The Annabel Loveday case was closed; all loose ends tidied up, or, as Billy saw it, swept under the carpet. The lawyers, the coroner, the police, the establishment, had finished with the old lady. Society was screwing the lid firmly down on her life, and on her death too. Suffering a sudden surge of panic, Billy decided he had to get

107

inside the house for one last look around. And as far as viewing the sideboard was concerned, he had to do that too – no matter what. There was no time to lose.

With two slices of bread and pork dripping in his hand for breakfast, he dashed out of his house and ran to the chapel, stuffing his mouth on the way. He felt sick with panic. He had no idea how he would get inside. As the chapel came into view, his heart soared. A skinny old mare, harnessed to a small float, stood at the chapel's basement entrance. Two men were struggling to get a bulky wardrobe down from the cart.

'Hey, can I help thee carry it?' he blurted out, bulleting up to them, jettisoning the last bits of bread and dripping to free his hands.

The one visible man looked him up and down. 'Tha can if tha wants, but tha'll get nowt for it.'

'I don't want nowt.'

The other man, invisible behind the wardrobe, spoke up. 'Well get hold of a corner sithee. Them as wants to work for nowt will always find willing Mesters.'

Billy grabbed a corner and struggled hard to make his presence felt on their burden. 'What's tha do then?' asked the visible man. 'Are tha like a boy scout or sommat? Is it Bob-a-Job week?'

'Nay he's on the scrounge for a copper or two,' invisible man suggested. 'He thinks we're going to change us mind and give him sommat. I hope he asks thee for it, cos if he asks me he'll get chuff all.'

They drummed and bumped into the chapel's huge basement. Billy gazed around astonished as he crab stepped alongside the tottering wardrobe. Nut-brown furniture of every shape and size stood in tight ranks. Every item bore a label with its lot number written in purple crayon. How would he find the sideboard in this lot?

'To me - to me - to me - and down.'

'Hey, well done young en – now chuff off home before tha gets locked in.'

'Can I have a look round a bit first?'

'No tha can't,' said the invisible man, making an appearance from behind the wardrobe.

'Please mister. My granny's just died and her stuff's in here,' lied Billy, whining pathetically. 'I just wanted to see it one last time before it's all sold off.'

'Tha bloody liar! Thee granny's that old bird who lives on Orchard Road. And I know thee an' all. Thee father's a brickie at Hadfields steelworks.'

'Furnace mason,' Billy corrected indignantly.

'Lerrim have a look round, Farewell. What's it matter to thee? We'll be another ten minutes yet.'

'Farewell? Is that his name?' asked Billy, ridicule seasoning his tone.

'Aye it is. Tha sees, when he were a chabby, his dad were always trying to get rid o' him, so they called him Farewell, hoping he'd buggar off.'

Unmoved, Farewell took off his tweed cap, and ran a palm over his sweating baldhead. 'Hilarious,' he said dryly, adding in stilted monotone. 'Never-before-in-my-culturally-impoverished-life-have-I-heard-such-biting-wit-and-repartee.'

The other man laughed and winked at Billy. 'It's alreight mi-owd. He likes thee. Tha can stay a bit.'

As the two men went back to their cart, Billy turned his attention to the mass of furniture jammed into the great room. The task seemed impossible. How could anybody find anything? Luckily, the auctioneer's need to provide access to each lot for inspection, made the task easier than he had imagined. He was able to squeeze along the narrow gangways and soon found the old lady's sideboard. Its flame mahogany doors burned out from a dim corner like a tiger, casting a rich glow onto the dusty items around it.

A sudden swell of emotion gathered in the pit of Billy's stomach. There it was at last, the old lady's pride and joy; the only thing in her house of any value. How often had she waxed and polished it? Had she, as a young bride, gone with her new husband to buy it from the cabinetmaker all those years ago? Did they run their fingers along its smooth surface and think of the years they would share in its company? Did they imagine the children who would search its shelves for birthday treats?

Two roll front drawers separated the sideboard's lower cupboards from its flat top, where the old lady had kept a vase of wild flowers. He'd been told that the left hand drawer would be the one with a secret compartment. He pulled it out with little effort. As expected, it was empty, making it easier to reach deep inside. Far at the back, a panel gave slightly when he pressed. It felt spring loaded, but did not open. His fingers traced the panel, sliding along its face and edges, searching for something to trip, unlatch, press, or pull. There was nothing: no hooks, no levers, no buttons, no crafty springs, or pendulum locks. He pulled the drawer out further and bent to peer inside to the back. Nothing useful revealed itself. Frustrated he prodded and poked randomly. The panel suddenly popped out with a sigh and gently pushed his fingers away to reveal its secrets. There was enough room inside to hide a book, or even a gold bar, but there were no gold bars, no books, no papers, not even an old rent book. The secret drawer was empty.

. . . .

CHAPTER TWELVE

Saturday lunch from Bottomley's chip shop restored Billy's spirits. As usual, his mother insisted on removing the chips and fishcakes from their newspaper wrapping, and arranging them carefully on oven warmed plates. She served them with bread, butter, and tea at the table, set with a clean white cloth.

After lunch she sent him on numerous errands, punishment, she explained, for running out of the house that morning without telling her where he was going, or when he would return. 'It's not a hotel,' she told him. A well used declaration of hers, which he failed to see as being in any way relevant.

It was mid-afternoon before he finally had the chance to go to the Star Woman's house. He would miss the build up to sports report and the half time scores of the important football matches on the wireless, but this was more important. It could be his last chance to get inside the house for a look round.

Orchard Road was quiet, its pavements deserted. He jogged quickly to the old lady's back yard wall and flipped himself over it, commando style. Thankfully, the back door had not been resealed. The padlock and hasp still hung uselessly from the splintered doorjamb. He pushed the door open and entered.

The ceiling seemed lower than he remembered. The room felt damp and gloomy. It smelled like wet feathers and soot. The stone flags, swept by Yvonne after they had cleared the house, showed the marks of centuries of use; the imprint of the woven coconut fibre matting, the waxy outline of the sideboard, and beside it, a scrubbed patch where the old lady's blood had pooled. Next to the stone sink, the ivy, with its roots outside in the backyard, clambered up the wall. With nobody to clip it, a bright green tendril had reached out to grab the brass tap over the sink, and the narrow slit of window had almost disappeared behind new growth.

Billy ran his fingers through the polished leaves and smiled at the eccentricity of the old woman who had welcomed and groomed the interloper. A grubby twist of blue silk between the shiny green leaves caught his eye. Parting the foliage, he found a brass hook screwed into the wall. The ribbon, looped through a small key, hung from it. He teased it out greedily, his heart pounding. Suddenly he felt panicky and wanted to get away. It was as if discovering the key had changed everything. He had no idea what it would fit, but he knew he had to keep it. It could be evidence; a new clue, but what? He had no idea. Without a further glance he dashed for the door, slammed it shut behind him, and scrambled over the wall, the key gripped firmly in his hand. On the other side of the wall, he found Arnold Pearce, but too late. Gravity was already in charge of his descent. Nothing could prevent him from crashing into him.

They bounced off each other. Pearce's shoulders hit the pavement just a split second before Billy landed on top of him. Clawing hands reached out, grabbing at Billy's collar. They slipped to his jacket sleeves and tank top, scrabbling to grip, stretching the knitted wool to twice its size, before he broke free, shirttail flying, sock dragged to his heel. Pearce was yelling and struggling to regain his feet. 'Come back here! What've you stolen? Come back you little sod. I'll kill you when I get hold of you. What did you find? Come back.'

Billy was running madly. Pearce was up and after him, coat flying, trilby hat skimming into the road. Billy was terrified. He fled in utter panic. Pearce was so wild with fury, he had no care for who might see him chasing a small boy through the streets, screaming at him.

As he rounded the corner of the street, the Co-op shop came into view. Billy thought of Yvonne's sister Marlene, perched high up in her glass cashier's kiosk. In that moment, she seemed the perfect ally. She was bossy and in charge of the shop. He felt sure she would not allow Pearce to tear him limb from limb in the Co-op without some protest, even if it was only don't mix red meat with boiled ham on the same counter. He dived for the Co-op's door. Pearce followed, hard on his heels, breathless and shouting.

Yvonne was at the dairy counter, a full string bag of groceries in front of her. She was paying her bill. With everyone

112

else in the shop, she had turned, alarmed as the door burst open and Billy and Pearce skidded into view. She saw Pearce lunge at Billy, dragging him back by the collar. He was reaching out trying to grab something from Billy's hand, and she spotted the loop of scruffy blue ribbon. As she tried to work out what was going on Billy tossed the ribbon to her. She caught it, and stared blankly at the little key. Pearce shoved Billy aside, and followed the key. Yvonne saw him coming towards her. His face was red with fury and exertion. He was snarling like an animal. She popped the key into the little brass cup into which the counter assistant had just placed her payment and sales note. Bunty Griffiths saw her moment of glory arrive and seized upon it. She screwed the brass cup to its cradle, pulled the lever, and sent it rattling across the store, high on its wire above the counters. It shot across the cheeses, over the dry goods and into the kiosk where Marlene, seated in her splendid isolation, waited to receive it.

Pearce sagged miserably. He knew the game was up. Whatever Billy had found in the Star Woman's house, was now out of reach. Feeling stupid and caught out, he turned to leave, casting a last furious glare at Billy on the way. 'I'll get you,' he snarled. 'I'll have the police on you.'

*

'Can I stay out late tonight?'
'No.'
'I have to.'
'No.'
'But it's important and I won't stay out too late.'
'No.'
'I have to see the vicar.'
'What?'
'I have to see the vicar.'
'We're Catholics, Billy.'
'But he's the editor of the life story she was writing. I've got an appointment with him. I did it properly; I rang him up and everything, but it means I can't get back home until about eight.'
'No.'

*

Half an hour later Billy was walking up the gravel drive to St Mary's vicarage. It had been a tough job wearing down his mother, but she had eventually relented.

The vicarage was a large, grey house with gothic stone mullioned windows. A cluster of ornate chimneys poked out of its grey tiled roof. High gabled attics with tiny windows, harked back to an age of servants and grooms. Standing in large gardens, surrounded by mature trees and overgrown shrubs, it seemed in need of some urgent care and attention.

At the front door, Reverend Hinchcliffe greeted him stiffly. When Billy had telephoned him earlier, he had expressed reluctance about a meeting, and now, on his front door step, his beaming smile faded as soon as Billy announced himself.

'Come in. I'm sorry, but I don't much welcome this meeting, young man,' he said, noting Billy's apologetic shrug.

Trapped in his studious gaze, Billy waited nervously, unsure what he should do next. The heavy lead glazed door clattered shut behind him, setting the vicar walking into the heart of his house. Billy followed along a wide entrance hall paved with mock mediaeval tiles.

'I can only give you a few minutes. Tomorrow is Sunday. However, I'm not sure I can fill even a few minutes, knowing as little as I do of the events you described to me on the telephone.'

'It's very nice,' said Billy.

The vicar peered at him over gold wire framed spectacles. 'What is?'

'Your house - it's very nice. It must be very old. It's just like my school.'

Reverend Hinchcliffe was in his late fifties, tall and slim. He had the bearing of a military man. His bald, freckled head seemed too large for his body. His face was cherubic with cheeks that seemed to be saving food for the winter. His small mouth had probably smiled so much professionally, that it could no longer relax. It smiled now, even though the vicar was far from happy.

'It was built about 1885. So, not that old really: though the architect clearly wanted people to think it was. It implies authority I suppose. You can be forgiven for being fooled.' He

114

led Billy into a large room full of clutter and papers. Books lay around everywhere, some open facing up with pebbles weighting down their pages, some open face down, others stacked with book marks poking out of them. 'My study; it's rather untidy I'm afraid. Mrs Corbert never comes in here; not that I forbid it. The good woman simply refuses to enter. She tells me I'm hopeless - beyond care.' He sighed and looked about the room as if trying to remember why he was there. 'So, what can I do for you, Master – err - William Perks?'

'I was wondering, sir, what an editor does.'

Reverend Hinchcliffe looked surprised, and inflated his cheeks briefly, as if playing a trumpet. 'Well that's an odd thing to ask. Why is it so important to you?'

'You were the editor of Mrs Loveday's book. I wondered what that means.'

'Still am, my boy. I haven't finished. Mind you I don't suppose I ever will now.'

'Why not?' asked Billy.

'I enquired at the police station,' said the vicar shaking his big freckled head. 'They say the house was cleared and all the papers and things destroyed – burned. The manuscript was in four notebooks. I had edited three of them already, but I've not even begun the fourth. Never will now. There's no point without the others.'

'You have a fourth notebook?' gasped Billy.

The vicar eyed him curiously. 'Yes, why do you ask? Have you seen the others?'

'I have them,' said Billy. 'They were going to be burned, but I saved them.'

The vicar's cherubic face seemed to test several expressions before settling for quiet satisfaction. 'I think you and I should have some tea, or perhaps you'd like cherryade?' he said, suddenly warming to his visitor.

'Cherryade, please.'

'Mrs Corbert is not here so we must fend manfully.'

Billy took this to mean that he should follow the vicar to wherever fending manfully was to take place. It turned out to be to a large kitchen whose dark walls were hung with pots, pans

115

and strange gadgets, which to Billy looked like instruments of torture.

'Nip, snip, shorten, liquidise, rephrase, smooth out, annotate, discard, rearrange, check, rectify, strike out, revise,' said the vicar, delivering cherryade with all the sombre ceremony of communion wine. 'The editor's role. I read and ask myself, is this comfortable? Does it sit well? Is it true to the truth as I know it?'

Billy watched him and listened intently, then downed his cherryade in one.

'People can be funny about the truth,' said the vicar, tapping the side of his nose with a finger. 'Truth and roses have thorns about them – eh?'

Noisily hoovering the last dregs of cherryade, Billy dismissed the vicar's question and dived in with one of his own. 'Did you ever mention her memoirs to Mr Pearce? D'you know him – the boss at the chemists?'

The vicar smiled, his head nodding as if on springs. 'Ah ha! Mr Pearce,' he sang quietly, pacing his gloomy kitchen and stirring his teacup. 'You know what the Greeks said? "Truth lies at the bottom of a well." Believe me, Billy, there are many who would want it to be left there.'

. . . .

CHAPTER THIRTEEN

Billy sulked like a coiled hosepipe. It was the last Saturday before Whitsuntide. The city's pavements were bustling and his mother had bustled him on them. They alighted from the tram at the Cathedral and dodged past the Cutlers' Hall into the crowds of shoppers. Unnoticed, the tramp followed them. For over an hour, he watched as Billy trailed sullenly behind his mother from store to store.

Billy was taking part in, what he hoped, was the last expedition to be togged out for Whitsuntide. He was struggling to be on his best behaviour. He needed to keep his mother sweet, because this year, he was desperate for long trousers. He should be out of shorts by now. He was no longer a little kid. Nothing must upset her and ruin his chance of getting them. His pals had been strutting about in longs for almost a year. He would die of shame if he did not get them too.

He needn't have worried. At Stewart and Stewart's opposite the Peace Gardens, the young salesman was pushing long trousers. His faultless line in sales chat and flattery, so impressed Mrs Perks, that Billy was *blazored and flannelled* by an expert in record time. Pink and flustered, Mrs Perks thanked the young man and paid for the long trousers. Billy's heart was singing. With new, manly garb in paper bags, he skipped out of the shop and followed his mother.

As they battered through the crowds of shoppers on The Moor, Billy's path was suddenly barred. He peered over his packages into a pair of startled eyes set in a grimy, scarred face. A grubby tramp in an old RAF great coat and balaclava stood before him, seemingly frozen in panic. His face looked oddly familiar, even allowing for the scars.

Billy clumsily stepped right to get round him. The tramp moved to his left at the same moment, and the pair jinked to and fro, like clumsy dancers, until the man broke away and ran off through the crowd. He headed for a fence made of old doors and

117

floor boards surrounding a bomb crater where a department store had once stood. Finding a loose board, he squeezed through and vanished. Billy ran to the fence and bobbed along it, peering through splintered gaps and old keyholes, down to the rubble and slimy green water in the bomb crater. There was no sign of the tramp.

'Come back here, I don't want you getting lost,' his mother called testily. 'And don't get those parcels on that mucky fence. For goodness sake, have you no sense at all?'

He rejoined his mother, his head alive with questions. A shiver of unease shook him. Since getting off the tram, he'd felt as if he was being followed. Was it the tramp? Was this the man, whom Sergeant Burke had said, was sleeping in the tunnel? He remembered the old cardboard box of belongings and the newspaper cutting about Annabel Loveday. Had they belonged to *this* man? If so what was his connection to Annabel? Had he killed her? It was obvious he had recognised Billy, otherwise why had he looked so shocked, and run away like that? Who was he?

Yvonne had said she'd seen a tramp watching them at the greenhouse. Kick Morley was certain he had. But who was he, and why was he following them? Billy knew he would have to find out. Again he regretted that he had not taken more notice of the things he had found in the tunnel. Was one of the medals he had seen a DFM? He hadn't a clue. How can you find out what a DFM looks like? He didn't know. Do medals have labels on the back of them to remind people which is which? "This is your Victoria Cross, this is your DFM." He did not know. Detectiving, he told himself ruefully, involved more brains and hard work than he had expected.

'Do they have medals in the museum Mam? Can we go?'
'Don't be stupid.'

*

They found the photograph pinned to the MOM board. Kick had been the first to see it when he had arrived at the greenhouse. 'I didn't touch it, because – err … '

The others waited, wondering what gem of forensic science he was about to reveal.'

'... I don't know why.'

'It looks like some fly boys playing cards,' said Yvonne, not touching it either.

'I've seen it before,' Billy told them. 'It was in the tunnel.'

'Does it say who they are?' Yvonne asked, plucking it from the board.

'No, I looked when I was in the tunnel,' said Billy.

'Well it does now,' Yvonne told him. 'Bob Hinchcliffe, Tommy Loveday, Frenchie Cadell, Noll Pearce and Willy Glover, nineteen forty-one. It says Charlie Leedham took it.

Billy grabbed it and read, flipping several times from the faces in the photograph to the names pencilled on its reverse. 'Bob, that must be Robert Hinchcliffe, the vicar's son. He look's just like him.'

Kick and Yvonne leaned in to see the face in the photograph. 'That's Pearce, Yvonne said pointing. 'Noll must be his nick name. I don't know the others.'

'Me neither,' Kick said.

'I think I do,' Billy said cryptically. 'That one there might be the tramp.' He pointed to a face in the photograph, then flipped it to read the name. 'Frenchie Cadell.'

'Frenchie Cadell. I've never heard of him.'

'Well it looks a bit like him, but he's different here - all cleaned up like that. He's got burn scars now and he's scruffy.'

Yvonne, pointed to the two remaining laughing faces. 'If it is him, does that make this one Willy Glover, or ..?'

'So which's Tommy Loveday?' Kick interrupted.

'I don't know, but if I'm right about the tramp, Tommy must be one of these two.'

'I thought he might be in it – the tramp. I thought it might prove it was him that's been sleeping in the tunnel.'

'Is he helping us?' asked Yvonne. 'I mean, he's given us this photograph, and he even gave us their names on the back. He must be helping us.'

'It looks like it, but why?' asked Kick.

Billy sighed gloomily. 'I've gotta go. My curfew's coming up.'

*

119

Invisible in the gloaming and the flaking wreckage of an old garden shed, the tramp watched the friends file out of the greenhouse. Meeting Billy in the town centre had been a close call; a bad mistake. He would have to be more careful. It was not yet time. They mustn't know him yet. There were still too many unanswered questions.

*

As Billy rounded the corner of his house his mother appeared and grabbed him by the shoulders. Shoving him firmly against the house wall, she began brushing down his jacket and smoothing his hair with her palms. Then, glancing shiftily at the house window, she spat on her handkerchief and began wiping his face with it. 'The Vicar is here,' she hissed. 'He wants to talk to you. We're Catholics, Billy - for God's sake. What will Father MacDonagh say if he finds out? What've you done now?'

With difficulty, balancing cup, plate, paper serviette and a pyramid of scones, the Reverend Hinchcliffe rose from his chair as Billy was ushered into his presence. 'Billy, my dear chap. I hope you don't mind me coming like this,' he apologised, trying to ignore the excited little dog bouncing around Billy's legs. 'I waited until I thought you would have eaten, but I'm told your father is working nights. I do apologise, do you mind me coming when he's not here?'

Catching the bouncing dog and easing under the table, Billy shook his head. 'I'm glad, sir. It's very nice to see you.'

'More tea, vicar?' asked Mrs Perks.

Billy giggled and couldn't stop. "More tea, vicar," was a family in-joke used by his mother, should Billy or his father accidentally burp at table. Realising her error, Mrs Perks was herself now fighting not to join her son in nervous giggling.

The vicar was puzzled, but delighted to be among such cheerful people. 'Yes please,' he enthused, 'but – err - no more scones I think.'

After tea and pleasantries, Reverend Hinchcliffe at last broached the topic that had brought him. It was no surprise to Billy, but his mother listened intently, her jaw sagging occasionally as her young son thrust and parried with the vicar on seemingly equal terms.

'The other three books are safe, Sir,' Billy assured the vicar. 'I swear it. And when we know who killed Mrs Loveday, I promise you I will give them to the police, but not before. If I did it now they might just throw 'em away because they don't think she was murdered.'

'But my dear young friend, I've read them, and I can assure you they do not suggest a killer, nor even vaguely a possible motive.'

'You read them before they had pages torn out?'

'Ah yes, the pages torn out. Well - oh dear – that is a shame of course.'

'Book three has pages missing; possibly something about a Distinguished Flying Medal. They missed a word or two. Can you remember what it said?'

The vicar shuffled, clearly discomforted by the question. 'I must ask you to believe me, Billy, it is not what you're looking for.'

Billy had found pencil and paper. 'Can you say what it said?'

'I must be going. I have much to do. It's a big day tomorrow - a very big day.'

'Does it say anything about lies and a medal? Does it mention Mr Pearce?'

'It is not what you're looking for Billy, I can assure you. That is all I will say. Now I'd like you to return the books to me for safe keeping. They belong together.'

'He can't,' said Billy's mother, her sudden interjection surprising the vicar. 'I'm sorry Reverend, but my son can't do that. They were about to be burned, but he saved them. I'm sure you'll agree, upon reflection, that he is their rightful custodian, until he hands them over to the police. He's made it quite clear that he values and respects them. I think you and I can both feel that they are safe. However, perhaps you'll agree that the fourth book, which you have, should join the others?'

Brilliant, thought Billy. Go for it Mam.

The vicar frowned thoughtfully and studied his shoes. His small, pursed mouth seemed to be chewing some of the food Billy suspected he kept in his cheeks. Silence hung on the air. 'I can't quite do entirely that,' he said, straining to be agreeable.

'But you *are* right, Mrs Perks. The books should be given to the authorities, but not until we know they will be protected. I give you my firm promise to protect the fourth book.'

Billy sagged, disappointed, and tossed his paper and pencil aside. His mother seemed satisfied and began rescuing the vicar from his teacup and the plate.

*

Marlene Sparkes tilted her nose and sneered loftily as she approached Billy outside the pikelet shop. 'I'm reporting you to the Co-op committee,' she said sourly. 'You've no right using Co-op property for your silly games. That cash carrier is not a toy. You could have broken it.'

'You mess with it,' Billy huffed. 'I've seen Doctor Hadfield send you love letters.'

Marlene blushed and shuffled on her high heels. 'That was business. Anyway, here's your key, and don't let me catch you fooling with it again. You need to learn how to behave you do. You and our Yvonne are making us a laughing stop.'

'Stock. It's a laughing stock, not a stop. Trams have stops not laughs.'

Marlene gaped at him, her expression mixing alarm and revulsion, as if he were sloughing off his skin. 'You're weird, you are, Billy Perks,' she said with a shudder. 'Well anyway don't do it. You'll just get into bother. I've told Fergal not to encourage you.'

'Fergal?' hooted Billy.

'It's Doctor Hadfield to you. And you needn't think he'll be helping you anymore, not if he knows what's good for him.'

It was easy to guess what potent influences Marlene could bring to bear upon a spirited young man like Doctor Hadfield: Fergal. Her threat was not an empty one. It seemed more than likely that the forensic advice and adult access that the Doctor had provided would come to an abrupt end. Billy's face darkened with disappointment. Marlene shrugged, concerned to see his response. 'Well really Billy, you'll just get into trouble, or be disappointed in the end,' she cooed, as if doing him a big favour. 'Oh, and there *are* no photographs of the wound. So you can forget that too.' She spun on her tottering heels and swished away, honey coloured curls tossing on coral pink padded shoulders.

*

Whitsuntide: first to Mass at Saint Joseph's, then down South Road to Saint Mary's to join the proddys at their whit walk. Youth bands tuned up, smart Alecs played bits of Colonel Bogey until clipped on the ear by a scoutmaster. Huge, silken banners were unsheathed from storage and hoisted in the breeze. Shimmering tapestries of saints and martyrs, billowing proudly, cracking their gold tasselled cords like whips until brought under control. Solemn faced men slotted banner poles into shiny leather holsters, as the parade noisily jostled into place. Pretty little girls, the annual crop of May Queens, Rose Queens and Sunday School Queens, appeared in their regalia to head the march, their sheepish maids of honour and blushing page boys, shepherded into place to carry colourful trains of made-over curtains and ribbons. Then the bands struck up, uncertainly at first. They chased one another for a bar or two, before falling into key and tempo, as the parade moved off.

Billy swung his arms, tripping into step behind a particularly asymmetrical troop of the Boys' Brigaders. It was more of a stroll than a march. Along the way, folk gathered on the pavements, waving and clapping. Billy cheerfully acknowledged them and pulled back his shoulders in proud imitation of the be-medalled old soldiers up front. Occasionally people stepped off the kerb and joined in, others dropped out after a token few hundred yards. Box Brownies snapped, and whistles sounded amid the cheers of friends honouring friends.

Arnold Pearce was amongst them, gaily clapping like the rest until he spotted Billy. Then his face darkened. Beneath his new blazer and long trousers, Billy shivered, eyeing Pearce warily. Suddenly he lost sight of him and spun round searching the happy faces, but he was not there. Stretching up he searched around from one side of the road to the other, until he sensed him at his shoulder.

'You've got some explaining to do, my lad.'

'What d'yer mean?'

123

'You dare go near Miss Burkinshaw's door step again and by God I'll have you. Just who the hell do you think you are, asking questions about me and that spotless lady?'

'I'm sorry, I didn't know she was spotless – or that she'd get so upset.'

'No, well you don't know anything do you? You've been asking all sorts of questions about me and now you've started folk talking. You'd better keep your snotty nose out of my business in future, Perks. I shall be speaking to your father the very first chance I get. I shall tell him that if you don't stop it, you'll be in serious bother. I'll go to the police.'

As quickly as he had arrived, he vanished, leaving a gap in the parade's ranks, which Kick Morley immediately filled.

'Chuffin eck! What did he want? He looked like he were going to scutch thee reight then.'

Billy took heart from his friend's arrival. 'He was telling me off for asking old Burkinshaw if she were shagging him,' he quipped, trying to sound cool, though not totally sure what shagging was.

'Aye well, that'd do it I guess,' observed Kick.

*

In his hideout, the tramp listened to the distant drumming bands. His accidental meeting with Billy still worried him, and he tossed and turned on his mattress of newspapers and cardboard. The boy was so young, he thought. Too young to realise the danger he was stirring up.

*

Whit walks brought dusty churches out to smell the spring flowers. Congregations streamed towards the city's parks from every direction. Victorian bandstands and gazebos thronged with civic worthies: councillors, magistrates, and officials, their medals and chains of office glittering in the spring sunlight. Even the occasional MP, a rare sight in any community, might be spotted amongst the municipal fur and feathers. Tented altars and pulpits were raised. Scoutmasters, bandsmen, schoolteachers and clergy, jostled their charges into position, breaking off occasionally to mutter, one-two - one-two - one - into powerful, crackling microphones.

124

In the parks, colourful snakes of happy people merged into groups gathered on their standard-bearers. The brash discordance of the Boy Scouts and Boys' Brigade bands gave way to the velvet harmonies of colliery and steelworks' bands. Hymns were sung, and vicars' voices crackled from ex-army loud speakers whose huge microphones picked up every sound muttered, sung, coughed, sneezed or farted within fifty feet. You could legally stand on the grass on Whit Sunday, even if it said keep off the grass, which of course it always did.

Beyond the singing and the city dignitaries in their suits and regalia, the church showed itself alive and well. It showed itself at ease with the people, and vital and relevant.

'Hey, you got me into trouble.'

Billy turned to find Doctor Hadfield behind him. 'I did? How? Oh you mean Marlene?'

'I've been told not to encourage you,' he said winking.

'That's a pity,' said Billy. 'I was going to ask you who visits the sick people in their houses, is it mostly you, or old Doctor Greenhow?'

'Who do you think?' Hadfield laughed ruefully. 'Me, of course. I'm the hired help. I do all the house calls except for a few of his private patients.'

'Was Mrs Loveday a private patient?'

'No, she was a special old friend. The Doctor always treated her, himself.' It sounded odd, thought Billy, to hear him say, "The Doctor", with such hushed deference. 'Why?'

'Why what?'

'Why did he look after her instead of giving her to you like the other – not posh people?'

'I don't know. He took care of her during her pregnancy and I guess they just became good friends.'

They marched on a few steps in silence before Billy spun round to the doctor again. 'He can't have done. He was in the Royal Navy when she was pregnant. He told me he didn't come out until Christmas after the Great War.'

'No, that can't be right. I'm sure he told me himself. Believe me, he doesn't make mistakes, but I can check his old patient records. He's a real stickler for recording everything – every little detail.' He laughed and nudged Billy's elbow. 'It's one of our knotty issues. He tells me off because I don't record every little detail like he does.'

'Am I allowed to ask you one more question?

'Afraid not,' he replied glumly. 'And especially if you want to know if I've seen the autopsy photographs. I couldn't possibly tell you that I had a really good look at them yesterday.'

Not the sharpest knife in the drawer, Billy was unsure whether the doctor was joking or not. 'Marlene said there weren't any,' he said, giving him a sidelong glance. 'The thing is, I've got this thing. It's like a silver thing, like it's come off a silver thing, but not the toasting fork thing. I just thought if ...'

The doctor was grimacing as if in pain. 'Don't worry,' he interrupted. 'I checked it out for you. I did say I would, but I'm afraid I didn't see anything promising. There's nothing about the wound indicative of anything unusual. Look, I will keep doing my bit if you want, old bean. To tell the truth I enjoy a good mystery. Just don't tell Marlene.' He gave Billy's shoulder a friendly punch.

*

Whitsunday afternoon was the turn of the Catholics. They began their Whit walks as the Protestants' band music faded. Powerful shire horses, loaned by British Railway's, and tacked out with brasses, flowers and ribbons, drew drays up to the gates of Saint Joseph's church. Men nailed old school benches to the floats. Girls and nuns added more ribbons and flowers to the manes and tails of the horses. Then, with a stony-faced nun on each float, children from the catholic school climbed aboard. The draymen clucked at the big horses and set them off towards the city centre, down over Commonside's cobbles and past the chest hospital where the TB patients waved from the windows.

More children and parents, and dray loads of cheering kids from Saint Vincent's and other catholic schools and churches joined them along the way. They headed for Norfolk Park. There a great, open air alter awaited them, beneath a tasselled canopy that billowed and flapped in the breeze. Priests, resplendent in golden vestments, celebrated High Mass, struggling with microphones, incense, and wine. In the hot sunshine a beer tent was made ready for a busy afternoon; the cheerful chink of bottles and glasses, competing for the congregation's attention with the interminable Latin responses of the High Mass. Finally, hopes rose when the priest faced the congregation and recited the words, "Ete Missa est," which Billy's uncle had told him was Latin for, go and stuff your face with ale and pork pies.

*

Granny Smeggs fell asleep when Billy and Yvonne visited her to review their evidence and acquaint her with their latest notes. Even as they placed them on her table, her silver head was drooping. Billy nudged her and complained. She groaned, claiming she was only resting her eyes. After several attempts to keep her awake, they gave up, repacked their evidence into its brown paper carrier bag and tip toed to the cottage door.

'You could be wrong about the time she was killed,' Granny said suddenly, her eyes tightly shut. 'It didn't have to be early in the morning like you said. It could have been anytime after about eight-o-clock.'

Yvonne gaped in disbelief. 'But she had her nightdress on and her hair down.'

'Yes but she couldn't afford the coal, lovie. She often went to bed about eight to keep warm and save the fire.' She shivered theatrically. 'Now put some coal on before you go. I'm fair clemmed. It'd freeze soap to a badger in here.'

Billie placed coals carefully around the brightest part of the fire, his face tingling in the red glow. 'Gran?' he whispered tentatively, his gaze fixed on the glowing fire. 'Did Mrs Loveday have another baby – later - after Tommy?'

'Billie - shush!' she said, grabbing his upper arms tightly and turning him to face her. 'You're to say no more about that,' she urged him. 'D'you hear me? Don't ever mention that again.'

Billie nodded, startled by her intense reaction. He had no doubt whatsoever about the answer it indicated.

*

Enquiries at a nearby garage established that the car jack handle used to prize the padlock off the back door was similar to a type supplied in the tool kit of a Triumph car. Arnold Pearce owned a Triumph Mayflower saloon. Billy said this proved

Pearce had broken into the house, but Kick Morley disagreed. He said it was of a commonly used type, made by a firm called Lake and Elliot. Dozens of cars had similar jack handles.

Billy kicked a pebble despairingly, hurting his foot. 'Well I think we should check his car to see if his jack handle is missing,' he grumbled, hopping on one leg.

'How do we do that? He always parks it near his shop window so he can keep an eye on it.'

'Well we could creep into his garage at night and ...'

'No-no, I'm not doing that, but I know what we could do, and this is better still,' Kick interrupted eagerly. 'We could create a diversion, like they do in the films. You know, make something happen to distract him while we open his car and check the tool kit.'

'What sort of diversion?' asked Billy, warming to the idea.

'We can make some shelves fall over in the chemists, and while he's picking up all the jars and pills and stuff we can nip round and check the motor.'

Billy shook his head doubtfully. 'But he'll see us. The shop door bell will give us away.'

Yvonne groaned despairingly. 'You two are barmy.'

'Oh yeah, and what would you do, oh Miss Mighty Knickers of Knowledge? There's a chuffin bell on the shop door.'

'You don't need to go in to the shop, you wazzock! You don't need your stupid diversion either,' she cried. 'Anyway it's always full of mothers and babies and old folks. Do you really want to go smashing it up with toddlers and babies around. It's a barmy idea - you'd be locked up in a minute.'

'So what *do* we do then?'

'Just let a tyre down of course,' she told them. 'If we pinch the valve thingy so he can't pump it up again, he'll have to use the spare wheel – so he'll need the jack.'

For a second or so the boys gazed around trying to pretend this was not a brilliant idea, but found her logic flawless. 'Well I suppose we could try that,' Billy admitted grudgingly. 'I mean, if it'll stop you moaning on about it.'

Yvonne was furious. 'You're pathetic you two,' she cried, and stormed off. The lads watched the greenhouse door slam behind

128

her and flinched, preparing themselves for a shower of shattered glass. Luckily it did not come.

'Tha just never knows where tha stands with lasses,' Kick observed ruefully.

·········

CHAPTER FOURTEEN

Yvonne made room for Billy to join her on a crowded stone bench seat. They had met after school in one of the city's main Victorian squares, to do research. As time was short, they decided to split up and meet back at the stone seat later. They wanted to find out everything they could about Tommy Loveday's death in nineteen-forty-six. Yvonne would check the city library archive, while Billy went to Kemsley House, the offices of The Sheffield Telegraph, and The Star, newspapers.

Kemsley House overlooks Coles Corner, a busy city junction and favourite meeting place. It is a fine, Portland Stone building, whose clock had been watched by generations of doodling solicitors' clerks, bankers, and shop workers in the airless city offices around it. Billy pushed his way in through the glazed doors in its colonnaded entrance with all the confidence of a visiting celebrity. A woman receptionist, busily typing some document of little importance, ignored him. After what seemed a long time Billy coughed. With practiced ease, the receptionist continued to ignore him. Undeterred Billy coughed again, this time delivering his "Aaahem" with theatrical emphasis.

'Boots the chemist is across the road, young man,' the receptionist said icily, her typing fingers not pausing for a second. 'If you need cough syrup, I'm sure they'll have it.'

'I don't want none,' said Billy. 'I want to see the archive, *please*. I came all the way from Walkley on the tram.'

Lifting her glassy gaze, she swept it over him like a snake considering its next meal. 'But you're a boy,' she said, with deep distaste. 'Boys are not permitted to see the archive.'

'I'm sorry Miss, I thought we are. I've heard about it at school,' he lied.

'Do you have a letter from your headmaster? You must be accompanied by an adult, and have a letter from your school explaining the nature of your research.'

She has won, thought Billy miserably. No matter what he said, he knew she would trump it with another rule. Swinging round to leave empty-handed, he found himself looking up into a pair of sparkling green eyes set deeply in a man's weather beaten face.

'Archive eh? What're you after, lad; the most goals in a season, Yorkshire's best knock against Lancashire? I could tell you that now off the top of my head if you like.'

'No sir, I want to know who killed Tommy Loveday, cos I think the same one killed his mother an' all.'

The green eyes widened and their owner took a step back. 'Wow, old Annabel! Are you the kid who says ..?' He paused and studied Billy's face for a second or two. 'Yeah, I've heard about you, haven't I? I bet you're the kid who says she was murdered, aren't you? I thought about doing a piece on you, but I got side tracked.'

Billy gazed back at him willing him to help. 'It's a real mystery,' he said, 'I've got some clues, but I need to check out some things, cos having proof and just knowing sommat aren't the same thing ...'

'Huh, tell me about it,' groaned the man. 'If I could write what I know, instead of only what I can prove, things'd be a damn sight different in this city. How old are you?'

'Eleven,' replied Billy, adding hopefully, 'twelve next.'

'Really, twelve next you say – fancy that,' the man seemed surprised. 'Come with me, son.' He laid a hand on Billy's shoulder and started him towards a flight of stairs up into the building's clamorous heart. 'I think you and me can help each other. What's your name?'

*

The following morning Yvonne came to Billy's house, bringing the results of her research at the City's central library, neatly set out in her notebook. At the Perks' dining table, they compared their findings, ate toast smeared with pork dripping, and drank tea. By the time they had finished they could show that on that same day in October nineteen-forty-six, when Tommy Loveday had been found drowned under the Old Tilt's water wheel, Arnold Pearce was seen limping along South Road,

131

Walkley, dishevelled and muddy, and with one shoe missing. According to one newspaper, people said that he looked as though he'd been in a fight. A beat bobby had questioned him briefly, but left him to find his own way home.

Back then, Arnold Pearce lived with his mother, in a back-to-back house in a steep street, in the shadow of Saint Joseph's convent. Billy made a mental note to visit the area and ask around. Pearce, with his pinstripe suit and white-collar job, had always stood out like a pie on a coffin, amongst the poverty-stricken residents of Daniel Hill Street's claustrophobic courtyards. Even though five years had now passed, someone was sure to remember seeing Poshy Pearce with a shoe missing. It would be a sight to stick in the memory of poor folk, used to sharing the same washhouse and lavatory.

In Yvonne's notes, Billy found she had entered a reminder to the effect that, because Tommy Loveday was killed that very same day, the police should have been extra careful to record everything. 'You're right, Wy,' he agreed, thumbing through her notes. 'I bet they even recorded what the beat copper said to Pearce. It'd be in his notebook. I bet they keep all them old notebooks in a room somewhere.'

Yvonne chewed her lip thoughtfully. 'If you want to go and see Sergeant Burke again, you know that I'll come with you,' she offered loyally.

Billy sniffed cockily. 'I'm not scared of him,' he crowed. 'I'll go and see him anytime I like.' It was almost true, Billy thought on reflection. Confronting Sergeant Burke was not a cheering prospect, but it was certainly better than sitting in the old greenhouse waiting to be slaughtered by a mysterious killer.

Yvonne's notes mentioned a newspaper article about Pearce receiving the DFM, and a photograph of the award ceremony. Billy wished he had seen it. 'It's a pity you can't copy stuff with a camera or something,' he said. 'It'd be great for people who go to see archives and stuff to be able to make copies of it.'

'Well you'll have to invent sommat then,' she teased.

'Maybe I will.' He added inventor to the list of jobs he'd like to do when he left school. 'What else did it say?'

'It mentioned flight sergeant Jacque Cadell, a volunteer pilot from Canada, missing in action. It said they gave Pearce the medal because he had tried to save him.'

'My mam'll be back soon, she's only gone to Liptons. Let's scarper before she comes. I don't want her giving me a load of errands.'

'Aren't you going to wash these?' Yvonne enquired about their teacups.

'Nah, they weren't washed before. I'll just shove 'em back in the sink.'

'Ergh! Did you gimme a mucky cup, you filthy pig?' she cried, hoping earnestly that his mother had been the last to use the cup he had given her, and not his dog, or even worse, Billy.

Billy ignored the rebuke, concentrating instead on her notes. 'I'm going to see old Burke. He'll know what was recorded about Pearce and his shoe. You go and check out Doc Hadfield. Is he still sniffing round your Marlene? If he is ask him to find out what Tommy's injuries were. He can look it up in the Post Mortem records. But don't let your Marlene know, she'll stop his chocolate.'

'But that was five years ago. He'll never find out anything now.'

'Yes he will. I know all about ortosk - err- autopsies. They keep records forever and ever. I found that out yesterday.'

'What do you mean she'll stop his chocolate? What chocolate?'

*

'Sergeant, hold that boy!' Sergeant Burke boomed from his office door as Billy shuffled into the police station. The desk sergeant grabbed Billy and pulled him through the counter hatch into the main office area.

'What's up?' Billy gasped.

'Oh little Mr Innocent - butter wouldn't melt in his mouth,' sneered the desk sergeant, as Sergeant Burke stalked towards them.

'I'm glad you're here,' Sergeant Burke growled, knotting his eyebrows in a dark scowl. 'We've had another complaint about you, my lad. Haven't we Tom?'

'Yes we have, sarj, and it's a very serious one this time.'

Billy stared fearfully at his old enemy the desk sergeant, who was clearly enjoying the situation. 'I haven't done nowt,' he protested.

'Have you seen any medals, Billy?' Sergeant Burke asked him sternly.

'The young bloke asked me that already,' Billy huffed.

'You see, Tom. There he goes again,' Sergeant Burke explained to his younger colleague. 'You ask him a straight question and you get an evasive answer. He'll make a damn good politician - Prime Minister even. He never gives you a straight answer.'

'Well he did,' protested Billy. 'He told my mam I was helping him, and he asked me to look out for them.' He stared back at them defiantly, wondering what was going on.

'Oh yes, lad. I'm sure that's the absolute truth, but, watch my lips: have - you - seen - any - medals? Now answer that question, Just say yes or no.'

'When?'

'When! What do you mean when?' hooted Burke.

'When do you want to know about?' Billy explained reasonably. 'I saw some medals last week on the Whit walk. I saw some last Poppy Day at the Cenotaph. I've seen my granddad's medals in our sideboard drawer. I just mean - when?'

Sergeant Burke turned to the desk sergeant and blew a sigh of frustration. Turning back to Billy, he leaned slowly down towards him until his nose almost touched Billy's. 'Right, young man. I'm going to spell it out for you so that no matter what you do you can't fail to understand the question.' He fixed Billy with a cold, determined stare. 'Some medals have been stolen from a house at Dore. The owner has suggested ...'

'You mean Poshy Pearce, don't you?' Billy interrupted. 'I knew it'd be him. He lives in a posh house at Dore.'

'It doesn't matter who it is,' snapped Sergeant Burke. 'I'm asking you the same question that I'll be asking other slippery characters an' all.'

134

'I've not nicked his medals, and I'm fed up of him trying to get me into trouble. I'm going to tell my dad. My dad'll bash his brains in.'

'Well if he does, he'll be in one of my cells before you can say, up the Owls.'

The three stood motionless, staring at each other, fixed by the tension between them. The desk sergeant broke the silence. 'What did you want anyway?'

'Nowt! I'm going home,' Billy said, testily. 'All you do here is yell at me and say I did sommat what I didn't do. I'm trying to find somebody who killed somebody, but you don't help me. You just yell at me and say I nicked Pearce's rotten medals which he lied about and never should have had in the first place.'

The two officers patiently folded their arms across their chests and looked at Billy, clearly amused by his outburst.

'I help the police I do,' Billy went on. 'I might have come to tell you about a man who robbed a bank and all you do is shout at me.'

'Who was it?'

'What?'

'Who robbed the bank?'

'I don't know who robbed a bank. I was just saying.'

'Hahaah! so you're making false accusations about a nonexistent bank robbery, wasting police time, and coming past the front desk hatch without handcuffs. That's a crime that is, isn't it, Tom?'

'Twenty years hard labour at least, sarj.'

'Have we got any biscuits left, Tom?'

'I think so, sarj.'

'OK, let's drop the charges and give him a cup of tea and a garibaldi instead.'

Billy shrugged and sullenly followed the sergeant to his office as the desk sergeant went off in search of tea and biscuits.

'Go on then, the floor is yours,' said Sergeant Burke amiably, settling back in his creaking chair. Billy looked thoughtfully at the fishing pictures on his wall. The subjects' beaming faces and rural settings had a calming effect on him and he began to tell of his visit to Kemsley House. Tea arrived, and the sergeant sipped quietly as Billy told his tale.

......'He's a journalist. That means he writes what you read in the paper,' Billy explained. 'He showed me an article about Pearce losing his shoe in the river. It was on the same page as one about 'em finding Tommy dead. Didn't anybody think it was funny him losing his shoe and Tommy being drowned on the same day? I mean, it made me suspicious straight off.' He crammed a garibaldi into his mouth. Sergeant Burke sipped and waited. 'Don't you think it's just too much of a coincidence, Sergeant?' Billy asked, spraying crumbs. 'If you drowned somebody in that mill, you'll get all mucked up and you could lose a shoe. I bet if you looked you could even still find it in them grinding pits. Five years is not all that long, a shoe could still be there. They found Tutankhamen's.'

'Down Rivelin?'

Billy sagged despairingly and returned his cup to its saucer. 'Nobody ever believes me,' he groaned. 'I know it was him. He killed Tommy and I think he did Mrs Loveday as well.'

'OK lad, I'm sorry – I am listening. And I'll tell you sommat else an' all - I do take notice of what you say, Billy. But we're not stupid, you know. Of course we check things out. We check everything. Mr Pearce was not in the mill, and he can prove it. There were witnesses - very reliable ones.' The sergeant stood up suddenly. 'Come with me.' He sped round his desk and out of the office door before Billy could offload his cup, and had to scramble to follow him.

'You've got to stop all this suspicion, Billy. Let sleeping dogs lie. You're a bright lad, but you're just stirring up trouble for everybody.' The sergeant led him through a doorway at the far side of the open office area.

Billy followed onto a gloomy, concrete landing with a flight of steps going to an upper floor and one going down. The sergeant descended into a basement store. Dimly lit and low ceilinged, it smelled dusty and dry. Wooden shelves filled every available space. They were crammed with box files, and brown paper parcels tied with string. Billy watched him walk slowly along one of the racks, his head tilted to one side, mumbling as he read the labels. Suddenly, he straightened up and pulled out a heavy, leather book. It was as big as a tea tray. 'This is it.'

Billy shuffled along the narrow aisle to where the sergeant had opened the battered book. 'This is the day book that was being used in nineteen forty-six. And there - see this entry? That's the date Tommy Loveday was found.' Billy peered at the page. Columns showed the date and time for each entry. The neat, pen and ink writing recorded the events at the front desk for each day.

'Here it says Tommy was found, and here you've got the report. You've also got the constable's notebook reference so we could find that too if we need it. Now, believe it or not, we're not daft in the police force. We get suspicious about coincidences just like you do. And, when we do, we check 'em out.'

Billy shuffled uncomfortably in the sergeant's stern gaze.

'Now I've rechecked all this recently. Do you know why, Billy?'

Billy shook his head, shamefaced.

'Because of what you said to me,' he growled, staring hard at him. 'You see we don't just ignore what people tell us. We do sommat about it.'

'I'm sorry,' mumbled Billy.

'Aye well, seeing as you're a detective an' all, I'm going to break a rule. In fact I've already broken about ten rules bringing you down here and showing you this book. But I'll tell you what's in these reports.' He moved to the end of the row and pulled out a thin folder containing a few hand written pages. 'I made these notes a couple of weeks ago. I've been saving 'em because – just like you - I had my suspicions about poor Annabel, so I checked them out.'

Billy peered at the papers as the sergeant read from them. 'Mr Pearce was questioned by the beat officer on South Road. He'd lost his right shoe when he fell in the river near the Walkley Bank Tilt Wheel. He told the constable he'd slipped on the stepping stones because a car's loud backfire gave him a start. He was crossing the river going towards the mill, not, coming away from it. He got wet up to his knees.' Sergeant Burke closed the folder and turned to face Billy. 'Now normally, that would

137

have been that. The incident would have been noted and closed, but because Tommy Loveday was found dead on that same day, the constable, quite rightly, thoroughly checked every detail of Mr Pearce's story.'

He began leading Billy back up the steps and into his office. Billy took his seat at the sergeant's desk and waited calmly for the rest of the story.

'A good detective checks everything – even the shadow of a shadow. Remember that.'

Billy returned the sergeant's gaze, struggling not to wilt beneath it. 'Yes I will, sergeant,' he croaked. 'And I am checking everything.'

The sergeant nodded thoughtfully tapping his large fingers on the file. Opening it, he sorted through the papers to find the one he wanted. He read aloud from it. 'The constable cycled down to Rivelin Valley - questioned potential witnesses - found corroboration for Pearce's story. Yes, it says, he'd been observed from some garden allotments on the river bank. Two gardeners at different allotments had seen him. But better still, there's a statement here from the angling club's water bailiff. In fact the bailiff even spoke to Pearce and tried to find his shoe in the river.' The sergeant straightened up and sighed. 'You see, check the facts and it soon begins to makes sense, no matter how strange it may seem. It was all true – every word.'

'What about the bang?' Billy asked. 'Did he ask 'em about the bang?'

Sergeant Burke laughed softly. 'I knew you'd ask about that. When you grow up we'll have you in the force. You'll make a good copper.'

'Well did he?'

'Yes of course he did. What did I tell you? "Check even the shadow of a shadow." He asked them all. One of the gardeners said he'd heard a loud report like a gun shot, but he said the farmer across the river was always shooting rabbits and he put it down to that. The other bloke said he thought it was car's back fire. The water bailiff said the same.'

'But it might not have been,' said Billy.

'Yeah, but it doesn't matter does it? Nobody was shot! And anyway, the bailiff is an ex-marine commando, if he couldn't tell a gun shot from a backfire – nobody could. He swore it was a car backfire that made Pearce slip on the stepping stones, just like he'd told the constable. A lot of blokes who've seen action, Billy, like Mr Pearce - they are easily startled by a loud bang. It's quite common among ex-service men.'

Billy released a sigh. 'Well I suppose that's that then.'

'Look lad, leave Mr Pearce alone. And keep your eyes open for them medals. I know you didn't burgle his house, but when he makes a complaint, I have to follow it up. We've got enough work here without looking for more. Keep your nose clean and forget poor old Mr Pearce.'

....

CHAPTER FIFTEEN

'Early morning's not a valid clue anymore. We should rub it off,' Kick ruled, pacing restlessly in front of the MOM board.

Yvonne shot him a disapproving glare. 'Why?'

'Cos his granny said the old girl could've went to bed at eight at night, so it doesn't matter anymore if they were on the street at dawn, unless we also include them who were out there at eight-o-clock at night as well.'

'We can't – there'd be too many, and any road up, it were dark by eight.'

'Oh leave it as it is,' Billy groaned, tired of their bickering.

'It's not getting us anywhere,' Yvonne moaned.

Sensing her frustration Billy moved to the MOM board and set about trying to rescue the situation. 'OK – so we know that your dad, the milkman, and the old doctor were all near Annabel's at round about five in the morning. As far as we know none of them saw nowt unusual. Any of them could have nipped in and killed her.'

'Not my dad!' Yvonne cried.

'I know, I know, but I'm just saying ...' Billy shuffled and gathered his thoughts. 'Then somebody wrote Pearce's name on the board, and my gran thinks he was there that day as well.' He scratched his head thoughtfully, his hand poised to write. 'I think we should add Emily Burkinshaw to the Opportunity column.'

'What for? She didn't do it!' Yvonne cried.

Billy fixed her with a steady gaze and wagged his finger. 'You don't know that for certain, Wy. And don't forget she would have been wide awake at that time, up and around in her house, which's only a few yards from Annabel's front doorstep. She could've easily nipped across the road and done it.'

'Yeah, but why would she?'

'Well, let's see shall we?' he turned to the MOM board. 'Out of this lot who had the best motive?' he asked dramatically, and immediately answered himself. 'We know Pearce did, so that means Miss Burkinshaw did as well.'

'Why?'

'Because she's Pearce's bit of fluff. She might have done it thinking she was protecting him. She could have killed Annabel - for the sake of love.'

'Urgggh! Nah, never,' Kick growled.

'OK then, but who else might have wanted her dead?' Billy asked him.

'What about the vicar? He knew his son had lied for Pearce about the medal. And don't forget - he's read the memoirs. He'd know if Annabel was about to burst a story in her memoirs, that would hurt him – you know, for the sake of his dead son's reputation,' Kick suggested.

'Rubbish,' Billy snapped. 'He's the chuffin vicar. He's more like a chipmunk than a killer beast.'

'What about Doctor Greenhow? He was there. He could have done it?' said Yvonne.

'No – never, they were old friends,' Billy argued. 'Doctor Hadfield told me he even kept her on his special list of patients. They were friends from way back. Anyway, he'd have poisoned her. Doctors always poison folk cos they can get away with it.'

'Maybe you should question him anyway,' said Yvonne. 'If they were such good friends, he'll know about her from the olden days. It might give us some clues.'

'He'll not talk to him,' Kick sneered. 'He's a bad tempered old grump.'

Billy grinned. 'I bet he does. He likes me. He says I'm courageous and honest.'

Later that afternoon Billy went looking for the old Doctor. He didn't want to visit his surgery and have to endure him at close quarters in his consulting room, so he hoped to find him out and about on his rounds. He would pretend to have bumped into him accidentally. After combing the streets for an hour, he eventually spotted the doctor's car parked outside the Douro Wine shop. It should be a simple enough matter, he thought, to waylay him whilst he's loaded down with brandy.

141

As he approached the shop, the Doctor burst out through the door, a bottle wrapped in newspaper gripped firmly in his fist. He strode to his car, and ignoring Billy flung open its door and bustled inside. Billy panicked, fearing he was about to lose his prey. 'Hello, Doctor,' he cried, somewhat goofily.

'Ah Billy, Old Stick,' the doctor boomed warmly. 'Why aren't you studying? You're a bright boy, but you need to hone your God given wits, my lad. You should be studying.'

'I will, sir. I will. I'm just doing an errand.'

The doctor eyed him wryly. 'How's the investigation going?'

'Oh we don't do that anymore,' he lied. 'As I said before, we couldn't find any proof, so we stopped. But we know who did it – well probably did it - but there's no way we can prove it.'

The doctor wound down his car window before pulling the door shut. 'Oh you do, eh? And who would that be then?'

'Well, I'd better not say, sir, if you'll excuse me. I might get into trouble again.'

'Again?'

'Yes. I told the police, but they just gave me a telling off. They said it's a crime to say things about people when you can't prove it. I had to promise to leave – err - this certain person alone, and not to say any more, but they know I didn't steal his medals.'

The doctor chuckled, rumbling like distant thunder. 'Ah haa, so you think it's our venerable chemist? That's who you mean isn't it? I heard he'd had his medals pinched. Poor Mr Pearce. So he's your murderer. Does he know?'

Billy tried not to show his satisfaction. Telling the doctor who they suspected had been Yvonne's idea, but making it appear to be a slip of the tongue was all Billy's own work. 'Yes, that's why he complained to the police.'

The doctor seemed delighted with the news. 'Well I have to say, my boy, I can't really blame the poor chap. I mean to say, you can't go around saying ...'

'But he says things about me, sir. He told the police I'd pinched his medals.'

'Hum, well that was very wrong of him, I'm sure, but I'm quite certain Mr Pearce is far from being a murderer. If you'll

142

take my advice, Billy, you'll look no further than poor Mrs Loveday's hearth for a killer. I'm afraid she fell, and that's all there is to it. It's a terrible thing, but even a simple fall can be fatal under certain circumstances. And that's what happened to her.' The doctor stretched out a hand and gave Billy's forearm a patronising squeeze. 'Forget it, Old Stick, and go and do some revision. I expect to see you pass for grammar school with flying colours, but I can tell you for sure, you will not do so, if you don't study.'

'Sir, you were her good friend I believe? Did Mrs Loveday have any enemies?'

'Indeed yes, we were very good friends. Old friends. We'd known each other many years. Her husband was killed you know, a fine man I believe. It broke her heart. They'd only been married a few weeks. I attended her after he died.' The Doctor stared through the windscreen at some remembered scene, his eyes shining with moisture. He blew his nose on a red pocket-handkerchief. 'No, she had no enemies,' he said, 'except perhaps her own stubbornness. In the end, she'd almost no friends either. She could be a difficult woman - very difficult at times.'

Billy wasn't sure what that meant, but saw clearly how it saddened the old man.

....

CHAPTER SIXTEEN

There have been water mills in Rivelin Valley at least since the sixteenth century. The Walkley Bank Tilt Wheel stands at a bend of the River Rivelin below a steep, crumbling cliff, topped with woodland. The valley squeezes the peaty waters between polished rocks and massive tree roots before splicing with the river Loxley.

The old Tilt was a rectangular building standing across the base of its triangular millpond. Ivy clung to its sandstone walls. Alder rooted in its decaying floors and reached for daylight through dark windows. Wind and rain have pecked at the ancient stone roof, carving holes here and there for owls and bats to find shelter. Large lime trees and horse chestnuts stoop over its millpond, shading shoeless boys fishing for sticklebacks. Barbed wire has coiled around the Tilt mill since its closure, but a canny millwright with a keg of grease and a crowbar, could probably have the wheel turning again with a few days of hard work.

Billy approached it from the millpond along a narrow cinder path several feet above the rushing river. His mind was full of images of Tommy Loveday and his little dog. Halfway along the track he spotted the stepping-stones across the river, where Arnold Pearce had fallen, losing his shoe. On the far bank lay the garden allotments Sergeant Burke had mentioned, neatly planted and staked, guarded by the occasional scarecrow. In a few of the gardens, men bent over raked beds of rich black earth, or patiently plaited young runner bean vines to poles.

The valley pressed in warmly overhead like a big sister, sheltering and calming, as the river raced noisily by, crashing into black and amber rocks, worn smooth in its ancient torrent. Beyond the allotments, a bosky strip rose up steeply to cornfields dotted with an occasional cottage or beast hovel.

At the old Tilt Wheel, Billy lay flat on the ground and slid under a scribble of barbed wire. A few seconds later, he was

144

inside listening to the randy clamour of sparrows above his head and the urgent rush of water beneath his feet.

Scored by ancient utility, the main tilt floor was laid out like a plan drawn in sand. Iron tools and old bits of equipment lay around, as if dropped only moments ago by workers who have just stepped outside for a breather. Strange machinery hung in the air like dragons frozen in flight. Slender alders and elderberry, rooted in cracks in the stone floor, struggled towards the light of glassless windows. A scatter of owl pellets betrayed a roost in the rafters. Billy could not resist picking up one. He sat on a stone step and began unpicking its outer case of mammal skin. Inside he found a tiny shrew skull, all the little teeth and bones stripped clean enough for a museum display case. Laying them out beside him, he had almost a complete skeleton when he stopped and reminded himself abruptly, that this was not why he had come to the mill. He put the tiny bones aside and thought of Tommy Loveday.

Tommy had survived a terrible war. He had flown countless missions over enemy territory, suffered burns and flack injuries. Then on a day of strange coincidences, he had died in this curious, redundant shell. If only, Billy wished, he could unravel the mystery as easily as he had the owl pellet.

How did Tommy fall? He examined the stone floor and tried to imagine how he could have lost his footing and fatally plunged to the water below. The floor was like a maze, made up of different stone levels, steps, ridges, and channels. Two vertical shafts big enough to hide a coffin, were open to flowing water beneath. Certainly, he had to move with care, but every feature was obvious, none concealed or deceptively drawn. The more he looked, the more he failed to understand how Tommy could have fallen accidentally.

'So there you are, still poking your snotty nose in to other people's business.' The voice belonged to old Sutcliffe. He was standing in the Tilt's broken doorway, a steaming silhouette, drawn in sunlight, tinted green by the canopy of limes above him. 'I knew I'd eventually get thee by the sen. I knew it. I just needed to wait.'

'Whaddyer want? Leave me alone, I've done nowt to you.'

145

'Maybe, but you know who did, you little shit. You know who killed my Stan.'

'I don't. I've told you the truth. I saw nowt, heard nowt. If I knew, I'd tell you.'

'Somebody paid him fifty quid. He had it on him when they found him. The coppers showed it me in the envelope. Not a penny spent. Why? Who gave it to him? Where'd he get fifty quid that I didn't know nowt about? We was a team. We shared everything.' He stalked menacingly towards Billy, an insane spark glowing in his eyes. 'You know sommat. You're covering up for somebody. Who is it?'

'I'm not. I don't understand it myself. I'm as keen as you to get to the bottom of it. That's why I came here today.'

'Why do you care? What's in it for thee? If you think there's more cash – well there isn't.'

'I know that. This's not about money. I just want to find out. I came here to learn something, anything, some clues - anything that'll ...'

'Liar,' Sutcliffe screamed, looking about wild eyed and shaking. He grabbed an iron bar from an old work bench and advanced on Billy. 'You know who killed my Stan. Somebody shot him. Somebody, who was not man enough to fight him fair and square. I think it were the same one that got him into this mess - then killed him to shut him up. And you know who it is. You're not leaving here until you tell me his name.'

Billy backed away as the old man came towards him brandishing the iron bar threateningly. 'Honest, Mr Sutcliffe, I swear, I don't know what's going on. If I knew I'd tell thee.'

Grimy tears stained Sutcliffe's face as he advanced. Misery glazed his eyes, adding to his crazed look. He drew back the metal bar like a baseball player about to strike. Tears welled in Billy's eyes. He could see the old man was mad with grief and hungry for revenge on somebody – anybody.

Sutcliffe drew back the bar and swung it with all his might.

The floor disappeared beneath Billy's feet. He felt himself tumbling backwards as the iron bar swept passed his head. The light vanished as he plunged. An instant later, he was in the water splashing around trying to find something to hang onto. His fingers clawed at slimy stonework, pulling off skeins of thick green algae. The river dragged him under the building and slid him out through a stone-sided leet, slippery with algae and a smooth iron stained accretion. Then he was outside blinking at the bright sky through the woodland canopy leaning over him. Buoyed along unceremoniously he threshed his limbs trying to gain a foothold.

At last the current pushed him aground. He lay on a shingle bank under the curious gaze of a cow. The animal blew steam from its nostrils as it reached through barbed wire for the sweetest grasses. Billy stared back at it. He heard the distant sound of a heavy truck labouring along the valley road beyond the old Tilt, and was struck by how far away it seemed, yet how clear, like the muted sounds in a street after snow has fallen.

'Are you all reight?' Billy spun around looking for the owner of the voice. It was a skinny old man standing above him on the river bank. He had a garden rake in one hand and a sooty kettle in the other. 'Tha's picked a rum day for swimming.'

Billy stumbled to his feet and looked about, hoping to find some plausible excuse for his situation. 'I fell,' he said weakly. 'Somebody was chasing me and I fell.'

The old man chuckled silently. 'Nay lad, tha were weshed out o' that leet. I saw thee shoot out like a shuttle. Tha's been laiking about inside. You're not suppose to go in there you know. They don't put them signs up all over telling thee to keep out for nowt. A bloke were killed in there a bit back. You're lucky the same thing didn't happen to thee.' The old man took off his cap, wiped his face with it, and replaced it on his baldhead with practised precision.

Billy shivered, inwardly agreeing with the old man. Water lapped around his thighs. Cold drove control from his limbs and he swayed, shivering. Gazing around, he looked for a way up to dry land. The tall banks were sheer and slippery.

'Here grab this. I'll give thee a pull up.' The old man extended his rake. 'I use it to fill me kettle. I can't reach the watta otherwise. These banks are just shale. They give way as soon as you step on 'em.' He leaned out extending the rake as far as he could. 'Grab hold, sithee.'

Billy scrambled up the crumbling shale onto firm ground. 'Oh thanks, Mr.'

'Eyup, tha looks nithered,' said the old man, peering over spectacles held together with silver wire. 'Come wi me. I were just going to mash. Tha's dropped in just at reight time.' He started laughing soundlessly, setting his scrawny body shaking. Billy eyed him sideways wondering if he was having a fit.

'Did tha hear that?' the old man spluttered, laughter turning his face bright red. 'Dropped in. Huh, I said tha dropped in. Dropped in watta more like.' Laughter turned to coughing, ending his gleeful outburst for lack of air.

Billy worried the old chap might expire before he got his cup of tea, but luckily, he recovered quickly and led him away to his allotment.

In a shed, constructed from a variety of old doors, bits of air raid shelter and patches of tarpaulin and canvas, he found a comfortable rocking chair, a kitchen table with two stools drawn up to it, and a warming, pot bellied stove. A battered kitchen dresser occupied one corner. On its worktop a spirit stove, tea caddy and a bottle of Camp coffee stood at the ready.

'I can do thee a bacon banjo if th' art hungry,' the old man offered, tears from his near death laughter experience still rolling down his sweating face.

'No thanks, tea will be champion,' said Billy. 'Can I help thee to mash it?'

'Nay lad, sit thee sen down. I'll do it. I've to be reight careful with this paraffin stove. It's bloody jiggered. I burnt me chuffin eyebrows off yesterday.' He whipped off his cloth cap and held it under Billy's nose for inspection. 'Sithee, it even set me cap alight. I thought I were a gonna.'

Billy watched the old man as he made the tea. It was done with enough thoroughness and ceremony to shame a geisha. The kettle's position on the stove was accepted only after several minute adjustments. Enamel mugs from the dresser, were brought out and polished on a rag. A brown teapot was warmed up with a swirl of hot water, which was emptied out through a window. Milk, in a Tizer bottle, appeared from a cooling bucket of water under the table. Finally, a teaspoon on a string, was plucked from a nail in the wall.

'I hope tha dunt take sugar, cos there is none. I stopped taking it cos of rationing.' He adjusted the position of the cups unnecessarily on the table and waited for the kettle to whistle. After eyeing Billy critically for a moment, he moved to the dresser and rummaged to find an army blanket. 'Here, get thee things off and dry 'em. Put this round thee sen. Tha can hang thee clothes in front of t'stove. They'll soon dry in that heat.'

Billy blushed and tried to stop shivering. 'I'll be OK,' he said, unconvincingly, not quite ready to strip off in front of a stranger.

'Don't worry thee sen,' the old man said, understanding the boy's predicament. 'I waint look at thee bare bum. But if tha don't get dry tha'll be dead before tha get's home and thee mother'll kill thee.' He opened the top of the cast iron stove and added a few sticks of firewood and a piece of coal. Billy slipped out of his clothes and wrapped the coarse blanket around him.

Soon the cosy little hut was even warmer. Billy's dripping clothes hung from a sisal line, stretched in front of the stove. They were soon steaming in the fierce heat. He had stopped shivering and was now watching the old man quietly roll a cigarette. 'My dad smokes Wills Stars,' he told him.

'Stars – oh does he? Blimey, he must be a millionaire, thee father.'

Billy cast him a bewildered glance, which the old man seemed to think was hilarious.

'I like this Virginia. I've smoked it for years. It's cos if I have to roll it mi sen, I don't smoke as many. It's a mug's game smoking tha knows. It costs thee a fortune, and all it does is make thee cough.'

Silence settled on them again as the old man licked the cigarette paper with the tip of his tongue and stuck it down, gently stroking the seam.

'You said something – err - about a man who was killed in the old tilt,' Billy probed tentatively.

A small flame erupted in the old man's cupped hands, as he lit his cigarette. 'Aye, a few years back. He were a local lad. I knew him a bit- err - Tommy sommat,' he said, through clouds of blue smoke.

'Loveday,' Billy prompted. 'Tommy Loveday.'

'Aye that were it - a Walkley lad. I remember it ever so well. I were digging up at the top end near the river. It's horrible to think that while I were up there that young fella were gasping for his last breath, just thirty yards away on t'other side. He never shouted nor nowt. I'd 'ave heard him.'

'Did the police talk to you about it?'

'Nay, they come and saw him next door, but he's as deaf as a bell rope. He wouldn't even know if it were thundering, if it didn't come with lightning built in.'

Billy gasped, astonished. 'I heard they talked to two gardeners?'

'Oh aye they did, but not to me,' he said dismissively. 'They went to see Patrick, a bit further up an' all. He came round here afterwards, telling me all about it. He's never got any fags, old Patrick. He's always on the 'scrounge for a smoke. He loves an excuse to come and chat and get a fag off me.' He laughed and shook his head. 'I don't mind. He's a good sort old Patrick. He always buys me a pint in the Freedom House. We go in there for her pies, tha knows.'

'Can you remember what happened?'

'Of course I can. I'm not daft tha knows.' He eyed Billy huffily, drawing deeply on his cigarette. 'A young bloke were shot over in the old Tilt.'

'He wasn't shot.'

'He was tha knows, I heard it!' he argued fiercely. 'Believe me lad, I know what gun fire sounds like. I were in South Africa. I went reight through from Rietfontein to Ladysmith. Lance Corporal Francis Simmons, that's me. I were killed twice and wounded more times than tha's had Yorkshire Pudding. By God, them Boers could shoot. They could hit a threpny dodger in a jar of tanners from a hundred yards, dead easy. Believe me lad, I know what a gunshot sounds like.'

'But he wasn't shot! There were no bullet wounds,' cried Billy. 'He fell and banged his head. He died of drowning.'

'Look lad. I heard the shot. And so did Patrick.'

'Did he tell the policeman?'

'Of course, why shouldn't he?' He gazed at Billy, clearly annoyed that he had not been believed. 'Come wi me, we'll go and see Patrick. Tha can ask him thee sen, since tha dunt believe me.' He stopped himself suddenly, and peered at Billy wrapped in the old army blanket. 'Oh no, tha can't can tha? Thars got nowt on. Well, we'll go and see him when thee clothes are dry. He'll tell thee.' He turned to the stove, mumbling under his breath, and began testing the dryness of Billy's clothes. 'Mark my words lad, that poor bloke were shot, no matter what nobody tells thee.'

. . . .

CHAPTER SEVENTEEN

After school, Billy pushed his bike up steep, leafy streets, approaching with some trepidation, Doctor Hadfield's curious octagonal house at the gates of a grand Victorian villa. The last time he'd been in the area, old Sutcliffe had jumped him, and tried to crush him beneath his bicycle. The incident was still fresh in his mind, especially after his latest encounter with the crazed old ruffian.

The doctor's Austin Ruby Saloon was not in its usual parking spot, but he was not concerned. It was barely four-thirty; the doctor would not arrive home for his brief break before evening surgery for another half hour or so. Billy settled on the doorstep to wait.

Sunlight slanted across well-kept lawns and sparkled on the polished leaves of holly, and rhododendrons that twitched to the antics of foraging wrens and blue tits. It felt good to rest. His fall down the Old Tilt's shaft had raised painful bruises. Sunning himself eased them. He watched a pair of red squirrels flick about the lawn. Sunlight created a brilliant nimbus around them. Drowsiness weighed on him as the creatures jerkily chased each other, seeming to switch on and off like the electric toys they had in glass cases at the seaside.

Billy's eyes blurred, his lids felt heavy, and his mind drifted in the warmth. .....Tommy Loveday clutched a bloodless gunshot wound and toppled backwards into pitch blackness. Billy felt the hot burst of the gunfire in his hand, but there was no gun. The weary, incessant drone of a Wellington Bomber filled his head - then Doctor Hadfield's voice intruded, at first squawking from the pilot's radio, but then pushing in upon his daydream.

'Hey wake up! What's wrong? Are you waiting for me?'

Bemused, Billy groped to recover his senses. There was something he needed to remember. It was vitally important, but it had gone, flushed out of his mind by waking. He knew its crucial importance, but he could not recall it. Rubbing his face, he peered up at the doctor, silhouetted against a golden afternoon sky. 'Sorry – I must 'ave ...'

'Come in - I'm late. If you don't mind, we'll talk while I change?'

'OK, I'm sorry. I wanted to ask you ...'

'Can you make tea without scalding yourself? There's a tin of beans somewhere. Is the milk sour?'

Billy found the milk jug beneath an incongruous crocheted cover, held in place by three little china cows. He sniffed the contents, glaring disapprovingly at the girlie cover. 'It's on the turn a bit, but it should be OK.'

The doctor had vanished into an adjoining room leaving him alone in a semi-circular space, furnished with what he could only think of as junk shop rejects: a battered settee, sagging arm chair, garish aquamarine kitchen dresser with a matching sink unit, both stained like a map of the American states. A table covered with books occupied the middle of the room.

'I'll have to get a fridge. Does your mother have one? You can keep milk three or four days,' said the doctor, an odd note of wonder in his tone. 'I swear I have not had decent milk since I went up to Oxford. I barely recognise a cup of tea unless it has curdled floaters on it.' He appeared briefly in the doorway, lathering his face with a silver handled badger. 'Are you any good at beans on toast?'

Billy wanted to say no, but the doctor had gone again. 'I'll try,' he mumbled lamely.

'What is it that you want, old boy?' called Hadfield. 'Forgive my bluntness, but I realise this is not a social call. How did you know I'd be here anyway? Have you found the bread? There's a grill thing in the Belling. It's a bit fierce but works OK.'

'Somebody said a shot was fired when Tommy Loveday was killed ...'

'*Tommy Loveday*! Crikey, you're doing him now are you? I thought it was Mrs Loveday's death you were investigating.'

'They're linked - well – err - possibly.'

'Wow, you are certainly worth that old hat, my boy. Where is it by the way - still under arrest?'

153

'I want to know what the post mortem said,' Billy called at the open door. 'Can you look it up in some records, or something? It's only five years ago.'

'Five years? Crikey! Have you any idea how many people have died in the last five years? Absolutely squillions!'

'Maybe, but they didn't all need a post mortem. I looked it up in the library. You only need a post mortem if you die a bit funny.'

'A bit funny eh?' said the doctor, appearing in the doorway. He looked scrubbed and shiny, and was putting the final touches to a pink tie. 'You mean in a clown suit or something?'

Billy ignored the quip. 'It's important,' he said. 'There's a killer loose out there.'

Doctor Hadfield looked at him and scowled. 'Crikey, Billy, are you sure you're not forty-eight years old and my father in disguise?' He bent to look at his reflection in a spotty mirror, and fiddled with his tie. 'Oh I don't know, Billy. I'm a bit busy.'

'Of course, there's no *need* for me to tell Marlene,' said Billy, with cold deliberation.

The doctor turned and stared at him. 'Wow, that's a bit Machiavellian,' he gasped. 'You are my father aren't you? That's the sort of blackmailing mind game he plays.'

Billy held his gaze while working a can opener around the doctor's tin of beans. Hadfield eyed him thoughtfully then shrugged with amused resignation 'Well for your information – father dear - I might not be seeing her anymore. So, veiled threats, or even stark naked ones for that matter, won't work.'

'But you are still seeing her,' Billy contradicted firmly, 'and it wasn't a threat. I just meant to say that I won't tell her.'

'Who says I'm still seeing her?'

'Well you aren't getting all dolled up to do evening surgery. You pong like Boots' scent counter and that *pink* tie – well ...'

'What's wrong with the tie?'

'It's like them my Mam buys for my dad and he tries to lose behind the wardrobe.'

'Toast's burning.'

*

154

The dairy at the end of South Road made its own ice cream. You could have white or pink. The pink had a different, but equally unidentifiable flavour to the white one. Both colours contained tiny flakes of ice that you could crunch and were delicious.

Billy bought a tuppenny cornet, bit the bottom off it and started sucking out the ice cream from underneath. It's a very good way to eat ice cream, so long as you don't need to see where you're going. With his head back, gazing at the sky, the several people he collided with were luckily quite nice about it, but not Sergeant Burke. He threatened to arrest him for endangering life, property and senior policemen.

Billy apologised, but then quickly got down to business while he had the sergeant's attention. 'Look, I know you asked me to stop blaming Mr Pearce, but you've got to listen to me, sergeant – please. I've some new evidence.'

The Sergeant crossed the road heading for the police box. He tried to ignore Billy following close at his heels. He tugged at a silver chain dangling from his uniform pocket, and flipped a brass key into his hand, ready to open the police box door.

Billy drained the soggy ice cream cornet and shoved the whole thing into his mouth. 'It won't take a minute,' he spluttered, wiping his fingers on his tank top.

The sergeant unlocked the police box door and retreated inside. Billy stuck his foot in the doorway and waited sullenly as the sergeant lowered himself on to a stool and produced a newspaper from under his tunic. 'Go away, Billy, or I'll nick you for loitering.'

Billy danced nervously from foot to foot unwilling to give up. He watched the sergeant fire up a little spirit stove and place a kettle on it. With great ceremony, and glaring at Billy all the while, the sergeant unfolded his newspaper. 'Can't I get any peace from you?' he groaned. 'Have you any idea how much extra work you've caused me lately? If you're not stirring up paperwork at the station, you're bothering me up here. What the devil is it now?'

The little kettle began to steam and splutter. The sergeant struggled to turn the stove off, scalding his fingers and mumbling incoherently.

'I think Tommy Loveday was shot at. I think the constable was wrong when he reported a car backfire. It wasn't - it was a gunshot, and I've got a witness.'

'Billy, he fell down a hole in the tilt mill floor. There was no wound, no blood, no gunshot, and guess what - no bullet in him. You're talking nonsense lad.'

Billy pulled a toy gun from his belt and aimed it at the sergeant. 'If this was a real gun, Sergeant, what would you do now?'

'Don't be stupid. Put it away.'

'Please sergeant, tell me what you'd do?'

'I'd grab it off you and clip you round the ear-hole.'

'No, you're not being serious. You wouldn't grab it because you'd be scared it might go off,' Billy argued. 'If this was a real 'en, you'd be backing away and trying to talk me out of shooting you – all calming and quiet like.'

The sergeant poured hot water into a mug and stirred it. 'What's your point?'

'You'd back away. You'd put your hands up - and you'd back away.'

'Where's this going, Billy?'

'And you'd fall down the hole in the floor because you were walking backwards, because somebody was pointing a gun at you.' Billy raised the toy gun's barrel to his lips and blew across the muzzle. The sergeant stared back apparently transfixed by the vivid image Billy had painted.

'The killer fired a shot, maybe accidentally because he was startled to see Tommy move suddenly when he lost his balance and fell down the hole, or maybe - because he wanted to kill him. Whatever the reason, there was definitely a shot fired. Several people heard it. Even in the notes, it says one man thought it was a farmer shooting rabbits. That's the same as saying, it sounded like a gun shot. And I met a man who will swear it definitely was a gun shot.'

'My God, Billy,' breathed the sergeant. 'You get some weird ideas, lad.' He uncorked a small medicine bottle and poured milk from it into his mug. 'So you want me to believe that Tommy fell down the hole because he was scared by somebody pointing a gun at him? And I suppose you're going to say that it was poor old Mr Pearce, eh?'

'Yes. He was there, wasn't he? He lost his shoe in the river. It's in the policeman's notes.'

'Yes, and you've read them yourself, though I obviously wasted my time showing them to you. They clearly state he was on the stepping-stones and fell because he was surprised by the loud bang from a car exhaust backfire. You read it yourself. It's all in the notes,' argued the sergeant.

'Yes, but sergeant, if you wanted people to think you weren't in the mill when that gunshot was heard, don't you agree that it helps if you can make a big fuss about being somewhere else? Like falling in the river and losing your shoe?'

'No I don't. Pearce is just like lots of men who've seen action. They're as jumpy as kittens about loud bangs. That's why he fell in. Not because of some evil scheme.'

'So you don't believe me?'

'Of course I don't, lad. It's a smashing bit of deduction, and I admire you for that, but you are completely up the wrong tree.' He thumped him playfully on the shoulder. 'A copper is supposed to be suspicious about everything. He's supposed to question everything – even the shadow of a shadow, and by eck Billy, you certainly do that. But the evidence is against you. There's no way that Mr Pearce did it. He was never in the Old Tilt and he can prove it. Obviously, we had him down as a prime suspect. He was in the area, he was wet and muddy, and he knew the victim. But his alibi is solid, Billy. Plus, it was a copper who confirmed it for him. We did everything by the book, and the coroner agreed with us.'

'But there was something that was not checked,' Billy said solemnly. 'And you just said a policeman has to suspect everything, and check everything. Well I know something that wasn't checked - something right important.'

'Everything was checked – everything was covered – you mark my words.'

'Excuse me, sergeant, but no. You missed something. And if ever it came out in some sort of enquiry, or legal type of thing with big-wigs and lots of paperwork and stuff, they'd blame you for it. They'd say it was you that missed it. They'd say you made a mistake.'

The sergeant stared at the boy. 'What the devil are you talking about?'

'We have one witness who says he heard the gunshot. He thought it was a farmer shooting rabbits. It's in the copper's notes. But you never checked to see if a farmer really had been shooting rabbits – and yer dint look for a bullet. I bet I could show thee where that bullet went into inside that old mill. And sommat else, I found out that lead doesn't go rusty, so I bet it's still in there in that wall.'

'By eck, Billy Perks!' the sergeant gasped. 'You're challenging me, aren't you?'

'No, Sir. But I was once told that a good detective will check everything, even the shadow of a shadow.'

*

After school the following day, Billy went to the surgery hoping to see Doctor Hadfield. If his little Austin Ruby was parked in the coach house yard, he would know he was still taking afternoon surgery. He planned to climb in to the car and wait for him. But, as he arrived the Ruby was nosing out through the gates. Luckily, it's not a vehicle noted for rapid acceleration, and Billy was able to catch up with it.

'Hey Billy! Are you after me again? Get in, we can chat as we go.' The little Austin whined and chirred, emitting a blue mist as it pulled away up the steep street. 'You were right, Billy. Just as you said, my esteemed employer and principle tormentor in life, did not join this practice until the early spring of nineteen-twenty. Apparently, like me, he too came as locum. However, unlike me, six months later he married the boss's daughter and before the year was out was a full partner. Praise be the Lord. If it weren't for nepotism Billy where would we all be?'

158

Not having the faintest what he meant, Billy ignored the question and waited for him to calm down and speak English.

'Working for much brighter employers my lad - that's where.'

'I can go now,' said Billy flatly. 'You can let me off here. That's all I wanted to know.'

'Oh charming. Remind me one day, Billy, and we'll discuss social skills.'

*

This was going to be a big day – a really big day. And after all that had happened in the last few weeks, Billy sat on the tram between his parents as quiet as a mouse, keen to avoid setting events in train that might spoil it.

The tramcar bucked and tried its best to unseat everybody as it crested a cobbled hill and plunged down towards the city. The conductor showed off, mystically balancing, hands free, as if gyroscopically maintained in position, as he collected fares. The lower saloon was about half full, enjoying the lull between the rush of steelworkers off to their early shifts and the later, white collar crush of scholars and clerks.

The Perks were off to London, to the Festival of Britain. Since his curfew and grounding, Billy had given up all hope of this day. Then, quite unexpectedly, he'd been told to clean his shoes before bed, as he was off to London in the morning.

London, capital city, centre of empire, home of the King. He'd seen it on the Pathe News, burning, and bombed with defiant pearly kings and queens doing the knees up outside blitzed pubs. And though he had never set foot there, Tower Bridge, the Mall and Big Ben were as familiar sights to him as Sheffield's Snig Hill, or the Wicker Arches.

The steelworks where Billy's dad worked had organised the outing. First a luxury Pullman train to London, then a taxi to the South Bank and the festival's gates.

Still as invisible as he could make himself, Billy disembarked in the city and followed his parents to the Railway Station. Beneath its Victorian portico, three wheeled Scammels whizzed around between taxis and buses and horse drawn carts, loaded with parcels. Great heaps of newspapers, like grey

159

haystacks, leaned against iron pillars, waiting to be harvested by small red vans.

Inside the station, Billy's father recognised some of his workmates with their families and followed them to the London platform. There was lots of teasing and flipping of neckties as men who usually only ever see each other in muck and sweat faced up in their trilby hats and Sunday best, as slick as Jimmy Cagney. The steelworkers' wives looked like so many Doris Days in short jackets and big floral skirts of stiff, waffle cotton. Mothers wiped children's noses, and kept cleaning their faces with spit and handkerchiefs. Youngsters of all ages who had never met before, stared sullenly at each other, the younger ones swinging on their parents' hands, their older siblings trying to look bored and disinterested. A couple of proto-teddy boys with greased back hair and drainpipe trousers moved in on a pair of scowling Jane Russells and smoked violently, desperately pretending not to be children, forced into spending a day with their parents.

The train thundered in under the station's glass roof, gouting steam across the platform. The ground shook and the air swirled hot and cold. The chattering chorus rose to a high-pitched babble and Billy found himself borne along to the train in a cheerful crush of excitement. Harassed officials checked tickets. Billy and his parents were directed to the dining car and a table sparkling with cutlery and white linen. A minute or two later the rhythmic slamming of the train's doors thumped along its length, signalling that they would soon be off to the old imperial capital to see the wonders of modern science.

As the train pulled away a smiling waiter appeared, seeming so pleased to see him that Billy felt certain he must know the man. With a flourish, a menu appeared before him. He'd never seen anything like it. Every wondrous food known to mankind appeared to be listed there, even orange juice and smoked haddock. When the waiter returned Billy ordered the fish, and received a kick on the shins under the table from his mother. 'You can't have that,' she whispered hotly, as though he'd ordered the coddled testicles of the Dalai Lama.

160

'Of course he can,' said his dad. 'I paid extra for the full breakfast. We can have any damn thing we want – even him.'

'But fish for breakfast?' She seemed horrified.

'You 'ave kippers – them's fish,' he argued softly.

'But not like haddock though.'

'It's smoked like kippers are.'

That appeared to do it for Mrs Perks. She lifted her face to the waiter, smiled sweetly and said, 'My son will have the 'addock with a poached hhegg.'

Except for the dining car, the train had a separate side corridor along each coach. Billy set out to explore as soon as he had finished his breakfast. Steelworkers and their families filled two coaches and most of the dining car. The rest of the train, had its usual mix of travellers, and was much quieter. In the corridor of the first class coach Billy came face to face with the Reverend Hinchcliffe.

'My word! Billy isn't it?'

'Hello, Sir. Are you going to the festival an' all?'

'Festival? Oh, oh no, I'm afraid not Billy, though I would certainly like to. I'm only going as far as Nottingham.' He seemed agitated, and peered about as though uncertain what to do next. 'I say, Billy, since you're here, have you a moment? I'm really very glad we met like this. You see, I have something I need to get off my chest - so to speak. Let's find an empty compartment.' He led Billy away, peering into compartments as they passed them until he found an empty one. 'In here, old chap. Sit down - sit down.' He slid the door shut and chose the seat opposite Billy. 'This's been on my mind ever since we had our chat, so I'm really very glad to have this opportunity to make a clean breast of it.'

The Reverend took a moment, chewing on his chubby cheeks as Billy sank slowly into the deeply cushioned seat. Lines furrowed the Reverend's forehead and he gazed nervously at the floor, as he began. 'You see, sorry - I say sorry, but I lied.' His voice was sibilant and tremulous. 'I'm really very sorry, my boy. No excuses. I simply lied to you.'

Billy gaped, wondering what terrible lie he had told. 'What do you mean, Sir?'

161

'I err - stole – yes stole, that's the word for it, some papers from Mrs Loveday's house.' He paused shifting his gaze briefly to meet Billy's, then dropping it to his fingers, which were squirming around each other. 'I was concerned about my son – his reputation. I know it was wrong, but I was so afraid she might've had letters that could harm him. He can't fight back you see - my poor son. He was killed in forty-five, you know. Right at the very end. Terrible. Tragic. He was shot down over Wolfsburg. One of his friends brought me his footlocker. It was quite untouched. He shouldn't have, at least not without his CO's permission. Anyway, I couldn't bring myself to open it for years. I put it in his room, at the end of his bed. I like to see it there as I pass by his open door on the landing. It's as if he's just gone out – could be back any minute for something locked away in there: camera, book, photographs.' He paused, unfolded a neatly pressed handkerchief from his pocket, and blew his nose. 'Then when Annabel Loveday died, I recalled how Robert had been good friends with her son, Thomas. They flew together for a while you know. They were split up after they were shot down over France, but remained good friends. Well, finally I opened it up, the footlocker. Sure enough, there was a letter from Thomas Loveday. It was about something that had happened, something, about which they were both very upset. They wanted to change it – to put it right.'

'It's Arnold Pearce and that medal,' Billy said. 'It is isn't it?'

The reverend lifted red-rimmed eyes to meet Billy's. 'Thomas Loveday had written that he wanted the two of them to meet with Arnold Pearce, to persuade him to go to the RAF and own up to what had happened. I was scared that if my son had replied to the letter it might be amongst Annabel's papers. You see, I naturally thought she would have received all Thomas's papers and things upon his death. I was afraid that my son might have replied to Thomas's letter. I had to find out what he had said. You know, even an innocent remark can sound bad, if taken out of context. Of course, I fully expected he would have said the right thing, but sometimes people can attach quite the wrong interpretations. You - you can never be sure how things will appear, you know - out of context. You do see what I mean, don't you? You do understand why I did it?'

Billy nodded, trying to understand. 'So you stole them?'

'Yes. I know there's no excuse for it, no matter what. However, I know that God knows my heart.'

'Is that where you got the exercise book?'

'Oh no, no no, she really did give those to me. I edited them one at a time. I never saw all four together. I returned them each time. That was how she wanted it.'

'So, how did you steal her stuff? It was all locked up and padlocked.'

'I'm ashamed to say, I broke in like a common thief, which of course is precisely what I am. It was the day after you had found her body. I climbed over the back wall, and found the door padlocked. I couldn't get in. There was nothing useful in the yard, so I had to climb out and fetch a bar. I took my …'

'….jack handle from your car,' Billy interrupted, 'which just happens to be the same as the one in a Triumph Razoredge, like Pearce's car.'

'Ah, you found it? Yes, I'm afraid I'm not a very good burglar. I tend to leave clues scattered around everywhere.'

'Don't worry the cops don't have it yet - I do.'

'Well anyway, I searched. She had a secret drawer, you know. I was worried I might not find it, but I didn't need it. I found a folder in the very first drawer I opened. It had all her special – err - important papers in it. It was just lying there for anyone to find. Just as I suspected there was a letter from my son to Thomas. It wasn't incriminating at all, but I suppose some people might have raised an eyebrow, but nothing more. It discussed doing the honourable thing. Perhaps I'm oversensitive, but I felt it would be best if I got rid of it.

'What about the exercise book, was that you?'

'You mean the missing pages? Yes, I'm afraid it was. I began to think that maybe I'd panicked a little, but you must realise, I had already seen what she'd written about Pearce. I'd already suggested to her that she should remove those pages. After consideration, she agreed with me – for the sake of both our sons. That's why I felt it would be all right to tear them out.' He

163

gazed about sadly. 'God knows, I'm not proud of all this Billy, but please don't judge me harshly.'

'And you burned the torn out pages in the cold grate using a match. What about the secret drawer, did you look inside it?'

'Yes I did, and I found something truly awful. Something that will clear up everything, and prove you were right all along. I'm afraid I can't tell you about it yet. I need some advice first. That's why I'm on the train. I'm going to Nottingham to see my brother. He's a barrister. I get off in a few minutes.' He looked at Billy, his expression sad and thoughtful. 'There's a tin box too. It's locked. It feels as if it's got papers or photographs in it. I haven't been able to get at them. However, now that I can prove who killed her, there's no need to trample further through the poor lady's secrets. For her sake, I shall leave the tin box and its contents untouched. I think they're probably letters from her husband, because I didn't find any elsewhere, and I'm sure she must have some.' He sighed and shook his head. 'Oh Billy, what a poor example I am for you. A thief and a liar; and in God's house. Please don't think too badly of me.'

'I don't, sir. You did it for your son. Then you owned up about it, and that shows you care about what's right. It was a brave thing to do, and anyway, you said you're going to the cops, so that makes it all honest and not sneaky. I bet God's pleased with you – even though you are a proddy.'

'Thank you, Billy. I pray you're right.' He took out his handkerchief again and blew his nose noisily. 'There is something else.' From his inside jacket pocket he pulled out some folded sheets of paper and opened them up, smoothing them out on his knees. I was not sure what to do with this. It's from my son. It's his account of the night over France when they were shot down. I'd like you to read it – err - if you have a mind to. I think Robert would have liked that. You can return it to me at the vicarage.'

Billy accepted the pages carefully. 'Thank you. Did you keep the folder that the other papers were in?'

'Yes, but I shall give everything to the police. You needn't worry, Billy.'

'What's it like? What sort of folder is it?'

The reverend shook his head. 'I don't know really – just a home made cardboard thing.'

'Did it have a bird and lion on it?'

'I don't recall.' The train suddenly started to brake, almost tossing the Reverend Hinchcliffe into Billy's lap. He recovered and peered out of the window. 'This is my station. Don't worry, Billy. I'll be seeing Sergeant Burke just as soon as I get back to Sheffield. I intend to tell him everything.' He extended his hand and took Billy's, shaking it warmly. 'You're a good boy, Billy. I'm proud to know you. I owe you more than you can imagine.'

. . . .

CHAPTER EIGHTEEN

As the train pulled out of Nottingham station Billy closed the compartment door and pulled the blinds. Cocooned in first class, he unfolded the letter the Reverend Hinchcliffe had given him and began to read. The deep soft seats, polished wood and warm light from the reading lamp above his head felt luxuriously soporific. There was little comfort however, in the words penned by the young RAF sergeant, now dead and buried in some distant war cemetery. Tears glossed his eyes as he read the story of a crew's last flight together, and the death of their aircraft.

His eyes grew heavy as he read. He remembered the photograph he had found. How young and happy they had all seemed, playing cards in the sunlight. Now at least two of them were dead. And what about Pearce? He was one of them. He too had been wounded and traumatised by war; his cheek bore the scars to prove it. Did it really matter about a bit of shiny metal on a coloured ribbon?

Billy read the pages, his eyelids drooping; the words swimming before him and gently rocking to the rhythm of the train's wheels on the track. When he had done he sagged back, and closed his heavy eyes, trying to imagine the fear and horror of that night …,

………ragged strips of fabric lashed the Wellington's woven ribs. Icy wind tore through the fuselage, whipping away shouted orders, spraying them out into the black sky through dozens of shrapnel holes. Front gunner, Charlie Leedham, was dead - gone - blown away by the last shell. The skipper ordered them to bail out; Lana, was dying.

To the very last moment, they had battled with flack and flames, bouncing around the sky like a leaf in a gale. Coaxing her, nursing her, praying she'd make it to the English Channel where, if they ditched, there was at least some hope of rescue, and home. Ditching over France, they'd be killed or captured in

166

hours. If they survived, they'd be incarcerated in some German stalag for the duration. Seeing home again might be years away.

Jacque (Frenchie) Cadell, the skipper, put it to a vote. Nobody wanted to leave Lana to die in France. For what seemed hours, they struggled to keep her in one piece, steadily losing altitude as they edged towards the Channel.

Wellingtons don't give up easily. The cross weave structure of their fuselage can take a lot of punishment, but the shell that had blown away the front gunner had been the last straw. Lana shook and shuddered, control was impossible. It was over; they had to bail out.

One by one they jumped. Frenchie saw them off, grinning, yelling encouragement. First Tommy Loveday, the sparks, then Hinch, helping Willy Glover the tail gunner. He was out cold, his left leg like a twist of blood sodden rag. Frenchie wanted to give them the thumbs up, but he dare not let go of the controls. The French coast was barely ten miles ahead now, but he knew Lana couldn't make it. She was bucking and twisting as though trying to shake them loose to save their necks.

Terror had overcome the second pilot, freezing him in his seat. Frenchie risked reaching out a hand and tried to make him move, but he screamed and fought. Again he tried tugging at his co pilot's jacket. It was useless. He daren't release the controls. Lana was screaming now, falling faster every second. The two men struggled as pointers swept dials. The skipper knew there was nothing left to do but abandon the controls, free his hands to drag his comrade to the hatch. Still the man fought him madly, wild eyed and screaming. The skipper slapped him hard and shook him. At last he moved, seeming to waken in blundering confusion.

At the hatch, Frenchie pushed him out and watched with relief as the parachute blossomed. Now he must jump but the ground was hurtling up towards him. He knew it was too late. There would never be time for his parachute to open. Flames suddenly exploded along the aircraft engulfing him, ripping the breath from his body. There were no choices left. He dived in to the blackness to escape the flames, and filled his burning lungs on the icy wind. Yanking the rip cord he prayed to feel the jerk of

167

the canopy filling with air. At last it did, but too soon he hit the roof of a farm building and crashed through on to an earthen floor, roof tiles and debris showering down on him.

Ten minutes later Hinch found his skipper unconscious, his parachute still attached, his face blistered on one side like pork crackling. The others arrived, carrying Willy Glover, unconscious and bleeding. Gathering round, each tried to assess their comrades' injuries. Hinch applied field dressings. Tommy found some water and dribbled it onto the injured men's lips before handing it round.

Hinch looked for orders to Noll Pearce the second pilot, now ranking officer. He told them to check the other buildings to see if the farm was occupied. If it was, the farmer was sure to be wide awake after the explosion caused by Lana crashing in a fire ball not half of a mile away.

Flight sergeant Arnold Pearce remained kneeling beside his unconscious skipper, as his comrades left to carry out his orders. He stared sourly at both the injured men. Willy Glover looked almost dead, but the skipper was not much better. Pearce feared escape would be impossible with the two of them in tow. By now every German soldier in the area would be looking for them. How could they hope to get away carrying two unconscious men?

Willy's leg was virtually unattached. His blood was pooling on the ground around him. Pearce loosened the tourniquet that had been applied to his thigh and watched the spurts of blood it released. He considered leaving it off and letting poor Willy slip away peacefully, while the others were searching the farm.

'You need to tighten that again now,' the skipper croaked weakly. 'Loosen it again in twenty minutes for another two.'

'That's what I'm doing,' Pearce snapped, wondering how long the skipper had been awake and watching him. 'How do you feel?'

'Huh terrific. I've just stepped off a burning plane two feet before it hit the ground thanks to you,' he croaked. 'How do you think I bloody feel?'

168

Pearce felt his colour drain. He glanced around shiftily to see if any of his comrades had heard the skipper's reproach. 'I don't know what happened. It was just ...'

'Forget it. You're not the first to freeze under fire.'

Tommy Loveday returned with some eggs. 'The place is all in darkness, but it looks occupied. I think they must be hiding.' Seeing his skipper awake, he beamed a broad smile at him. 'Frenchie, how do you feel?'

'Great, just like a bloke who's fallen ten thousand feet into a barn full of horseshit and house bricks.'

'Oh – well, that's OK then.'

Hinch returned panting excitedly. 'There's a road and a couple of houses. The sea's that way. It's only about a mile.' He pointed energetically, as if to make the shore seem even nearer. 'You can see a harbour with small boats from the end of the farm's lane. It's all down hill. We could make it – I mean all of us.'

They started making stretchers with any old timbers they could find, a rake and a pitchfork handle, some stall rails. They whispered excitedly as they strapped them together with parachute cord and silk. They worked with a positive air of eager anticipation. They had survived the flack and the bail out from a burning aircraft. They were almost at the shore. There were boats to be had. Home and freedom seemed achievable.

Sporadic gunfire announced the enemy's approach, and the mood suddenly nosedived. 'They're on their way, boys,' croaked Frenchie, wincing as pain wore through the screening adrenaline rush, he had felt on leaping out of the aircraft. 'Take Willy first, and then come back for me.'

Tommy glanced at Pearce and Hinch, his concern revealed on his soot-smeared face. It had just dawned on him that there were only three of them to carry the two stretchers.

Hinch used the last of the morphine to inject Frenchie, the two of them exchanging whispered words.

'What's he say?' asked Tommy, as Hinch came out of his huddle with the skipper.

'He wants us to take Willy first.'

'But we should take the skipper first,' Tommy whispered. 'I hate saying it, but I don't think Willy will make it. The skipper still could.'

'We must help Willy first,' whispered Pearce, joining them. 'The skipper is the strongest. It could be a couple of days before we can come back and pick him up, or maybe HQ can get the resistance to do it. You know what the Marquis are like, they don't take unnecessary risks. They'd take one look at Willy and probably finish him off themselves before the Germans got him.'

The skipper turned his head towards them, evidently he had overheard Pearce. 'Noll's right,' he said. 'Take Willy first, get me later, when it's safe. You'll have to hide me. Leave me some water and the pain killers.'

The men looked at each other in silent consultation, then Tommy spoke. 'We could do it in stages,' he suggested. 'You know, move you down the lane a bit, then come back and move Willy, then move you again. It's only a mile at the most. We could get you both out like that.'

Frenchie had passed out, he heard nothing.

Pearce stepped in. 'No, we'll move Willy first, then come back for the skipper. Just like he told us.' He looked his two comrades squarely in the eyes and ....

....The ticket inspector leaned over Billy laid out on the deeply upholstered bench seat, a sneering smile on his mouth. 'Oh excuse me, Prime Minister. I didn't know you were on board today, Sir,' he said, sarcastically. 'Eeer, just a minute you're not Mr Atlee?'

Billy woke up sharply and sat up blinking. 'Err – no – err - I'm sorry.'

'If you're not Mr Atlee get them feet off my cushions and show us your ticket.'

'I don't have one. It's with my dad.'

'Your dad? Well, let's hope he's the Prime Minister then, cos if he's not, you're in big trouble, my lad.'

'He's not a prime minister,' Billy said weakly, adding, as if it might explain everything, 'He's a furnace mason.'

'Oh, a furnace mason. Oh thank God for that. Now you had better tell me why you're asleep with your feet up like the Prime Minister, in a First Class compartment, with the blinds down and no ticket?' The inspector's succinct summary, helped Billy to assess the precise depth of doo-doo, in which he now found himself.

*

Two police Wolsley's and a dark blue van drew up beside the barbed wire stretched around the old Walkley Bank Tilt Wheel. A constable climbed out of the leading car, drew on a pair of industrial leather gloves, and began tugging at the wire fence. A colleague carrying a set of wire cutters joined him. They chopped, snipped and folded the deadly barbed wire, to clear an access. Sergeant Burke climbed from the second car and oversaw their efforts. When it was done, three men in civilian clothes climbed stiffly from the blue van. One was evidently the driver. He lit up a cigarette and leaned back against his vehicle to watch proceedings. His two passengers shook out crisply pressed brown warehouse coats and pulled them on over their dark suits. The overalls were so stiffly starched that the men moved over the rubble strewn approaches to the old mill with a penguin like gait.

*

By promising to thrash Billie to within an inch of life, his father was able to placate the ticket inspector. The man went away, content on Mr Perks' assurance that Billy would soon be lying in a London gutter, like a blood sodden rag.

*

Late that evening as they returned after their day in London, Billy sat beside his mother. He felt dusty eyed and weary as he watched the lights of the city slide away into the darkness. Almost everyone in the carriage was asleep. Billy pulled out Bob Hinchcliffe's letter to his father and began reading.

..........A German patrol turned up at the farm. Frenchie and Willy Glover were unconscious, so Pearce was ranking officer. Willy was in a bad way. We couldn't stop the blood. The skipper had burns to his left cheek and hand. We'd dressed them OK, but the worse thing was his feet and legs. He seemed to have broken

171

every bone. We splinted them and did the best we could while he was unconscious. We used Tommy's shirt and the field dressings I had grabbed as I'd bailed.

Pearce was an arse. Sorry dad, but he was. He ordered us to hide Frenchie in the barn. He said we could get him picked up by the resistance. He argued that his fluent French would make it easier for him to escape once he could walk again. We didn't like the idea much, but it sort of made sense at the time. And anyway, we knew the Germans would not help Willy. I'm afraid he was too far gone. They'd have shot him to finish him off – so would the resistance for that matter. So we took him with us.

We made a sort of lean-to of some old timbers and junk and hid Frenchie behind it. We piled hay over it to finish it off. Next we threw open the barn's double doors as wide as they would go, in the hope that Gerry might assume nobody would be hiding in there with the doors wide open.

Tommy and I set off to the harbour carrying Willy on the make shift stretcher. A couple of times we thought he was dead and we had to check him out. Pearce stayed behind. He said he was going to hide and watch the Germans. He said that if the patrol passed by without giving the farm much attention, he would come and tell us so we could go back and get Frenchie.

Tommy found a boat. A clinker built lobsterman's, about ten feet long. It had oars and a mast. He swam out and hauled it in. We put Willy aboard and waited for Pearce. It was a working harbour full of fishing equipment. It reminded me of Cornwall. You remember that summer we had before all this nonsense began? We couldn't tell if people were awake, watching us from behind their windows or not. I just know it felt as if they were. Any moment I expected some angry Frenchman to come out waving a shotgun and yelling at us for pinching his boat. Tommy said that if they did see us they'd guess it was our plane that had crashed. He said they'd leave us to get on with it. Tommy always thinks the best of people. He's like you, Dad.

Next there was an explosion on the hillside. Flames flared up above the trees but quickly died away. A few windows lit up briefly, before their black-outs were drawn again. We heard voices and dogs from the houses.

Pearce arrived breathless. He said the German patrol had tossed a grenade into the hay in the barn where Frenchie was. He said he saw it catch fire. Tommy and I were puzzled by that, but too busy trying to get under way before we came under fire too. We didn't think about it until later.

We heard shots and another grenade up in the trees. When we spoke of it afterwards, we realised we both had our bearings wrong. Our impression was that both explosions had been some distance from the barn. Pearce was furious when we quizzed him about it. He went berserk. He called us lying rats and insisted we were wrong. He said he'd seen it happen and barely got away with his life. I'm ashamed to say that at the time, I was reluctant to argue with him more strongly.

Well dad, you know the rest, poor Willy died just before we were picked up by Air Sea Rescue. What I never told you was that at his debriefing, Pearce told them he had actually seen Frenchie killed by a German grenade. He said he had stayed and watched as the barn caught fire. This of course meant that the resistance would not be asked to go and look for him. We didn't know about this until Tommy and I were debriefed the following day. They asked us if we had seen Frenchie alive after the hand grenade attack. Of course, we had not, and no matter what else we told them they weren't interested. I couldn't say that Pearce was a liar because I had no proof. In any case, they never tell you if the resistance will pick up your crew mates or not.

Tommy was posted to a porridge loving place, and me to this bleak dump, I'm not allowed to say where, but they eat clangers as well as drop them.

Well they say the war will end soon, Dad. When I get out, I shall do something about this dirty business. I've written to Tommy because I know he feels the same way. Pearce made us into liars, and the longer it goes on, the harder it will be to undo. I know we'll be in big trouble for not speaking up sooner, but you see dad, I asked myself what you would do, and that's why I will face up to whatever they throw at me.

*

173

'Are you crying, Billy?' his mother asked. 'What's that you're reading?'

'No – I – err - I was just thinking what a great day, Mam,' Billy croaked, wiping his eyes on his sleeve and stuffing the Reverend's pages into his shirt front.

Mrs Perks leaned over and hugged him fondly. 'Ah bless him,' she cooed. 'I'm glad you had such a good day. At least you can stay awake for it. That's more than can be said for him,' she added sourly, eyeing Billy's father, snoozing peacefully.

Billy turned to the window. He could see little but his own reflection. It was black outside and the train was speeding along, streaking the windows with water and soot. It thundered past odd lights and bells, leaving traces of them on his senses like fading dreams. The bogies clattered rhythmically beneath his feet chanting to him, secret words that had no voice except inside his head. He closed his eyes and leaned his head on his mother's shoulder, loving her perfume.

Pearce killed Annabel,
Pearce's the one.
Pearce shot Tommy.
Find Pearce's gun.
Pearce stole the medal.
Pearce is a rat.
Tramp has the medal?
Cops have my hat.

. . . .

174

CHAPTER NINETEEN

'Are you sure you're old enough for potted meat on toast?'
Doctor Hadfield asked earnestly. 'I didn't discover it until my
second year at Oxford.' Kicking off his shoes, he grinned and
chuckled to himself.

'It's just potted meat - what's to discover?' Billy said, with a
pitying frown.

'Speaking of discovery, anything fascinating in the Dome of
Discovery?'

'No.'

Hadfield sat bolt upright in his sagging armchair and shot
Billy an incredulous scowl. 'D'yer mean to say the Government
spent eleven million quid of our hard earned taxes on a Dome of
Discovery that can't even excite your curiosity a tiny jot?'

'I don't know what you're on about,' Billy said dismissively.

The doctor cut the last slice of toast in half to share with him.
Billy accepted his half, and began loading potted meat.

'Surely there's something about it you can tell me. I mean,
should I go? Is it worth the trip? Would a certain female of our
mutual acquaintance appreciate me making such a financial
sacrifice if I were to take her?'

'There's the Skylon,' Billy replied phlegmatically.

'What's that?'

'Nobody knows.' Billy delicately picked crumbs from his
tank top. 'The Dome is massive. It's the biggest in the world.
There's allsorts you can do in it.'

'Such as?'

'You can steer the radio telescope and bounce signals off the
moon.'

'Wow, what's that like?'

'I don't know. There was a long queue. We had to miss it.'

'Huh, pity.'

'There were special sticks of festival rock.'

'Excellent – can I see some?'

175

'We didn't get any. There was a long queue.' He looked round for more bread to toast. 'You could get special soap with the festival embossed on it.'

'But the queue, I suppose - eh?' Hadfield queried, eyebrows arching theatrically.

'Yeah, we didn't wait.'

'It's beginning to sound as if the excitement would be too much for me,' Hadfield said, pushing the breadboard across the table with a sock covered toe. 'Anyway, just like you, I too also don't have either festival rock, or soap, and have never steered the radio telescope. Unlike you however, I've achieved all of this without spending hours on a train to London, so I reckon that's one up for me.'

'Did you get my Post Mortem results yet?'

'Sorry, I didn't know you'd died old thing.'

Billy giggled. 'Come on, stop messing about - my PM results - that's why I came.'

'Oooh PM results,' Hadfield cried, 'Soon slipped into the old police jargon eh?'

Billy felt his face colour and pretended to concentrate on the toasting.

'Don't worry, I checked it out for you. There was nothing about Tommy's death to suggest it was anything but a simple fall. Death by drowning. It doesn't look at all suspicious. If I'd done the post mortem myself I would have come to precisely the same conclusion.'

Disappointment briefly marred Billy's face, until smoke from the grill made him drop everything to rescue toast. 'I know I'm right,' he said, as if trying to convince himself. 'I'm sure he was threatened with a gun, and frightened, so that he fell backwards down that hole. And I think that if he'd not fallen, he would have been shot. It was a lucky accident for the killer, and it's hidden a murder all these years.'

'I know that you really care, Billy,' said the doctor. 'And believe me, I checked everything I could think of. I even talked it over with my arch tormentor himself. He remembers it very well. He was *almost* there when it happened.'

'Doctor Greenhow?'

176

'Yes he was watching some ducks or vultures, or something. He claims he's a bit of an ornithologist.'

Billy stared blankly.

'Well he was there. He remembers seeing Pearce there too. The police took a statement from him. Maybe you should have a little chat with him. He quite likes you, you know. He's always asking me how you're doing.'

Billy glowered. 'I've told him I stopped doing it. Why doesn't he believe me?'

'Because it's a bare faced fib, old lad, and everybody knows it.' The doctor helped himself to blackened toast and spread the last of the potted meat on it. 'Shares?'

Billy accepted the offer and watched grumpily as Hadfield jokily pretended to make much of measuring the toast before cutting it in half.

'A certain Miss Sparkes and I were walking down Rivelin yesterday,' he said casually. 'We saw the gendarmes crawling all over that old mill of yours ...'

Billy dropped his toast and leapt up suddenly. 'I knew it,' he cried. 'They're looking for a bullet.' He ran out of the house leaving the doctor cheerfully bemused.

'Yep, definitely need to buff up the old social skills,' he said, reaching for Billy's untouched toast and potted meat.

*

Kick Morley jinked to one side and slipped behind Billy, pushing him towards the surgery door. Billy twisted trying to turn on him. 'Why don't you? Why is it always me first?'

Kick was about to make his excuses when they heard the old doctor shouting at them from the coach house. 'Surgery is closed. It's Sunday! Am I expected to be at your beck and call twenty-fours hours a day and weekends too?' They turned to find him striding angrily toward them. He had his sleeves rolled up and a large screwdriver in one hand. 'When the devil am I supposed to get a break?' He stopped suddenly and peered as if through fog. 'Goodness, is that Billy? Oh, welcome, Old Stick, good to see you. Who's he?'

'Michael Morley, sir. My friend.'

'Best friend,' corrected Kick, feeling his credentials warranted greater emphasis.

'The doors keep jamming. I can't get them to close properly. One of you can climb up and give the screws a turn or two. That should do it. Come along, step lively - this way.'

Billy followed him back to the coach-house. He was shown to a stepladder and handed the screwdriver. 'We – err – we're sorry to disturb you, sir, but Doctor Hadfield said you wanted to speak to me.'

'Hum, did I? Can't recall why.'

Billy began climbing the stepladder. 'He said you were a witness, five years ago, when Tommy Loveday was killed.'

'Oh did he really? Well he should know better than to gossip.' The doctor peered up and pointed to the offending hinge. 'Tighten that one first,' he instructed. 'I assure you I was certainly not a witness – at least, not in any legal sense of the word. The police took my statement, but didn't use it. But yes, I suppose it does appear that I was in the area at the time. However, I was not witness to anything, as the police will happily confirm.'

'Doctor Hadfield seemed to think you'd seen Mr Pearce crossing the river.'

'Really! Well he should keep his thoughts to himself. I can see I will need to have a word with that young man.'

'Did you?'

'As a matter of fact, yes I did. The damn fool spoiled everything for me. I was watching a kingfisher's nest. It came out of its hole, flew to a twig over the water, dived, caught a fish and took it back to its hole. Absolutely fascinating. Few people ever see that you know. It sticks in my mind, a wonderful sight. I watched it for a while, but then that idiot Pearce blundered across the river, and scared it away.'

'Did he come out of the mill, and then cross the river?'

'Turn the damn thing, don't just wave the screwdriver at it. You'll never tighten it like that,' Greenhow grumbled.

'Did he come out of the mill?' Billy persisted.

'I think so. I don't know - I wasn't watching him. I was watching the kingfisher. As far as I can recall he went both ways, over and back again. The idiot had lost his shoe you see.'

'Was this in the police report?'

'No, of course not. I already told you, they didn't need me. They had the water bailiff and some gardener chappies as witnesses.'

The old doctor was becoming more bossy and grizzly. He paced about impatiently, pointing and grumbling, angrily picking up tools and dropping them again. Kick's patience with the old grouch quickly wore out. He told him he had to go to football practice. Billy seized on the moment to escape too.

While he had been struggling with the doctor's garage door, Billy had decided to check on what the police had been doing at the old mill. He also wanted to pay another visit to the old soldier, who had pulled him out of the river just a week earlier. He was troubled by the doctor's story. In particular he wanted to check something he had said about kingfishers. He was guessing that the old man would be the perfect authority.

*

It was a cool day under a leaden sky. There was not a breath of wind in Rivelin Valley and the birdsong in the great limes echoed from tree to glorious tree. The river was full and fast, bubbling noisily over the smooth rocks. Beyond the millpond, on the opposite bank, a few men were busy in their allotments, backs bent, faces close to their planting.

At the old Walkley Bank Tilt, there were no obvious indications on its grey exterior that the police had been there just a few days before. Taking a good look round to ensure old Sutcliffe was not around, Billy scroamed under the barbed wire into the derelict building.

Once inside the damp silence, everything seemed just as it had been the last time he'd been there. He moved slowly round the old machines, and scanned the walls and floor, ears alert to any new sounds. He could see nothing new or unusual. Disappointed, he was about to leave when he spotted a postcard-sized label, pinned to the furthest wall. Around it, was a circle drawn with yellow chalk.

The sudden, noisy fluttering of a pair of pigeons in the rafters made his heart stop. Sutcliffe was somewhere. Sweat popped out on his brow. He felt weak and his hands trembled.

179

Hiding behind an old forge bellows he listened for sounds of Sutcliffe's approach. He waited for what seemed ages, but heard nothing more. Eventually, plucking up courage, he peered through holes in the rotting leather bellows to the doorway where he had last seen Sutcliffe. There was nobody there. The birds fluttered again and flew off through a window, leaving a few downy feathers to float slowly to the ground.

Releasing a sigh he came out of hiding and resumed his investigation, promising himself fervently, that he would get this bit of detective work finished quickly and get out of there.

Between him, and the label on the wall, was the sump hole that he had fallen down on his last visit. He gave it a wide berth, and feeling increasingly excited, ran over to the wall to read the label. Apart from the word, ballistics, nothing else written there made sense to him; just a few numbers and some squiggles, which he took to be the signatures of the investigating officers.

Cautiously skirting the hole in the floor again, he walked back to where he had been standing when he'd spotted the label. 'The killer could have stood right here,' he said aloud, raising his arm as if to shoot a pistol at the height of a man's chest. The trajectory lined up exactly with the label on the wall.

This was it. A shiver of excitement ran down his spine. He imagined the killer standing exactly where he stood. Tommy Loveday would have been just a few yards away. There was no way he could miss from that distance, unless Tommy had vanished down the sump hole, to escape, or because he fell. Maybe that was it. Maybe Tommy could see no way out and had dived backwards down the hole, or maybe he had just blindly fallen, because he was backing away from the gun.

Gripped by sadness for a man he had never met, he left the old tilt, feeling as if he had just witnessed Tommy Loveday's murder. It was as if Tommy had communicated with him across the chasm of death. Billy muttered a prayer, promising the dead man that he would do everything in his power to find his killer, just as he had promised to find Annabel's.

Outside he paused and looked back at the ruined mill. He thought of Tommy, happily watching his little dog yapping and

180

sniffing excitedly around the old stones. It made him feel even more determined to find out what had happened.

The stepping-stones across the river were old grindstones worn down from their original six feet diameter to little more than twelve inches. Set about a foot apart, they were easy to use, and provided safe access to the other side. It was difficult to imagine how anyone could fall in, except perhaps the odd drunk from the nearby Hollybush Inn.

Lance Corporal Francis Simmons was scattering blood, fish and bone along a row of infant plants. Billy crossed over to the garden allotments to talk to him, noting on his way, how every stepping-stone felt soundly bedded. The fact that not one rantied underfoot, strengthened his conviction that Pearce's fall had definitely been deliberate theatre, rather than an unfortunate accident.

The old man's face lit up when he saw Billy. 'Ayup sithee, look who's here, little Mester Questions. Are tha alreight mi owd?'

'Hello Mr Simmons. Aye, I'm champion thank you. Can I talk to thee a bit? I was wondering if you've had any visitors lately?'

'Tha knows damn well I have, lad,' he said, laughing softly, and dusting his palms on his trousers, led Billy to his shed, chattering all the time. 'Come on in - we'll have a mashing.'

Inside he commenced his tea making ritual, without pausing for breath. 'It were him, that big un – whassiz-name? Him who who lost his little girl? Tragic that were. He came with a young constable. He were here again yesterday an' all. Whadda they call 'im? Burke. Built like a brick shit house he is. He comes asking me if I'd heard a shot. I think he were just showing off for the young bloke. I told 'im "Tha takes thee time dunt tha? It were five years sin' that." I told him, "Tha goes to him next door who's as deaf as a spanner and as blind as a Chelsea boot, but tha never comes to me until five years later.".'

'But you *did* tell him though?' asked Billy, worried that the old man might have succumbed to injured pride and withheld his information.

'Of course I did. Then he says, were it a farmer shooting a rabbit?'

'I says no, it weren't a rifle, nor a shotgun. It were a pistol shot.'

'Do you ever watch kingfishers round here?' Billy asked, without explanation.

'Kingfishers? Tha needs to be up at Roscoe mill to see them, or down stream at Mousehole Forge. I've never seen none just here.'

'An ornithologist would know that wouldn't he?'

'By gum, that's a ten-bob word. Does tha mean a bird watcher?'

'I looked it up at the library. It means somebody who knows a lot about birds,' Billy explained.

'Tha don't say. Well he'd know then wouldn't he? But whaddya talking about kingfishers for?'

'Somebody told me he was watching kingfishers going in and out of their nest hole with fish they'd caught.'

'Aye well that'd be when they're feeding their young uns. They can have a lot of chicks you know kingfishers, eight at a time. It's a lot of work, when they've to dive in and catch 'em all.'

'This was October, five years ago, when that shot was fired.'

'There might have been some nesting here then, I can't swear to it, but they wouldn't have been feeding young.'

'Why not?'

'Not in October; May, June, July time, or even April, if it's a warm year. But it's all over by October. The young have fledged and flown off by then. The nest hole would be like a cesspit. The parent birds would abandon it. Whoever said they watched 'em feeding, is lying to you – or he's got his dates wrong.'

He suddenly froze with a new thought, and spun round to face Billy, his old eyes alight with promise. 'Here, I know what!' he cried, and moved purposefully to rummage inside an old army gas mask bag, hanging with his coat behind the shed door. Billy watched, wondering what miracle of evidence he was about to reveal. The old man pulled out a tin box, about the size of a house brick. It had a hinged lid and was decorated with pictures of a seaside resort. Billy gaped in awe, as Mr Simmons

182

opened it and set it before him. Inside were half a dozen fairy cakes. 'We can have 'em wi' us tea.'

*

That evening as Billy laboured wearily up Rivelin Street, a four thousand year old way out of the deep valley, his legs felt like lead. He wished he had one of the generations of pack ponies that had racked up and down the ancient road to carry him home. Behind him, the lime trees lining the valley road gently swayed their great heads as a slight breeze blew in from the High Peak moors. The sky was on the move too; a few small patches of blue were opening up in the west. There was not yet enough blue to make a sailor a pair of bellbottoms, as his mother would say, but the Man's Head rock was bathed in bright evening sunlight, putting a smile on its craggy face as it looked out over Rivelin.

Old Sutcliffe leapt out from the scrub beside the road and grabbed him, clamping his hard hand over his mouth. 'Don't worry. Th'art alreight. I'm not going to hurt **thee**,' he hissed into Billy's ear, his stubbly chin, grinding against his cheek. 'Listen th' art alreight. I waynt hurt thee. If I let thee **go, tha**'ll not run off nor shout, will tha? I want to talk to thee. I **waynt** hurt thee.' He gradually released his grip. 'See, th' art alreight. I've done nowt to hurt thee.'

'Whaddya want?' Billy was not convinced, and readied himself to run at the first sign of danger.

'Tha didn't go to coppers. I thought tha'd go to coppers after I grabbed thee in the mill. I've been expecting 'em to come for me, but they never did. That shows tha didn't tell 'em nowt. So that makes thee alreight to my mind.'

'I didn't do it for thee. Why should I? And when I grow up, I'm going to come for thee and give thee a chuffin good hiding as soon as I'm big enough. Tha'll be gerrin older and weaker, and I'll be gerrin bigger and harder, so tha'd better watch thee sen.'

The old man chuckled admiringly. It was a logic he understood perfectly.' Well tha's got me there reight enough. So I'd better get to be good pals with thee.'

'Is that it?'

'No I wanted to tell thee sommat. It's about that fifty quid.'

'Look, I've told you already, I don't know nowt about it.'

'I know, and I believe thee now, but you have to see it my way. I only saw it for a second. It was at the police station. They'd pulled me in – after Stan - and they showed me an envelope. I could see there were cash in it. "Had I seen it before?" they asked me. Well, what a question that was. I thought if I tell 'em yes and say it's mine, they might give it to me and I'd be fifty quid better off. On t'other hand they might've found it on some job that they wanted to finger me for, and I could get nicked for sommat I never did.' He sighed glumly, shaking his head. 'I had no choice, did I? I had to say no. It were the truth anyway, but I had to miss out on fifty quid. Anyway, I saw the mucky spatters on the envelope - like that sooty water in the boiler room where they found my Stan. And I guessed that's where they'd found it. Then I heard that you'd been in there, so I put two and two together.'

'And made five,' Billy growled sullenly.

'Well I reckoned you must have seen sommat. You were in there, and so were that envelope judging by the muck spattered on it.'

'But now you reckon you know who it was?'

'Aye I do. I can't tell thee yet, but it proves tha were telling me the truth. So I just wanted thee to know that I think th' art alreight. Tha needn't be scared of me again.'

'Who was it?'

'I've just said I can't tell thee yet,' he snapped. 'I need a bit of time. I've got to try to make a few bob out of this first. I'll tell thee after that.'

'Blackmail?'

'Call it what you like. I don't care. For me it's gerrin even. He paid my lad and caused him to get killed. I want sommat back for that. I'm entitled to dip me bread in that gravy, especially after all I've gone through.'

'But if he killed Stan, don't you want him punished?'

'Stan's dead. Hanging somebody won't change that. But getting my hands on some decent cash for a change – that'll make a big difference. My whole family will get sommat out of that. It'll be the best job our Stan ever did for us.'

184

'Was it Pearce?'

The old man walked away. Billy ran after him and asked again, but the old man refused to talk.

Billy gave up and let him go. He watched Sutcliffe stamping off in his personal haze of revenge, and decided to find Yvonne, instead. There was a lot to record and analyse.

*

Yvonne Sparkes lived in a stone house next door to the Perks. It was a small pleasant house in a garden with a spring fed pool that had watercress growing at its edges. The spring flowed from the old Walkley well on Camm Street, further up the hill. The same waters fed a well in the cellar beneath Billy's house. In the height of summer, it served as the Perks' refrigerator for milk, eggs, and butter.

Evening sunlight was slanting into the steep street, as he knocked on the Sparkes' back door. It was standing ajar as usual. Silhouetted against a window, overlooking her front garden, Mrs Sparkes sat at her kitchen table reading a newspaper. She rose as she saw him, and tip toed towards him with strange birdlike steps, a finger pressed to her lips. 'Hush, he's sleeping. He's on nights,' she whispered, ushering him into her narrow kitchen.

Yvonne arrived from another room as her mother returned to her seat. 'Have you seen this?' she asked Billy, pointing to an article in her mother's newspaper. 'It says.... "Police are understood to be reopening the case of Thomas Loveday, who drowned in the River Rivelin, in October nineteen-forty-six. Loveday's body was found trapped beneath the water wheel of the Walkley Bank Tilt Mill, having drowned in less than a foot of water." '

'Brilliant. That's because they found the bullet I told 'em to look for.' He read the article again his face glowing with satisfaction.

'Give us me paper back, Sherlock.' Mrs Sparkes complained.

Billy released the newspaper. 'Now, I want us to talk to that tea lady, Mrs Taylor,' he told Yvonne. 'I think you'll be better at it than me.'

·········

CHAPTER TWENTY

Mrs Taylor's house was one of a stone built row on Camm Street, a quiet, level street running across the breast of the steep Walkley hillside. She was mopping the stone flagged pavement in front of her door when Yvonne and Billy arrived. Yvonne eyed Billy sideways and sighed despairingly. Never pristine, his appearance on that day had suffered a severe set back during a brief interlude on the football field with Kick Morley. Standing on Mrs Taylor's scrubbed pavement, Yvonne supposed he was an affront to everything Mrs Taylor held dear.

'Mrs Taylor,' she sang hopefully. 'Your garden is lovely. There should be a prize.'

Billy was impressed with Yvonne's opening gambit and watched as Mrs Taylor visibly grew with pride. She would be as putty in Yvonne's hands after that, he thought.

'Oh it's nothing,' gushed Mrs Taylor, 'but I do like things to be nice.' Shifting her gaze to Billy her expression hardened into a curiously apprehensive stare. Her detailed inspection took in his scuffed shoes, muddy trouser knees, ink stained tank top, tangled hair, and the muddy imprint Kick's soccer ball had left on his face. 'What's he want?' she asked, unable to move her eyes from him.

'Err w-what's this one called?' Yvonne asked sweetly, attempting to distract her by brushing her fingers through the nearest flowers.

Mrs Taylor shuddered, and tore her gaze from Billy. 'It's just Aubrietia, love - trailing. It's still a bit early for it. What's he want?' she repeated, from the corner of her mouth.

'I wanted to ask you something, please. If you don't mind of course,' said Billy, aware he had a long way to go to reach the dizzy heights of acceptance that Yvonne had attained.

Mrs Taylor blinked and twitched her head several times, 'Oh, he talks nice though, doesn't he? You wouldn't think it though would you? I hate it when they thee and thou all the time - it's very common.'

'My mam doesn't like me to thee and thou,' explained Billy.

'Yes, and quite right too,' Mrs Taylor agreed. 'I know your mother. A very nice lady. She works at the Children's Hospital doesn't she?'

'I believe you saw Mr Pearce chasing Stan Sutcliffe?' Yvonne interjected quietly, as if it was the last thing on her mind.

'Oh, I did - yes. I hate to say it, him being dead, but, I didn't like that young man. He had a terrible mouth. And such a nasty way of looking at you.' She dropped her gaze self-consciously. Her head flicked a couple of times, though as usual she did not seem to notice.

'You'd better come inside,' said Mrs Taylor, 'but you'll have to remove your shoes.'

They followed her inside, kicking off their shoes at the door step. The room smelled of lavender and furniture polish. Miniature ornaments and crystal objet d'art covered every spotless surface. Mrs Taylor fetched a tea towel from an adjoining room and arranged it carefully on her settee. 'Sit there please, on this,' she invited Billy, a death threat clearly evident in her piercing gaze. 'And, please do not touch anything.'

'So what did you see?' he asked, not in the slightest concerned at being quarantined by a tea-towel.

'He had him down on the ground just outside my door. I was cleaning my transom – on the inside. I saw everything, a grandstand view you might say.'

'Did you hear anything?'

Mrs Taylor shot him a horrified glance. 'I don't eavesdrop, young man,' she hissed.

Billy sighed and tried again, determined to stay calm. 'Yes but, did they speak? I mean, you must have heard something.'

'I just told you, didn't I? I don't listen to other people's conversations.'

Yvonne patted Mrs Taylor's arm. 'Of course you don't, Mrs Taylor. He knows that perfectly well, but sometimes we all hear things, we never wanted to hear, don't we? I hate it when that happens. I'm sure you do too.'

Yvonne's intervention seemed to calm her. She looked at her fingers for a moment then spoke. 'What were you looking for?'

'Well, we need evidence,' Billy explained. 'We need to find out as much as we can. We need to know what was said …' His voice trailed off, distracted by Mrs Taylor staring at him, as if he were a lunatic.

'I just told,' she said, giving him a pitying look. 'What - were - you - looking - for?'

'Oh – you mean that's what he said?'

'Yes, he asked him over and over – "What were you looking for?" and then he said "Who's paying you?" or something like that.' She turned to Yvonne and nodded at Billy. 'He's a bit scatty isn't he?'

'Did Stan say anything?'

Horrified, Mrs Taylor shook several invisible corn seeds from her ears before responding. 'I la lard,' she said.

'La Lard?' asked Billy, mystified.

'Yes I put my hands over my ears and la-la-lard, so I couldn't hear his filthy mouth. All I can say is poor Mr Pearce did not get a civil answer.'

Billy sighed, fearing Mrs Taylor would be of little further use. 'Before we go,' he said, gloomily. 'Do you know why the Sergeant doesn't like the Doctor?'

'Well I must say!' she gasped horrified. 'I don't go round gossiping about people. Whatever do you think I am?'

'He's sorry. He didn't mean anything by it,' said Yvonne, despairing. They thanked her and took their leave abruptly. Mrs Taylor was reaching for the Ewbank carpet sweeper, even before Billy had made it to the front door.

Once in their shoes again, they took a backyard route, past the chip shop, and over a wall to get to Grandmother Smegg's cottage. They found her sitting on a low rockery wall, sunning herself in the garden.

'There you see? There really are fairies in this garden,' she cried happily, as she saw them. 'I was just thinking, I wanted a fairy to bring me a cool glass of water and here you are.'

Billy gave her cheek a peck and went inside her house. He returned with three glasses of water balanced on a library book. 'I couldn't find your tray.'

'D'yer mind!' cried Mrs Smeggs. 'That's a library book, young man. I don't think Mr Carnegie gave us our library for you to put water stains on all his books. And another thing, what makes you think I've got a tray? I haven't had a tray since before your grandfather was buried and we lived in Linacre Road.'

It never ceased to amaze Billy how rapidly he could find himself in the deep and smelly stuff when talking to a woman – any woman. He could spend hours with men, discussing everything from football through to cricket without ever insulting a Scottish American philanthropist, or accusing people of having trays they didn't possess.

He sat cross-legged on the lawn and waited for his granny to calm down before venturing a question, 'I've got to find out about Annabel being pregnant.' He was resigned to the inevitable tirade this would evoke. 'It was in nineteen twenty or twenty-one, five years after her husband was killed. Do you know who was the father?'

'I told you never to mention that.'

'Granny, she's been killed. Some things have to be mentioned whether we like it or not. Some things could be evidence.'

'Who told you it was nineteen-twenty?'

'It must have been because Doctor Greenhow treated her and he was in the Navy until then. He didn't come to Sheffield until Christmas nineteen-nineteen.'

'Yes you're right. It was the year before the old doctor passed away. That's how Doctor Greenhow came to get the Practice. He married the old doctor's daughter you see, and of course, when her father died it came to him.' Granny Smeggs took a glass of water from the library book, and stood up slowly. 'But I told you not to talk about it. And I certainly won't'. She stalked stiffly into her house leaving the pair staring after her. The door closed on her and they heard the key turning in the lock.

*

It was woodwork on Mondays. The boys in Billy's mixed class of forty five children walked in line up the hill to Western Road School to learn the mysteries of the yard broom holder. Billy wanted to make an acoustic guitar - a futile hope. Ahead lay the pipe rack, the dove tailed box, the sea-grass stool, and the finger crushing collapsible ironing board. Only when he had mastered these, would he be let loose on a guitar. In the boys' absence the girls went to domestic science. They were marched off with their rolled up smocks and brown paper carrier bags of mysteries. All were eager to ice buns, make toffee fudge, or cherry cakes. Instead they learned how to wash hair brushes and combs, boil flannels, and bake cheese straws that, impossibly, had be threaded through a pastry loop that always collapsed before *Miss* had the chance to mark it. Only in their final year would they tackle cakes and pies, most of which could safely be stood upon without leaving an impression in their crusts.

Billy couldn't wait for school to finish. He'd arranged to meet Kick and Yvonne at the old greenhouse. When the final bell sounded, he rushed out of school, wrested his bike from a heap and pedalled off like crazy, slowing only to toss his yard brush hanger over a wall.

He played heading tennis with Kick until Yvonne arrived, a merciful release for Billy, who was seriously outclassed by Kick's superior skills.

'Doctor Hadfield stopped me,' apologised Yvonne, as she climbed into the derelict garden. 'He wants to see you. He said tonight, but I told him about your curfew.'

'What's he want?'

'Don't know. He wouldn't tell me.'

'He's probably discovered aypenny ducks,' Billy said wryly.

Kick curled his lip and stared at him. 'What about aypenny ducks?'

'He thinks he's funny,' Billy said, disparagingly. 'He makes jokes about tripe and ferrets and being Yorkshire. I think it's sommat they teach 'em at Oxford.'

'What are we here for?' cried Yvonne impatiently, sensing the onset of a pointless discussion. 'You said you wanted to wrap it all up.' She jabbed a finger in Billy's direction. 'And you said you'd got some important new evidence.'

'I do an 'all,' he said dramatically. 'It's old Sutcliffe. He says he knows who paid Stan that fifty quid.'

'Who?'

'He won't tell me. I asked him over and over, but he says he won't tell me nor the coppers neither because he's gonna blackmail whoever it is.'

'Wicked old sod,' Kick growled. 'He'd rather fill his pockets than get who killed his own son.'

'That's Sutcliffes for you. It's in the blood,' said Yvonne. 'Why did he tell you? I thought he was going to bash you up.'

'Not any more. He likes me now.'

'But surely he knows we'll tell the police, and once we do *they'll* be after him to find out who it is.' She stiffened and gave Billy a dubious glare. 'We are telling the police aren't we?'

'Of course we are - eventually. We'll tell them everything, but not until we're ready. Sutcliffe knows it too, but he doesn't care. I think he's glad about it, because he thinks it'll put extra pressure on his blackmail victim.'

'He's a crafty old sod,' said Kick, more admiring than condemning.

'Any road up, I think it's time we took the cops all our evidence, and your notes,' Billy said. 'That's what I wanted to talk about. We should tell them everything and get them to – you know, reopen the case.'

'But have we got enough?'

'We've got as much as three kids are ever going to get. The rest of it is locked up in police files and medical reports, and all that other official stuff. We'll never get to see that because we're only kids. Let's face it, we wouldn't have got nowhere if we'd not had Doctor Hadfield on our side.' He paused, concerned by his friends' lack of conviction. 'Look, we need them to open the file again and to start a proper investigation. Our evidence should be enough to convince 'em. If they won't, we'll have to carry on and try to solve it ourselves, even if it takes us years.'

'What about Doctor Hadfield?' Yvonne queried. 'He wants to talk to you. Maybe that's about new evidence.'

192

'Well maybe, we'll find out tomorrow, but it won't change anything as far as I'm concerned. Are we all agreed?'

Kick sighed, disappointed. From the start he had wanted to see blood on the carpet. It would not be over for him until somebody was swinging from the end of Albert Pierrepoint's rope. Yvonne was disappointed too. She desperately wanted the killer to pay the price. Unknown to the others, she had recently discovered where Annabel had been buried. She had visited her grave several times to give the old lady progress reports. Each time she promised to keep on until they had the killer. She did not want to break her promise. And also, there was Doctor Hadfield, what might he have to tell Billy? Could that be the final piece in the jigsaw?

Perhaps the strongest feeling she and Kick shared was that their quest was ending, but not as they had expected. The killer was still out there - and may yet get away with it.

'No I can't,' said Yvonne. 'I agree we should go to the police and ask them to re-open the case. I think that part is a good idea.' She sniffed back tears. 'But I can't agree with the rest. Don't forget Billy, you and me made a promise to Annabel when we were in her house that time. We promised we'd find out who killed her.'

Billy studied his shoes. 'But what more can we do?' he asked weakly.

'I agree with Wy,' Kick put in. 'It's like being five nil down at half time. You don't just pack up and go home. That's not the spirit. You have to finish the job. You have to grit your teeth and go out there and cripple their centre forward.'

Billy eyed them in turn trying to gauge their opposition, 'OK, so how about this then - we go and tell the police everything, but we keep on the detectivin an' all?'

Heads nodded. 'Brilliant,' Kick said. 'And if they do re-open the case, they'll need us as expert witnesses and stuff.'

Yvonne was not sure she'd go that far, but she was confident that her notes and the evidence they had gathered would be useful.

'Right, that's it then. We meet here tomorrow after school and we'll all go to Hammerton Road Police Station together,' said Billy, keen to make sure they knew that he was not going to do this without their full support. 'I've got to go now. There's something I want to check at the library before it closes.'

....

CHAPTER TWENTY-ONE

Doctor Hadfield's neglect of the two feet wide strip of ground surrounding his strange octagonal house had paid unexpected dividends. As Billy approached it, the house was aglow in the late afternoon sunshine amid a cloud of ox eye daisies, dandelions and early poppies. The old Austin Ruby sparkled cheerfully beside the house. Yvonne had told Billy that Marlene had bought an old brass motor horn for it from a junk shop. It now graced the Ruby's door pillar. What a great gift, thought Billy, giving its big rubber bulb a squeeze.

'Please don't do that old son, you'll drain the battery,' joked the doctor, opening his front door to admit him.

Billy felt increasingly at ease with the young man. They had become firm friends over the past few weeks and might remain so, Billy thought, if he could only cure him of his compulsion to make fun of the Yorkshire accent.

'Ayoop Billy lad, thanks for coming, mi owd,' said Hadfield, contorting his vowels.

Billy turned on his heel and headed straight back towards the door. The doctor frowned and moved to stop him. 'Hang on old son, where are you going?'

'If you're gonna talk daft like that I'm off. I don't make fun of people's accents, but I could. And thine sounds like a Nancy boy's, but I don't say owt about it, do I?'

'Nancy boy?' hooted the doctor. 'Wow, that's a bit harsh, Billy. Surely not.'

'Well give over then. Tell me what tha wants, and no more Yorkshire accent or I'm off.'

Doctor Hadfield vanished into his bedroom. He returned in an instant with a small envelope made of dusty blue, sugar paper. He perched on an arm of his battered armchair and waited in silence as Billy sat down, and faced him across the dining table.

'What I tell you now, Billy, must remain confidential – a secret,' he said, gravely. 'You mustn't repeat it to anyone, not even to Marlene's sister. I don't know what this might lead to, but I have to tell you that I have discovered something extremely upsetting.'

Billy moved to the edge of his chair and leaned towards him.

'You alerted me to a discrepancy in something my boss told me about poor Mrs Loveday. He told me that he'd been treating her since her pregnancy. When I innocently mentioned this, you said such a thing was impossible – remember? You said he had not arrived in Sheffield, from the Royal Navy, until five years after Tommy was born. Unless he was mistaken or confused, this of course can mean only one thing.' He paused, studying Billy's face closely before going on. 'There must have been a later pregnancy.' He paused, fingering the blue sugar paper packet on the table, before going on. 'I decided to take a look at the old medical records. Something you may not know about my master and arch tormentor, is that he's nuts about notes. He writes down everything. He keeps the old ones in the coach house, wrapped in brown paper parcels. Everything is labelled and dated.' He brushed his palms together like a baker and pulled a slip of paper from his pocket and smoothed it flat. 'Well it took me a while, but I found his first entry for Mrs Loveday. I copied it and put the original back.' He showed Billy the paper and read from it silently before going on. 'He first saw her in January nineteen-twenty. He recorded it in his usual manner; every little detail in that scruffy writing of his. There's another entry for a visit to the surgery three months later, the same sort of thing. Then – nothing!'

'So? She wasn't sick anymore,' said Billy.

'No, not that kind of nothing, and that's precisely the problem. It began in autumn nineteen-twenty-one. You see, he entered the date of a home visit, but no notes. There was another date a week later, but again he made no notes. This happened four times in October and November.'

Hadfield paused to consult his page of notes before going on. 'Then on the twenty-sixth of November, his boss back then, a certain Doctor Samuel Howard - visited her and immediately

196

had her admitted to hospital. I couldn't tell which hospital, because Howard's notes had been scratched off the record card. Whoever did it made a thorough job of concealing all reference to the hospital and her treatment - except for one thing.'

'What?' Billy asked eagerly.

'I could still make out part of the name of the doctor who treated her at the hospital. It said "brams".'

'Brams?'

'I thought of David Abrams. The thing is, Billy, I know who he is – was – he's dead now. He was a leading authority on obstetrics. He wrote books. I read the damn things at Oxford, and I also knew that he worked here in Sheffield for a while.

Billy was frowning. 'What's ozplastics, and what does it prove?'

'Obstetrics, parturition, childbirth, babies, Billy, babies.' Hadfield was gleeful. 'We can also deduce from this that the hospital she was taken to was Jessops, the maternity hospital here in Sheffield. You see David Abrams worked there back then.' He sighed as if wearied by his revelations. 'It was an emergency admission and she lost the baby. Howard recorded everything in the normal way, but someone scratched out his notes to hide the facts.'

Billy looked doubtful. 'How do you know it was Greenhow who did it? Anyway, why not just rip up the card? Throw it away – burn it?'

'That, Billy, is precisely what makes me believe it was Greenhow. As you say - why not just burn it? Maybe Samuel Howard or someone else would have done, if they had been the ones wanting to hide the truth, but not Greenhow. He is obsessive about case notes. He couldn't bear to lose one. He just removed the bits he wanted to hide. Then, guess what? He started visiting her again when she was out of hospital and the notes start up again with every minute, boring little detail recorded, but not a word about her pregnancy.'

Billy listened, not sure what to think. It could mean that Greenhow had simply felt no reason to make notes on some occasions, or maybe it was kindness - he might have cooperated with her to conceal her pregnancy and miscarriage. In any case, it did not seem to have hurt anybody.

He sighed, wishing he understood such things better, or could talk to his Mam about them. She often said he should ask her if he didn't understand things about babies and sex and stuff, but when he did once, she almost fainted, and then demanded he tell her why he needed to know.

'At first, I was content to leave it at that,' said Hadfield. 'After all, it happened a long time ago and poor Annabel is dead now. Greenhow retires soon, so, what good would it do?'

'But?' queried Billy, sensing one coming.

Hadfield eyed him thoughtfully. 'Oh yes, there's a but, and it's a big one.' He sighed and slid down into his battered armchair forcing out a few more strands of horsehair stuffing from its split seams. 'This is the thing, Billy. And it's a very worrying thing, old son. Frankly I don't know what to do about it. If I tell you, I must have your solemn word that ...'

A knock at the door preceded the sudden eruption into the room of Marlene Sparkes. Their discussion was over. Hadfield leapt up and greeted her, embracing her warmly. Over her shoulder, he mouthed to Billy that he should go and return later.

Billy agreed and mimed in response, *I will see you tomorrow because I have to go to my auntie Emma's and uncle Reg's house on Bellhagg Road, to take their dog Judy, it's a border collie, to the vet's on Crookes Road, it has a dewclaw on its left leg and can't walk very well, especially on new carpets.*

The doctor gazed back, utterly bemused.

*

PC Handley gave Billy a friendly wave as he pedalled his police bicycle towards him. 'Hey Billy, it must be more than two weeks since we arrested you for anything,' he joked. 'How's the detective business?'

'Fine,' he replied guardedly. 'How's the cop business? I see you found a bullet, like I said you would.'

Handley shrugged. 'We might have, or maybe not.'

'You did, and you stuck a label where you found it.'

'Have you been in there? That's trespassing. I could nick you for that. You're not supposed to be in there.'

198

' … And I also know you went to see Mr Simmons at his allotment. You wouldn't do that either if I hadn't said so.'

'Well maybe – maybe not,' said Handley. 'But you know Mr Burke, as he's always telling me, "Check everyth …" '

' "…everything even the shadow of a shadow." ,' Billy interrupted.

Handley smiled, nodding. 'By the way, did you know we arrested that tramp who's been hanging around?'

'Why? I thought you said he was harmless.'

'We found his hidey hole. He had those medals that were nicked from Mr Pearce's house. It was me who found 'em.' He preened proudly. 'It was a good arrest. It should keep Mr Pearce off our backs for a while.'

'Where was he sleeping?'

'Oh you won't know the place. It's an old garden with a derelict greenhouse behind those big advertising placards in Heavygate Road. He had a hidey hole in there. It was full of his stuff. All we had to do was wait for him to came back.'

'Do you know his name? Is he called Frenchie Cadell?'

'Don't know. He won't speak to us.'

'Pearce never deserved that medal. He lied about it,' Billy said grimly.

'Hey steady on, Billy. He's only a tramp. He probably ...'

'He's a war hero,' Billy blurted. 'That's Jacque Cadell. He's a Canadian volunteer pilot. Check it out. I bet that's his name.'

'How do you know?'

'I just do, that's all. He's a war hero,' cried Billy. 'A real one too, not a liar like Pearce.' He ran off almost in tears as the story he had read on the train flooded back into his memory. Frenchie Cadell was a true hero. He had risked his life to save Pearce's. Pearce had abandoned him and cheated him out of his medal. It must be him, Billy told himself. Somehow, he had survived and come back. Now he was in jail, unjustly. Billy knew he had to do something. He couldn't just leave him there.

He set off to ask the Reverend Hinchcliffe. Surely, he would know what to do. And he would want to help Frenchie Cadell too, Billy guessed. He would want to do whatever he thought his son would have done in the circumstances, and Billy was sure

Bob Hinchcliffe would not have wanted his old skipper locked up in a police cell without a friend in the world.

*

Virginia creeper covered the front of the vicarage, sparkling in the sunlight as if each leaf had been individually wax polished. Mrs Corbert answered Billy's persistent rings on the doorbell. 'I can't disturb him, Billy. I told you yesterday,' she apologised, even before he had managed to speak to her. 'He's been deep in his studies for days. I've never seen him so upset. I'm very worried about him.'

'What I have to tell him will bring him back to his old self.'

'Will it? Oh I do hope so. Come in then, come in.'

'Don't worry,' Billy assured her. 'I'll go straight in. Is he in his study?'

Mrs Corbert nodded uncertainly, and dabbed her nose with a tiny handkerchief. 'He's not eaten. Do you think I should make him a sandwich while you're here? He might eat it. He had nothing yesterday but a garibaldi and I think that was the cat.' She looked around releasing a hopeless sigh. 'Do they eat them – cats?'

'I don't know. I don't like them.'

'Cats! Why not?'

'No, Garibaldi's.'

'I don't know what to do for him next.'

'Make the sandwich,' Billy said smiling. 'He'll eat it.'

Reverend Hinchcliffe looked up from his desk as Billy entered. His face was drawn and pale. A few days growth of stubble shadowed his chubby cheeks. The desk top was completely clear except for an empty tea plate. On the floor around the desk lay a scatter of papers and books. Billy imagined the reverend sweeping them off his desk in a moment of despair.

'Ah, Billy,' he said, trying to act cheerful, but missing the mark. 'How was your trip? Exciting place, London.'

'Fine, Sir. How about you?'

'Have you come to return my papers?'

'I gave them to Mrs Corbert yesterday. She said you weren't to be disturbed.'

200

'Yes of course, she told me - you and that nice young girl –
err – Yvonne. Yes I remember.' He stood up and walked to the
fireplace, and resting both hands on the mantle shelf stared into
the cold grate. 'I'm sorry, Billy. I have a great deal on my mind
today. Would you mind awfully if we talked another time?'

'Yes - no,' said Billy bluntly. 'We have to talk now.'

'But you don't understand, Billy. I must go to the police
today - as I promised you. But then, if there's a court hearing or
something - well, you know what the newspapers are like. They
love it when a clergyman gets into trouble. I rather think I might
lose my job, Billy. In fact I think I should resign.'

'Resign! What give your job up, d'you you mean? Why,
you're good at it. I mean - I'm not a proddy, but I've heard people
say you're really good at it; them with troubles and dead relatives
and things. And you go and see 'em in hospital, and all them
mucky tramps at the six-hundred-hostel. You help people all the
time. They need you. You can't give it up. My granny says, "It
doesn't matter what you think of yourself. It's what other folks
think of you that really counts." I think if you asked people,
they'd all say they want you to stay. So no matter how easy it
might be just to give up and leave, you can't resign.'

The old man looked at Billy. His words had shocked and
moved him. He stepped from the fireplace. 'It's cold in here I
think. This fireplace doesn't work. We had to brick up the flu last
year. It should be warmer, especially in May, shouldn't it?'

There was a rattle of china as the study door began to swing
open slowly. 'Yes it is cold, and you need to eat. Have a
sandwich.'

The housekeeper entered and placed a tray on the empty
desk. It bore a plate of ham sandwiches, a cup of tea and a glass
of cherryade. The reverend ignored the sandwiches, but picked
up the teacup. Billy helped himself to the cherryade.

'You're very kind, Mrs Corbert,' the vicar said softly.

'Someone needs your help,' Billy went on sternly. 'a friend of
Robert's.'

The Reverend pricked up his ears at the mention of his son's
name. Facing him, he listened closely as Billy explained why he
thought the tramp was Frenchie Cadell. Halfway through the

story the vicar selected a sandwich, took a couple of large bites, and had soon polished it off.

'Don't worry, Billy, you did the right thing,' Hinchcliffe said. 'I'll get down there this evening and we'll soon have him out and tucked up in a nice warm bed before you can say – err- I don't know what. I'll invite him to stay here. He can sleep in Robert's – err – old room.'

*

Sergeant Burke finished his call and gently dropped the telephone on to its rest. His hand remained hovering over it, his expression fixed like a waxwork.

Anxiously observing him from the office door were constable Handley and the desk sergeant. 'What's up sarj?'

Without moving, Burke replied softly. 'The bullet we took from the mill wall is no good for a positive ID. Ballistics can't prove it was from the same gun as the one that shot Stan Sutcliffe.'

'Bloody hell!' gasped Constable Handley, exchanging shocked expressions with the desk sergeant. 'Even so, the lad is still right. Somebody did wave a gun at Tommy Loveday and make him fall to his death down that hole.'

The desk sergeant nodded. 'Now five years later the same killer has shot young Stan.'

'Well we can't really say that can we, sarj?' Handley queried.

'Wow, a bloody serial killer - in Walkey.' The desk sergeant brightened. He seemed to like the idea until he caught Sergeant Burke's black glare. 'Oh, I mean, it couldn't be worse.'

'So, what about the old Star Woman then, Sarj?' Handley asked. He was thinking that if Billy was right about Tommy, he might also be right about the old lady's death?

'No! That's ridiculous,' Burke snapped. 'She fell and died. Don't go looking for murders everywhere, Handley. This is Walkley not the Wild West.' The Sergeant glared at the pair. 'What's up? Haven't you two any work to do?'

'Sorry, sarj.'

'Handley, you'd better find Billy Perks and his parents. We'll need every bit of evidence that lad has dug up, just in case anybody else is as daft as you are. We don't want them reopening the Annabel Loveday case. We've enough on our plates without that. We need to keep calm and do everything by the book. We do proper police work here. I don't want C.I.D. bouncing all over this. We've gone this far without 'em, we can finish it off ourselves.'

As the desk sergeant scurried away to his front desk, Handley stood pondering. He noticed it was now *we*, who had gone this far. Until then it had been Sergeant Burke alone who had ignored procedure and kept C.I.D out of their enquiries.

'Well don't just stand there gawping, Handley. Fetch the Perks. Use the boss's car,' snapped Sergeant Burke. 'I'll have a word with him.' He looked around his office as if taking his final look at it. 'He's not going to be best pleased to hear we've got a five year old possible murder on our hands.'

PC Handley shrugged, shaking his head doubtfully. 'I'll tell Mrs Taylor to bring you a cuppa.'

Burke smiled weakly and rose from his desk. 'Good lad. I'd better go and see him now.' He was not looking forward to it. There would be a brief flare up with cries of anguish and disbelief, followed by a call to the Chief Superintendent. It was not going to be fun, he told himself, as he straightened his tunic and brushed his cuffs with his finger ends.

The outer office fell silent as Burke marched through, without making eye contact. 'Get on now, please,' he told them all firmly. 'We've plenty to do.'

Fifteen minutes later Constable Handley ushered Billy and his parents into the station. All work stopped again as everyone watched the desk sergeant lead them to Sergeant Burke's still empty office. As the door closed behind them a buzz of excited whispering started up, causing Mrs Perks to look quizzically from husband to son. Constable Handley hovered by the door, unable to decide whether he should leave, or stay and explain the sergeant's absence.

'He'll be here in a minute. He's up with the boss.'

'What's going on?' Frank Perks asked.

Handley raised his eyes and tried to think of a simple explanation. Unable to come up with one he gave up and excused himself, claiming he had an important matter to deal with.

'I think they've found a bullet and it's the same as the one that killed Stan,' Billy said.

'Shut up Billy,' chorused his parents.

Ten minutes later Sergeant Burke entered the office. He smiled, sat at his desk, and blew a long whistling sigh. 'Thank you for coming.'

'Did we have a choice?' Billy's dad said querulously.

'Oh I know, Frank. I'm sorry, it's a pain in the neck, but there's been a development. It's something you need to know about.' He glanced shiftily at Billy as he mulled over how best to proceed. 'Billy, if you wouldn't mind, please go and ask the desk sergeant to give you a long stand.'

Billy jumped up cheerfully and went to carry out his errand. Sergeant Burke leaned across his desk confidentially. His visitors moved in closer too. 'While he's gone,' he said softly. 'I have to tell you something. We might possibly have a serious situation coming up, and I want to make sure it doesn't affect Billy. You see, it's these enquiries he's been making, well – err – they might have placed him in danger. I don't think it's too serious, but I believe you should be aware of the possible risk – err - however remote that might be.'

'What risk?'

'Well, as I say, we don't think there is a serious risk, not much of one anyway, but it's my duty to point out any sort of risk, no matter how unlikely and ...'

'If there isn't a risk, how can you point it out?' Mrs Perks said, unnerved by the sergeant's obfuscation.

'Look, don't be alarmed, but if there was a murderer and he finds out that Billy is ... It'll never come to that. I don't think there's any risk at all.'

'You think there really is a killer, just like our Billy's been saying all along? You think he might try to harm our Billy?' said Mrs Perks, her clenched fists pressing into her cheeks. 'Oh my God! There is a killer, isn't there? Our Billy was right, and now he's in danger.'

'I don't - I mean, I think it's not very likely. Let's just be sensible and take sensible precautions. That's all I'm saying. Keep him at home. Stop him doing this damned investigating. If he stops that, he'll be safe enough. '

The office door opened slowly admitting the desk sergeant. He looked pale and sick. Billy was bobbing about behind him trying to see round him into the office. 'I've just had a call from central,' said the desk sergeant. He leaned in close to Sergeant Burke's ear and whispered something. Sergeant Burke went pale, nodded his head, and stood up, gaping at his colleague. He straightened his tunic and sat down again, blowing a long thoughtful sigh.

He looked across his desk at Billy's parents. 'West Bar Central took an emergency call five minutes ago. Arnold Pearce is dead. He's been found shot at the back of his shop.'

. . . .

CHAPTER TWENTY-TWO

Arnold Pearce's death was front page news in the Sheffield Telegraph and The Star newspapers. The following day the nationals also carried the story of the war hero and prospective Tory party candidate, killed in his pharmacy.

Friends and neighbours were said to be stunned and saddened by the death. Sheffielders fear a gunman is prowling the steel city as the killing comes so soon after the still unsolved murder of seventeen year old Stan Sutcliffe, an unemployed labourer, shot in a Sheffield church. A Police spokesman could not confirm rumours that they are anxious to interview Mr Sutcliffe's father in connection with both killings.

Old man Sutcliffe was last seen happily drinking in the Rose House pub before word of Pearce's death. As the news broke, he vanished and had not been seen since.

A grave silence and stillness hung over Hammerton Road Police Station, like a chapel of rest. The city's C.I.D, had taken over the case. Sergeant Burke was suspended from duty, and now sat at home, his reputation and retirement plans in shreds.

The Ballistics Report confirmed that the same gun had been used to shoot both Stan Sutcliffe and Arnold Pearce, though it did not mention the bullet found inside the old Tilt mill.

In the greenhouse, there was deep gloom too. Yvonne, Kick and Billy sat at various corners gazing out at the sky through the white wash flaking off the windows. For a long time nobody spoke. Kick endlessly rolled a football down his legs, toed it back up to his chest, and let it roll down his legs again.

'At least they can't blame Frenchie. He's in jail.'

'Yep - anyway I know who did it,' Billy said quietly.

'You don't,' gasped Yvonne, eager to be convinced.

'I do, and I know how to prove it an' all.'

'Chuffin eck! Straight up?'

'Straight up.'

'Who is it? Is it Sutcliffe?'

'I need to see Sergeant Burke. I shall tell him who did it, but first I have to make sure.' He struggled out of his sagging deck chair and headed for the door. 'Kick, find Doctor Hadfield and tell him what I'm doing? Yvonne, I need you to come with me.'

They ran down to the police station where they learned that the sergeant was taking a holiday at his home. Yvonne said she knew where he lived, so they set off, jogging the mile back up the hill to his house.

'What if he won't talk to us?'

'Why wouldn't he?' panted Billy, as they pushed onward up the steep hill. 'Anyway if he won't, we'll have to get the Reverend, or the Doctor.' Billy scowled crossly. 'The cops won't believe me. It'll have to come from an adult.'

The sergeant's house was one of a fine terrace of Victorian villas, behind a screen of lilac and rhododendron shrubs. A glossy bay window, with leaded glass, pushed out from stout ashlars. Beside an ornate glazed door, a large brass bell push sparkled from a circular carved stone surround. Billy rang the bell. Somewhere deep inside the house a small dog barked, but nobody quieted it, or came to the door.

They tried again, and imagined the little dog going crazy, alone in some distant room. Again, there was no response. Billy moved glumly from the door and stepped down back into the street. 'I wonder if Kick's found the doctor.'

'Let's not wait,' said Yvonne. 'Let's go to the vicarage.'

*

Mrs Corbert answered the vicarage door. She was grave faced and edgy. 'Oh Billy, it's you. The Reverend's not here. He's taking a walk - for his head. Something is wrong, I can tell. He's really not himself. He's been lost somewhere ever since he came back from Nottingham. I don't know what to do for the best.'

'Drink lots of water, my granny says. Water cures a head full of worries.'

Mrs Corbert looked at him doubtfully. 'He could be back around five but I don't know. I finish at five on Saturdays. If he's remembered, he might try to be back before I go.'

'Will you tell him I have to speak to him – life or death. I'll come round first thing in the morning.'

'Not tomorrow you won't - it's Sunday. He'll be busy all day, and dog tired in the evening. You'll have to wait until Monday,' she said sternly. 'The poor man works like a slave. I'll not have him bothered when he's so tired.'

'OK Monday then - I'll come before I go to school. Will he be up?'

Mrs Corbert looked shocked. 'Of course he'll be up. He's always been up a couple of hours by the time I get here at eight.'

'Eight then,' Billy told her.

*

On Sunday morning as Billy was looking for Kick, the Doctor's old Austin Ruby pulled up beside him.

'Hey, get in, I need to talk to you.'

'Did Kick find you yesterday?' Billy asked him.

The doctor looked puzzled. 'No. Come on quick. Get in.'

'What's up?'

Rummaging in his jacket pocket he pulled out the blue sugar paper envelope Billy had seen at his house. 'You and Yvonne cleared the old lady's house, didn't you?'

'Well it was Mr Leaper, but we helped.'

'What did you do with her things?'

'Furniture was sold off: pots and pans, and most of her bedding and towels. She didn't have much. The rest was burned, or put in the dust bin.'

'What about medicines? Did you find any pills, or bottles?'

'Loads of 'em, mostly really old stuff. Mr Leaper said they'd be no good. We emptied full ones down the sink, then put 'em in the dustbin. Why? Was that wrong?'

'Did you see anything like these?' the doctor held out a cupped hand and shook a few greenish-brown pills into it from the sugar paper packet.

'Green mouse droppings,' laughed Billy, recognising them instantly. 'Yeah we saw some of them. There were only a few. We emptied 'em out so I could have the jar for – err – something else.'

'You're positive you saw pills exactly like these?'

208

'Yes,' he said firmly, 'We laughed because they looked like mouse droppings.'

'Can you remember what it said on the jar?'

'Yes, it was different to the rest. It didn't look like a proper label. You know, there was no proper printing on it, no chemist's name or anything. It just said three times a day. Nothing else.'

'How many were in the jar?'

'Hardly any; that's why I chose that jar – three, maybe four.'

Doctor Hadfield released a miserable sigh and stared at the steering wheel. 'Don't say a word about this, not even to Yvonne, or your parents. I mean it, Billy. You really must keep this to yourself.'

The Ruby revved up and pulled away from the kerb. Billy stared though the window as they drove. The doctor was belting along like a Wicker tram. The doctor swung the little car into Highton Street and plunged down its precipitous hill. The little Austin Ruby offering scant promise that it would be able to stop, but the doctor seemed unconcerned.

Outside his house, Billy thanked Doctor Hadfield for the lift and clambered out, surprised and relieved to still be alive.

His mother dismissively handed him a note as soon as he walked into his house. 'Here, I found this pinned on the door. It's terrible writing and spelling, it must be from Michael Morley.'

The note was unsigned and scribbled on the inside face of a cigarette packet. It read, *Meet me now wear you fellen. ERGENT!*

It was from old Sutcliffe, Billy guessed. He was the only one who knew exactly where he had fallen. It wouldn't be Mr Simmons, because he didn't know his address, and Kick would have signed it with the special new signature he had been practicing for giving out autographs when he achieves his ambition of playing for Sheffield United.

He volunteered to take the dog for a walk, so that he could get out of the house without raising his mother's suspicions. Preoccupied with her endless chores, she barely noticed his departure. Ten minutes later, he was in the old tilt mill looking for his one time enemy, old man Sutcliffe.

'Did tha get rid of my note?' the old man croaked, materialising from the gloom.

Ruff barked and snarled fiercely from behind Billy's legs. 'Well I didn't eat it if that's what you mean,' cracked Billy, fishing the note from his pocket and offering it.

Sutcliffe took it and tore it up before dropping it into a sump hole. 'I hear they've sacked Burke. Good riddance.'

'What do you want? I've not got much time. It's Sunday and we're going to Bradfield on my dad's motor bike and sidecar this afternoon.'

'Huh – all right for some int it? I've got to stay in this shit hole until the stupid coppers trip over the killer. It's the only way they'll ever find him. He's too clever to get caught.'

'Do you know who it is?'

'I'm not saying nowt about it.'

'Do you think Pearce knew who it was? Is that why he was killed?'

'I don't know or care neither. I just want him caught so they'll stop blaming me. It's always the same. If sommat happens they always blame me.'

'Why did you send me the note?'

'Thars got to prove it. Thars to get me off. There's nobody else that'll help me.'

'Tell me what you know and I'll do my best.'

Old Mr Sutcliffe breathed a sigh of relief and squatted down on an old wooden stillage.

*

In the little octagonal gatehouse Doctor Hadfield answered the telephone. The voice on the line belonged to an old university friend, now working for the City of Bath Police forensics department.

'Loafer! Great, thanks for getting back to me. What did you find out?'

'Where did you get these monsters from?' his friend asked.

'I can't say too much, Loafer old man, but I found them in rather suspicious circumstances. If they're what I think they are, I'll be taking them to the police, so if you don't mind, I'd better not say too much about it at this stage.'

'Well your suspicions are quite correct,' Loafer said. 'They're a particularly nasty herbal concoction. If a pregnant woman took these, as you suspect, they could certainly have caused her to miscarry. But that's not all, she would be playing Russian roulette with her life and certainly with her kidneys and liver. Some of the nasties we found in them are, pennyroyal, savin and wild celery seed, but there's also a toxic cocktail of other stuff too. Your joke about mouse droppings wouldn't apply. Any mouse nibbling one of these monsters would be dead in a squeak. Anyway, I'll write it all up and send you the report. I'll have to make it official, of course. I'm sure you understand. At this level of concentration, these are dangerous toxins - much too nasty to keep quiet about.'

'Of course, I quite understand, and thanks for your help, Loafer,' Hadfeld said, 'and give my love to baby Mark.'

*

Oliver Stark OBE, the Chief Constable of Sheffield was not pleased to be missing his Sunday afternoon golf, even for an old fishing pal like Sergeant Terrence Burke.

He'd sent for him as soon as he'd heard of his suspension from duty. He would have liked to talk as they played a round together, but Burke didn't have his clubs and appeared far too jumpy and sullen to play. The two had known each other for years, and often went on fishing trips, away from the city; Scotland and Ireland were their favourite escapes. Another senior officer often joined them. As young men the three had joined the Royal Horse Artillery on the same day and served together between the wars. They still wore identical regimental rings. After their demob, it was Burke who had persuaded the other two to join the police. Theirs was a deep-rooted friendship. It had even survived their widening social differences, as Burke had stuck as a sergeant, and the others had progressed to ever higher levels of seniority in the police force.

'Well what did you expect, Terry?' cried Oliver Stark, swinging a putter on his back garden lawn. 'You should have brought C.I.D in from the start.'

Sergeant Burke blew a sigh. 'There was no case to start with. It was down as accidental death. The Coroner called it just like

211

the doctor had said. Then this young lad started poking about and making a fuss. I was just trying to handle it. The last thing I wanted was the newspapers getting hold of it and saying we didn't care about little old ladies.'

'But what do I do now? Bob Simpson is one of the few of our graduate intake that we dared to promote. You know what a big song and dance I made about it when we made him Chief Superintendent. If I overrule him now and the newspapers get hold of it, what will that make me look like?'

'I'm not asking you for any favours. I know I messed up, but you know you can rely on me to give C.I.D all the help I can to make up for it. The thing is, I can't do anything if I'm sat at home listening to Mrs Dale's Diary.'

'And what do I say to Bob Simpson? Oh Bob that old pal of mine you've suspended for behaving like a plonker, I've overruled you – d'yer mind?'

Sergeant Burke's shoulders sagged.

When the two old friends parted, Oliver Stark reached for the telephone and called Bob Simpson. 'Hello, Bob. Sorry to disturb you on a Sunday afternoon - I hope it's not too inconvenient.'

'Not at all, sir - how can I help?'

'I just saw Terry Burke. He's pretty down as you can guess.'

'Oh yes – err- I expect he is ...'

'I just wanted to say that I think you did the right thing in suspending him, Bob. I bet it was a hard decision too, him being such a close friend of mine, but I want you to know that I support you a hundred percent. Terry and me go back a long way. We were in the Royal Horse Artillery together. There's a lot I would put up with from an old comrade like that. Especially such an experienced officer, but I have to say, I think you got it exactly right.'

'Oh, well - err - thank you, Sir. I'm glad you think so – err - but as a matter of fact, I was intending to call him back in on Monday. Yes – err - men of his experience are in short supply, and frankly, he would be more use to me at work right now rather than on suspension. I hope you think that's the right move.'

'Oh, it's not for me to comment, Bob, me being such a close personal friend of his. God, he was best man at my wedding. What would it look like if I interfered? You must do what you think is best, Bob – best for all of us.'

*

Glancing warily around, Doctor Hadfield knocked on Mrs Smeggs' cottage door, wondering why he felt so shifty and conspicuous. Noticing a small bead of blood that had formed on his finger end, he sucked it, making a mental note to be more careful in future, of the vicious spring on her garden gate.

'Doctor!' Mrs Smeggs cried, surprised to see him. 'I didn't send for you. Is it the Mester next door again?'

'Oh no, I'm sorry to disturb you, Mrs Smeggs. If you don't mind, I really would appreciate a moment of your time. Is it convenient? I can come back another time.'

'No, come in, come in.'

Granny Smeggs ushered in the young man and fussed and dithered until he was safely ensconced in the armchair facing her rocker. 'My word this is a surprise. Would you like tea, or I've got a bottle of Camp? I like to make it with hot milk.'

'You're very kind, but no thank you. I don't want to take up your time.' He coughed and scanned the room nervously. 'I – err – it's a delicate matter, Mrs Smeggs,' he said awkwardly. 'And one I fear you may prefer not to discuss at all. But I can tell you that it is a matter of the very gravest importance.'

Mrs Smeggs peered at him over her spectacles, her eyebrows almost hitting the ceiling. 'Good gracious. What ever can it be?'

'I believe you knew Mrs Loveday quite well, and helped her from time to time.'

Granny Smeggs chewed her bottom lip for a second and considered where he might be leading. 'Yes, I knew her. We were neighbours,' she admitted cautiously. 'My garden wall adjoins her backyard.'

'I'm sorry to press you, Mrs Smeggs, but I believe it went further than that.' He paused, studying her reaction. When she did not add to her admission, he probed tentatively. 'Before the war, I believe you sometimes laid out the dead for people.'

213

'Yes, I helped those who didn't have the money for an undertaker.'

'And you delivered many a baby round here too, I believe.'

She eyed him suspiciously and pushed her glasses up her nose. 'Ordinary folk couldn't afford midwives and doctors until Mr Bevan gave us the National Health Service. But babies have been coming since Cain and Able, doctor, without hospitals and doctors. I just helped along what comes naturally.'

'Would I be right in saying that you nursed Annabel Loveday during her pregnancy?'

Mrs Smeggs bristled and shook her shoulders stiffly. 'I don't want to talk about it. The poor woman's dead, God rest her. Nothing can be served by it now.'

Hadfield persisted. 'Have you ever seen anything like these before?' He fished in his jacket pocket, took out the blue sugar paper packet he had shown Billy and shook out a few of the little green tablets into his cupped hand.

The old lady squirmed in her rocking chair, her eyes sparkling with unshed tears. 'I told her not to take 'em. She'd got the crazy idea they would help form the child's bones. Her sister had rickets you see, and died young. A lot did in them days. She believed them things would be good for the child. I told her good food and exercise would do as much. I told her not to take them. I told her to drink milk stout, and eat eggs and fruit. She never had no herbal pills for her Tommy, and he was a lovely baby.'

'Do you know what they are?'

'Some old wives tonic I think - vitamins, or something I suppose.'

'Do you know where she got them?'

Mrs Smeggs gripped the arms of her chair. Her lips trembled, her eyes blazing with fury. 'Not from me!' she cried angrily, spitting her words at the doctor. 'I brought children into this world without witch's brews. Like I just told you: good food, milk and eggs, and don't drink strong liquor, but for a glass of stout now and again. That's what I always told my ladies.'

'I agree, and I am entirely sure you didn't give these to her.' He settled in his seat and tried to relax. 'Was she looking forward to the birth?'

214

'She was sick most of the time, but she was strong and didn't complain much. It was the old doctor, Doctor Howard, who took her into Jessop's hospital. You probably won't have heard of him. Anyway, it was a good job he saw her and took her to hospital. Even so, she still lost the child, but she nearly lost her life too.'

'I believe you fetched the doctor personally.'

She nodded.

'Did you always do that?'

'If need be, I did. Why?'

'No, I mean do you go to the doctor's house yourself instead of sending a boy with a note.'

'Sometimes, I can't say really. Sometimes it was different.'

'Would I be right in thinking that you particularly wanted it to be Doctor Howard that came to see her on that occasion, and not any other doctor?'

She bristled and avoided his eyes. 'I don't know what you mean.'

'Forgive me, but I think you do. What I mean is, I think you wanted to make sure it was not Doctor Greenhow. I think you had your suspicions about those pills, didn't you? I think that's why you tried to stop her taking them.' He watched her closely reading her reactions. 'You knew, didn't you? You knew what he was doing. Why did you keep quiet?'

Mrs Smeggs took a deep breath and sighed, staring into the embers in her fireplace, her lips trembling as she recalled things she had not wanted to think about for thirty years. 'She had nothing left, but her Tommy,' she told him softly. 'She'd lost everything. For a time he was a comfort to her, Doctor Greenhow. Why should I add to her misery by dragging it out for everybody to snuffle through like foraging pigs? She promised she would stop taking the pills, if I agreed to keep quiet about it. So I did.'

She blew her nose and dabbed her eyes. 'They started out with high hopes, her and her Noah,' she told him, a small smile coming to her trembling lips. 'He was a good boy, Noah, a saw-smith. They should have had a good life too, never too much nor too little — just right. He would have set up as a little mester.

215

Things would have been good for them. But the war stopped all that. It broke her, though she was still young - and very comely too, believe it or not. Those dark eyes of hers could fell men like a scythe through barley. But inside, it was different.' She paused and looked at the young doctor, studying his face for a moment. 'When people look at each other, doctor, do you know what they see?'

He shrugged, sombrely.

'They see skin, and that's all they see. Anything else is put there by their imaginations. In other words, they see what they want to see. Nothing more or less.'

'You know that you probably saved her life?'

'Only just. You'd have thought she was a ninety year old to look at her. She was younger than me, barely sixty. She's been sallow and sick all her life since them pills.' She gestured to the packet in Hadfield's hand. 'Greenhow kept her alive afterwards. He made sure he was the only one who treated her.'

Hadfield put the pills away in his jacket pocket. 'I don't know what to do about this,' he told her. 'Of course, you know it's a criminal offence to terminate a pregnancy. I've been thinking about it.' He looked up at her. 'It will have to come out – all of it. You do understand, don't you?'

'You must do what's right. But I just ask you to think of that poor woman when you decide what that is.'

. . . .

CHAPTER TWENTY-THREE

Monday morning was grey and damp. Trees dripped after overnight rain, and puddles floated May blossom. A chill mist clung to everything as Yvonne and Billy walked to the vicarage for their meeting with Reverend Hinchcliffe.

From the bottom of the vicarage drive, they saw Mrs Corbert on the front door step. She appeared to have just arrived for work and seemed to be having some difficulty unlocking the door. Stooped in concentration, she did not notice them, as finally, she opened the door and started inside. Billy hurried up the drive to try to catch her before she went inside. Yvonne yawned, and slouched along behind him.

As he reached the front door it suddenly swung open again. Mrs Corbert stood on the threshold, ashen faced, eyes wide with horror, her body hunched and trembling. She fell into Billy's arms wailing and gibbering. He struggled to hold her as she wept and shook. Yvonne ran past them into the house, returning almost immediately, looking grim faced and frightened. 'He's dead,' she cried. 'He's on the floor - there's blood ...'

Billy steered Mrs Corbert to a garden seat nearby and sat her down. Yvonne sat beside her, holding her. Gently relinquishing his hold on her Billy stepped cautiously into the house. He found the Reverend Hinchcliffe lying face down in a pool of blood in the entrance hall, near to his study door. There was a bloodstain on the back of the dark green cardigan covering his clerical black shirt and white collar.

Gasping for breath, Billy stood over the body. He found he was unable to stop repeatedly wiping his palms on his trousers. He told himself he must calm down and ring the police. There was a telephone on a hall table. He dialled three nines, and was soon explaining what he had found.

'Stay where you are. Officers are on the way.'

Police Headquarters passed the call details to Hammerton Road Police Station, barely a five-minute car drive from the vicarage.

Sergeant Burke was in his office, keeping his head down, after having his suspension unexpectedly lifted by the chief superintendent late on Sunday afternoon. So far, the officers at their desks in the main office had been unable to catch his eye. They were all itching to know his situation. There had been no formal announcement. Some were even wondering if he had any right to be on duty at all. Whispered speculation persisted.

Heads turned in unison from Burke's door to the door opposite, as the inspector was heard running down the stairs from his office on the upper floor. They watched, as he burst in, and dashed across into Burke's office. What on earth was going on? Was the inspector about to throw the sergeant out? The next moment Burke and the Inspector rushed out of the station together. They left in the Inspector's car, bells down, tyres screeching.

At the vicarage, Billy heard the distant sounds of police car bells. He went out into the front garden to join Mrs Corbert and Yvonne as he waited for the police to arrive.

Tears stained Yvonne's face, but she bravely tried to console the poor woman, whose wails echoed round the garden like wolf howls. 'She says it was Alexander,' sobbed Yvonne.

'What?'

'She said he was still alive. She asked him who did it and he told her, "Alexander," then he died.'

'I don't know who he meant,' wailed Mrs Corbert. 'I don't know Alexander.'

At the bottom of the drive the wooden gates of the vicarage scraped noisily on gravel as PC Handley pushed them back against wet, overhanging shrubs. He stood back and waved in a waiting police car. Another followed, and in the distance others could be heard approaching.

Billy was relieved to see Sergeant Burke, though the inspector with him glared around, grim faced and hostile. The sergeant adjusted his helmet and headed purposefully towards the vicarage's still open door. The inspector spun around, and pointing at PC Handley, stomped towards him. 'You – what's your name?'

'Handley boss ...'

'Cover the gate Henley. The press'll soon get wind of this. Oh, and keep your eyes peeled for the C.I.D. They'll be the ones that look like criminals.'

Handley gave a half-hearted salute and muttered under his breath.

The activity around her had quietened Mrs Corbert. She was now sobbing, staring about, and dabbing her nose with a headscarf. Billy and Yvonne sat either side of her. Yvonne cuddled her, watching patiently as the garden filled with police. At the gate, PC Handley began fighting off reporters and sightseers. A crowd was gathering. Traffic honked in the street as it slowed and wound its way past parked police cars, an ambulance, and several reporters' cars. A traffic cop appeared and started waving his arms. The traffic chaos eased miraculously. Another policeman booked the reporters' cars for traffic obstruction.

Two young men in dark suits hurried up the drive. The C.I.D had opened for business.

'Are you Billy Perks?' asked one of the young plain clothes men.

'Yes, but I want to talk to Sergeant Burke.'

The young man looked surprised. 'Look, I'm Detective Sergeant Wooffitt. I'm in charge of this investigation - at the moment. I need you to come with me.' DS Wooffitt clearly believed his tenure of the case would be short lived, but to be dismissed quite so soon, and by a schoolboy, was unacceptable. For Billy, it was simply a matter of common sense. The sergeant knew the history of the case. He could see no sensible reason why he should have to deal with someone who would need everything explained to him, and probably more than once.

'No I want to see Sergeant Burke,' he insisted.

'Look sonny, come with me, or you'll be in deep bother.'

'I don't care. I want to talk to the sergeant. He knows what's going on. Me and him have solved this case together.'

'And me,' cried Yvonne, digging Billy in the ribs.

The detective sergeant stomped off to the doorstep where Sergeant Burke and the Inspector were in earnest conversation.

'Excuse me, Inspector, we're ready to interview the witnesses and we …'

'I'm talking – wait.'

Detective sergeant Wooffitt swallowed, set his jaw and tried to smile politely, resisting the impulse to batter his superior officer. 'I need to talk to them now, sir, and would like the sergeant to join me. He knows the young lad and we feel it'll be helpful if he sees him there.'

'Baby sitting?' queried the inspector, turning to smile sarcastically at his sergeant. 'They want you to baby sit them, Sergeant Burke. How do you feel about that?'

Sergeant Burke looked at both men in turn. 'That man in there was my friend,' he said quietly, nodding towards the open door. 'The folks round here loved him. I think we should do whatever it takes to find out who killed him'

Between shuddering sobs, Mrs Corbert told her story to a detective. A young constable gave her a cup of tea, which she did not drink. The sergeant, Billy and Yvonne waited for their turn to come.

A slight commotion at the bottom of the drive sent a ripple of change through the proceedings. The two C.I.D officers looked at each other, concern showing on their eager young faces. They turned to Sergeant Burke as if to see how he was reacting to this new situation.

'It'll be the Chief Superintendent,' Burke suggested calmly. 'The vicar was a much loved public figure, and we've had more than our fair share of murders just recently. The public will expect to see at least a Chief Super., on the case. Just carry on as though nothing special is going on. That's what he wants to see, not a pair of his officers standing to attention like tailors' dummies.'

Chief Superintendent Bob Simpson, strode up the drive ahead of a small posse of uniforms and civilians. He touched his hat with his baton and nodded in turn to every officer and civilian in sight, coming to the sergeant last. 'Ah, Sergeant Burke, good to see you. Nasty business this,' he said. Only a few hours earlier he had been yelling down the telephone, threatening the sergeant with the sack. 'A very good man, Reverend Hinchcliffe. He'll be missed.'

'Yes sir, very much so.'

'Right, so what do we have so far?'

Detective Sergeant Wooffitt swallowed hard and stood to attention. 'White male aged fifty-eight ...'

'And you are?' interrupted Simpson.

'DS Wooffitt, sir'

'Carry on DS Wooffitt.'

'Erm – a white male aged fifty-eight ...'

'Sorry Wooffitt, but isn't it the Reverend Hinchcliffe?' Simpson interrupted again.

'Yes sir,' answered Wooffitt, terrified.

'Then why not say so?'

Wooffitt shuffled his feet and grabbed a sheaf of papers from the garden seat where Mrs Corbert sat, still sobbing quietly. He leafed through them as if they would somehow help him to cope. 'The reverend is dead sir; gunshot wound in the back. He was still alive at – err ...' He shuffled through the papers.

'Eight,' his quaking partner prompted.

'Eight this morning, when this lady, err - Mrs Corbert, the housekeeper, arrived and discovered the body - err - the reverend – he was not the body then - he was still alive.'

'And time of death?'

'Eight oh five, sir.'

'Is that it? Thank you Sergeant. Well done. Err, the reverend was a popular man, very well liked, so please be careful Sergeant Wooffitt. I know you will be, but you know what the press are like.'

DS Wooffitt smiled, looking relieved. His little ordeal was over and seemed to have gone quite well. He watched, relaxing slightly, as Simpson turned to Sergeant Burke. 'So Sergeant, what do you make of all this?'

Sergeant Burke cleared his throat. 'I haven't spoken to DS Wooffitt yet sir. I was about to tell him that there was a call from the Reverend on Friday afternoon. The duty sergeant took it, because at the time - you see - I wasn't able to be there.'

'Yes - yes we know all about that sergeant. Get on with it please,' said Simpson annoyed.

'He wanted to come in to the station. Err – specifically, he asked if he could come to see me. The duty officer recorded the message, and I found it this morning when I – finally - got to my desk.'

'Any idea what he wanted?'

'It would only be a guess sir, no more than that,' replied the sergeant.

'I do,' Billy interjected, stepping forward.

Chief Superintendent Simpson peered past Sergeant Burke. 'Is this the lad?' he asked, not taking his eyes off Billy.

'It is sir. Billy Perks.'

'Bring him over. Let's have a word.'

A young constable eased into the circle of faces in front of the vicarage's front door. 'Forensics are here, sir,' he announced. 'And a doctor's arrived.'

Simpson nodded to DS Wooffitt and his colleague, releasing them to attend to the forensics team. 'Give me the headlines Wooffitt, as soon as you have them. Oh - and ask the doctor to hang on when he's finished.'

Billy was ushered forward. 'I've heard a lot about you,' said Simpson warmly. 'You did a good job getting that case reopened – the man in the water mill, very interesting that. Do you want to be a policeman when you grow up?'

'No sir, I want to be a tram driver.'

Simpson nodded, seeming to understand completely. 'Right. So, what can you tell us about this sad business, Billy?'

'He was going to give you some evidence,' Billy told him. 'It's about old Annabel – err, Mrs Loveday and her son, and Pearce and the lot. He'd found out who did it, but he was scared.'

'Scared of the killer?' asked Chief Superintendent Simpson.

'No sir, scared he'd have to give up his job because – because of something he had to do to get the evidence. I told him it didn't matter, but he was very upset about it.'

Sergeant Burke leaned in closer. He was more interested in the actual evidence than how the reverend had come by it, and wanted to hear more. 'What evidence Billy?' he asked.

'I don't know Mr Burke. I never saw anything, but he said it would change everything and prove what I'd been saying about the murder.'

'Do you think he knew who killed Mrs Loveday?' asked the Chief Superintendent.

'Yes, I do, and her Tommy too.'

'But *you* don't know?' Sergeant Burke queried.

'Well not exactly, but I know who killed Pearce for certain. And because of that I think I could soon prove that the same person killed Tommy and Mrs Loveday. And when you get the bullet out of the reverend, I bet that's from the same gun that killed Stan Sutcliffe, and Mr Pearce. Just like I said.' He looked into the faces of the sergeant and the chief superintendent. 'That bullet will tie it all up.'

'OK, young man - so tell us, who do you say killed Mr Pearce?' asked Bob Simpson.

'Doctor Greenhow.'

The sergeant and the chief superintendent gasped in disbelieve. 'For Heaven's sake don't repeat that, Billy,' said Sergeant Burke. 'You got it all wrong about Mr Pearce - didn't you? You said he was the killer, and we all know that was wrong. Don't do it again. I've told you before, proof positive before you say a word.'

'But he did it,' insisted Billy. 'He killed him because Pearce found out that it was him who gave Stan Sutcliffe the fifty pounds. I can prove it if you show me the money envelope.'

'What good will that do?'

'If it's got ink splatters all over it, like I bet it has, that'll prove it came from Doctor Greenhow's desk. Pearce knew this too, because he was always getting envelopes just like it at his chemist shop with prescriptions in them. When he saw that money envelope when you were questioning him, he recognised it as one of the doctor's.'

'That's not proof of a murder,' said the chief superintendent, 'but in any case why would Doctor Greenhow pay this - err - Stan Sutcliffe fifty pounds?'

'Because there was something he wanted from the old woman's house. He paid Stan to break in and get it. That's what

Stan was doing when I found the police notice blowing about in the skittle yard. That's why he beat me up. And he stole my Easter egg. And afterwards, we found the nail bar he'd been using to break in. I knew it was his because it was painted with red lead like the garden tools he and his Dad have been nicking. And that's also why Pearce said he never recognised Stan when he chased after him. He knew very well it was Stan, but he wanted to protect him, just long enough to find out what he was looking for. That's why he kept him out of trouble.'

Chief superintendant Bob Simpson removed his cap and scratched his head. 'But how is this connected to the Reverend?' he asked.

'I think the Reverend had already discovered whatever it was that Doctor Greenhow had paid Stan to find. I still don't really know what it is, but whatever it is, he killed Annabel to get his hands on it. He hit her with his walking stick. That's probably where the little silver thing broke off from.'

'What silver thing?'

'You've got it now, with my other clues. It's got blood and hair on it. You should have tested it by now, but nobody ever believes me. People never believe kids.'

The three exchanged glances. 'I'll check with forensics sir,' Sergeant DS Wooffitt volunteered.

'It's probably nothing,' said Sergeant Burke. 'We can check all that stuff later, if we need to.'

'So now you're saying Doctor Greenhow killed the Reverend too?' queried the Chief Superintendent. 'But that's ridiculous, Billy. He's given us the name of his killer. It was his very last word to Mrs Corbert. "Alexander". Mrs Corbert asked him who shot him and he said, "Alexander". You can't have it plainer than that.' He looked to the sergeant for support, but Burke appeared distracted by some other thoughts. 'Once we find Alexander,' Simpson went on, 'everything will fall into place. Frankly, Billy, your evidence amounts to little more than a few ink spots on an envelope. I'm afraid that's not proof of anything. It certainly won't convince a jury, that an eminent doctor and leading member of the community is a serial killer.'

·········

CHAPTER TWENTY-FOUR

Doctor Hadfield joined the group of police officers gathered around the Chief Superintendent in front of the vicarage door. He was pale and frowning. Seeing Billy, he greeted him with a vague nod before taking Sergeant Burke to one side. 'May I have a word please, Sergeant?'

Bob Simpson nodded his permission to the sergeant. 'I'm going to see what forensics are doing,' he said. 'Catch me up when you're finished here, Sergeant. You too, Doctor, if you please.' He moved off smartly to where forensics inspectors, were overseeing the removal of the Reverend's body.

Billy moved to stand with Yvonne, leaning on the back of a garden bench. 'They don't believe me,' he growled. 'What do we have to do to get 'em to see what's under their chuffin noses?'

'Didn't they say owt about our evidence?' Yvonne sat down.

He joined her on the damp seat. 'Nowt. They should have tested the silver bit thing by now, but I don't think they've even seen it. It's probably still in Sergeant Burke's office. I'm getting really fed up. The Reverend was killed to stop him talking. It could be our turn next.'

Doctor Hadfield and Sergeant Burke talked in urgent whispers for some time. Billy watched them closely, trying to eavesdrop, but the garden was noisy with people and vehicles coming and going, and he could not hear them. They finished as Chief Superintendent Simpson joined them, his voice loud and authoritative.

'So, Sergeant, I have to go now. I've asked Inspector Fletcher to keep an eye on DS Wooffitt and his friend. I dare say some C.I.D top brass will dain to turn up eventually.'

'Very well, sir.'

'So, find out who Alexander is, and that should do it – eh?'

'No.' cried Billy from his seat. 'Alexander isn't a person.'

Bob Simpson smacked his baton impatiently against his leg. 'What?'

'It's not somebody,' repeated Billy. 'Alexander is not a person, it's a cardboard folder. I think it must have the evidence in it.' Everyone around them suddenly fell silent. Billy rose from his bench and walked towards the officers. 'It's a cardboard folder that Tommy Loveday made at school for his mother, years ago. It's gorra – a - cartouche painted on the front of it.' He turned and looked up at the sergeant. 'I looked it up in the library,' he explained. 'You see, I heard that Annabel had a folder with a picture of a bird and a lion on it. My granny told me Annabel kept only her most important papers in it. I found out that Tommy once did a school project about Alexander the Great, and in the library, I found out all about cartouches. That's what you call the picture writing the ancient Egyptians did for the names of the pharaohs. The one for Alexander the Great has a bird and a lion in it. Reverend Hinchcliffe told me that he – he – err – *borrowed* some papers from Annabel's house. I was pretty certain that the folder must be amongst them, because she only used it for her most important papers. I think it has the evidence in it that the Reverend was going to give to the police. When he said "Alexander", he meant for us to look in that folder.'

DS Wooffitt and his partner did not wait for orders. They rushed towards the house, followed closely by the Chief Superintendent and Inspector Fletcher.

For a second or two, Sergeant Burke stood rooted to the spot, watching them all go, before he followed, with a sideways glance at Billy.

Yvonne looked at Billy, and raised a cynical eyebrow. 'Hum, don't tell me they actually believe us at last.'

'Come on, let's see.'

'I'm coming too,' said Mrs Corbert. 'I need to get back inside. I have things to do.'

Yvonne stopped herself from reminding the housekeeper that she now had no employer. She decided it would be better to let her come to terms with her new situation in her own good time.

The Reverend's body had been removed from the entrance hall. A wet stain marked the spot where the floor had been disinfected. A rubberised ground sheet lay over the threshold.

227

The telephone rang. A constable, posted beside it, answered it immediately then ran off on some errand.

Billy led Yvonne into the Reverend's study. It felt damp, and smelled of smoke. Through the crush of policemen he could see a cardboard folder open on the desk. It was empty. Wooffitt examined it. It was battered and dirty, but on its front cover, beautifully painted by Tommy Loveday, Billy saw the cartouche of Alexander the Great.

'Well, whatever was in it has gone,' growled DS Wooffitt.

'If I'd been at work on Friday, this would never have happened,' said Sergeant Burke. 'By now we'd have the evidence and our killer too. And the Reverend would be alive.'

The back of Chief Superintendent Bob Simpson's neck glowed scarlet. Billy could almost feel its heat from where he stood. 'I have to go,' Simpson croaked quietly. 'You and I need to talk, Sergeant. Tomorrow, first thing, my office.' He smacked his baton against his leg, turned and marched off stiffly.

DS Wooffitt and his partner exchanged nervous glances and began fishing around in the fire-grate, trying to read the writing on a couple of sheets of paper ash. Billy remembered that a mirror was useless in such circumstances and glanced sheepishly at Yvonne. She seemed to have read his mind, and flicked an eyebrow triumphantly.

'The killer broke in,' suggested Wooffitt's junior partner. 'There was a struggle and the vicar was shot. Then the killer came in here looking for that folder. He took the contents and burned them here. He left the folder and ran off.'

'Or I suppose it could have been the Reverend that burnt the papers,' said Wooffitt. 'We heard from Billy that he was worried about losing his job. Maybe he changed his mind at the last minute.'

'It wasn't the Reverend,' said Mrs Corbert. 'That fireplace doesn't work. The flu is bricked up. He'd never burn anything here, it'd smoke the place out.'

'The killer was somebody he knew,' said Billy, scratching invisible stubble on his chin. 'You can tell that because the Reverend let him in.'

'Why do you say that?' asked Wooffitt, with a derisive sniff.

'This morning, I saw Mrs Corbert struggling with the door lock. She was trying to turn the key and open ...'

'Yes, that's right,' she interrupted, 'the key wouldn't turn, and I realised it was already unlocked, you see?'

'That shows the killer didn't break in. The Reverend unlocked the door for him, and because he was shot, he never relocked it. That's exactly how Mrs Corbert found it. So, he almost certainly knew his killer. Another thing is, he probably walked ahead of him towards the study. That's how he got shot in the back.'

'But how did the killer know where to look for the papers?' asked Wooffitt, waving a hand at the crowded shelves around the study walls.

'This house is cleaned by Mrs Corbert,' said Billy, pointing her out like a conjurer doing a lady in the cabinet trick. 'She does everywhere in the house except this room. The Reverend told me that himself. He often left things out, knowing she would never move them. It would be the obvious place to look. And because he was worried about taking his evidence to the police, he probably already had it out on the desk where he'd been sitting, thinking about it. The killer found it straight away.'

'Well whatever the evidence was we'll never know now,' Sergeant Burke said, dismissively.

'There may be sommat else,' said Billy cryptically. 'When I met him on the train, the Reverend told me he had some other papers that he'd not read, because he couldn't get at them.'

Wooffitt again looked around the walls lined with books and untidy heaps of files. 'Blimey it'll take a month of Sundays to find anything in this mess,' he groaned.

'Or maybe we could just look in that tin,' Billy said, pointing to a painted, tin plate jewellery case, wedged between a row of books on a shelf.

'It's like the clock,' Yvonne cried, pointing to the tin box.

Wooffitt stared blankly.

'When we cleared out Mrs Loveday's house,' she explained, 'we saw a strange tin clock. It was a really cheap looking thing, painted to look like a posh antique, just like that box. I bet the two of them were a matching set.'

229

Wooffitt pulled out the tin box. It was about the size of a shoebox. He shook it gently next to his ear. 'It sounds like papers.'

He set it down on the desk. Painted to look like an antique jewellery box, its ornate decoration was faded and scratched from heavy use. Nevertheless, Billy was certain it would match exactly the tin clock he had seen in Annabel's cottage. A fancy key plate escutcheon was painted on its front.. Around the keyhole, the paint was worn away to bare metal.

'It's locked, we'll need a screwdriver,' said Wooffitt.

Billy fumbled in his trouser pocket for the key he had found hidden in the ivy in Annabel's cottage. 'Try this,' he said, tossing it on to the desk.

'You said you'd given me everything,' said Sergeant Burke angrily.

'I forgot that,' said Billy, feeling smart, though in truth it really had been a simple oversight. His mood changed as he watched DS Wooffitt fit the key in the lock. He remembered how Reverend Hinchcliffe had said that box probably contained private letters from Mrs Loveday's husband, and how he had feared them becoming public property.

'Stop!' cried Billy. 'Whatever we find in there, we shouldn't just read everything. It's private. Some are probably letters from her husband.'

Sergeant Burke was looking at him. 'You're right, Billy. Perhaps we should slow down a bit,' he said. 'I'll take it back to the station and we can study them properly, later.'

'No I don't mean that. I mean it's just letters from her husband ...'

'Noah,' said Yvonne. 'They should be secret and not read. You should only read any other papers, but not Noah's letters. That would be all right, I think.'

'Yes, they're right. They belonged to her. We shouldn't be reading them. They can't possibly have anything to do with the murder,' said Sergeant Burke.

Yvonne threw her arms round him and kissed him on his cheek. He blushed and shuffled awkwardly.

Wooffitt stared at the Sergeant as if he thought he was losing his mind. 'It's all evidence, until we know it's not,' he argued. 'We can't just ignore stuff. You know that, Sergeant.' He turned the key and unlocked the box.

As he lifted the lid, Sergeant Burke sniffed loudly and pointed a threatening finger at him. 'Well it's on your head.'

Wooffitt scowled but went ahead. He pulled out two bundles of letters tied with wool yarn. A loose roll of papers held together by a loop of string, and an old sock. He examined the two bundles of letters. 'I'm guessing these could be the letters from her husband,' he said, and put them to one side. He held up the sock, and showed that there was something heavy inside it. He shook it gently to tip out the contents. Two gold sovereigns fell out and rolled on to the desk. Wooffitt slipped them impassively into a manila envelope and licked the seal. 'Two coins – gold,' he dictated to his partner. Finally, he picked up the loose roll of papers. 'These look like a bit of an odd assortment - could be anything.'

Billy watched spellbound as the detective slipped off the string and allowed the papers to unroll on the desk. Everybody moved closer and peered down at the uppermost document. It was a letter from a skin specialist at Sheffield Children's Hospital. It was about Tommy's impetigo. The second page was from the war office and attached a letter from Noah Loveday's commanding officer. Wooffitt read it in silence, then said softly, 'It says he dragged his wounded sergeant all the way back to their trench before he was killed on the wire.'

'Here son, let me,' said Sergeant Burke, taking the papers from DS Wooffitt, whose hands were now trembling. 'This one is unsigned.' Burke read the letter to himself, dismissed it and pulled out another. 'So is this.' Again he read it in silence and put it aside.

'May I see that, Sergeant?' This from Doctor Hadfield. He reached over and took the paper from the surprised policeman. 'I think this could be what we're looking for.'

Burke looked perplexed and for a moment seemed about to snatch the paper back from the doctor.

Hadfield took a step away from him and looked at each person in turn before speaking. 'I spoke to the sergeant earlier about a most serious matter I have uncovered, thanks to Billy here. Officers have been sent to my employer's surgery and I believe, Doctor Greenhow may now be under arrest.' He looked to the sergeant for confirmation.

Sergeant Burke nodded and recovered the papers from Doctor Hadfield. 'I think that with what the doctor has discovered and this letter, it completes the story.'

'Read it, Sergeant,' said Hadfield.

'I have read it, Doctor and I think that with the children here, we can save all this for later.

Hadfield took the papers from the Sergeant. 'I'll read it then,' he said impatiently, and looked around the group, noting their agreement.

He read

'Darling Bell, it breaks my heart, but if you come on Sunday you will spoil everything for us. You must remain my secret love. You surely know it's you that I love. Nobody will ever take your place. Believe me Bell, what I do now, I do for you as much as for myself.

H, thinks I will marry his daughter Iris. He will make me his partner. We must keep our love secret for a little while longer - until the right moment. You know my heart is yours, dearest Bell. Our lives will blossom when I am a partner in the practice, but you must surely see that a child now is out of the question. This is entirely the wrong time.

Beloved secret, do this for us both, and one day we will be free and happy.

Your true and eternal secret love'

'The bastard,' Wooffitt hissed.

Hadfield coughed and handed the letter to DS Wooffitt, who placed it in an evidence envelope under the watchful gaze of Yvonne and Billy.

'I have evidence that he caused her to lose the child. Whether she knew and agreed to it, I can't be sure, but I am almost certain that she was tricked. Luckily, Mrs Smeggs, Billy's Grandmother,

232

alerted old Doctor Howard. Otherwise – who knows what could have happened ...'

Yvonne went to close the lid of the tin box. She put the bundles of letters back in it and locked the lid with Billy's key. DS Wooffitt watched her, and for a moment seemed set to take the box away as evidence. Then he pushed it towards her. 'There's nothing we need in there. You can put it back where it belongs.'

Yvonne nodded gratefully and left with it under her arm.

PC Handley entered into the room. He looked pale and tense. He sidled up to Sergeant Burke and the Inspector and whispered to them. The sergeant looked relieved, the inspector perplexed.

'Did you find him?' asked Doctor Hadfield.

'He's dead,' the sergeant said stiffly. 'He shot himself. Constable Handley found the gun. It's with Forensics now. It's a Webley Scott .455 calibre Mk VI Navy revolver. It seems likely it's the gun that killed Pearce and Sutcliffe. It's certainly the right calibre.' He looked around brightly. 'So, that's that then! We have our killer. The Doctor.'

'Is that it?' queried the Inspector.

'Yes it's obvious isn't it? Greenhow heard Annabel was writing her memoirs. He went to see her, to plead with her not to disclose anything about the child and the abortion. She probably refused. You know what a stubborn old woman she could be. The doctor lost his temper and killed her. He looked for her memoirs or her papers, but couldn't find them, so he paid Stan Sutcliffe fifty quid to break in and get them. Pearce probably found out and challenged him about it, so he was shot to shut him up. He probably killed the vicar for the same reason.'

The inspector looked relieved. 'Excellent! That wraps it all up nicely then.'

'No it doesn't.' This from Billy, who had moved to stand close beside the young doctor.

'What do you mean, Billy?' the Inspector asked.

'Doctor Greenhow didn't kill Annabel. He couldn't have.'

Hadfield bent close to Billy's face. 'Look, old chap. It's all over now. You were right all the time. The killer has already paid the price. You can let it go now, Billy.'

233

'He didn't do it. He could not have killed Annabel.'

'Well who did then, Billy?' he asked.

Billy turned to face Sergeant Burke. 'A good detective always examines even the shadow of a shadow.' He looked at the old policeman, and around at the others in the room. The doctor patted his shoulder warmly.

'In our gang den, we have something called the MOM board,' he told them. 'We write on it who was there and could have killed her. Then we check up to see what those people did and where they went. We know that in the very early morning after Annabel was killed, Doctor Greenhow was seen in the street near her house. At first, we thought that made him a suspect, so we investigated him. We found out that the barmaid who lodges at the Rose House pub had a baby that night. Doctor Greenhow was with her all night because the midwife was on another birth and Doctor Hadfield was out on other calls. Old Dr Greenhow couldn't have done it. He was at the Rose House all night, delivering a baby.'

The inspector looked perplexed. 'But he shot ...'

'Oh yes, he killed Pearce and Stan and he probably shot the Vicar too. But, that was because he feared the incriminating evidence Annabel might let out about him. But the thing is, he was not the only person who wanted that evidence killed off.'

'Who else wanted it?'

'The person who killed her.'

The inspector bobbed impatiently. 'For goodness sake, boy, who is that? Tell us who killed her?'

'Someone was blackmailing Doctor Greenhow. That same person, also killed Tommy Loveday, and messed up the police investigation into his death so that it wouldn't look like murder.'

'Who?'

'I think Tommy Loveday found out that his mother had almost been poisoned to death by the old Doctor.' Billy looked around at the room full of police officers. Every face was turned to his. 'She might have told him herself, or more than likely, he found the evidence accidentally, when he was getting ready to go to the RAF about Pearce's DFM. Tommy had letters from his RAF comrades that he needed to show to the RAF. He knew his mother kept all the really important papers in that old folder. He could easily have looked in that, or maybe he did what we just did, and opened that tin box of letters. Once he found out what had happened, instead of being violent and wanting revenge, or blackmail, he did the right thing – the proper thing. He went to the police for help.'

First Wooffitt's eyes, then the inspector's swung towards Sergeant Burke, as Billy continued. 'You killed Mrs Loveday, Sergeant. I suppose she refused to keep quiet about the old Doctor, and you knew that once that came out, everything else would have come with it, like the fact that you have been blackmailing him for years, ever since you found out from Tommy and scared him into falling down that shaft in the old mill.'

'Billy, this is rubbish! Have you gone mad?' the sergeant cried. 'Why would I do such a thing?'

'It wasn't for the money,' said Billy. 'Not at first, any-road. But you hated the Doctor. Anybody could see that when the two of you had to work together. You hated him, cos you thought his drinking had stopped him saving your little girl when she was ill. You blackmailed him to punish him for her death. It was later on that it was for the money, because your friends got promoted, but you were still a sergeant.'

'It would certainly explain how you can afford all the salmon fishing and golf trips,' Hadfield put in, drawing Billy close to his side.

Stunned, the inspector gaped at his sergeant. DS Wooffitt stepped in between them. 'You're under arrest, sarj. You'd better come with me.'

. . . .

235

CHAPTER TWENTY-FIVE

The graveyard overlooked Rivelin Valley. It sloped steeply and had fine views over pastures and woodland, out to the Man's Head Rock and beyond to the wild moors of the Peak District. Yvonne led Kick and Billy through the rows of gravestones past the newer graves, some still without headstones, some with simple wooden crosses. Annabel Loveday had been laid to rest under an existing headstone of white marble. Her name had been recently added, carved below that of her son Tommy.

Annabel Lillian, mother of Thomas, beloved wife of Noah Cyril.

'We're all here, Mrs Loveday: Billy, Michael and me. We know all about it now,' Yvonne said, resting her hand on the polished stone. 'They found out that the little bit of silver fitted into a hole in the sergeant's regimental ring. He just confessed then. It's strange, because I really liked him. I never thought ...'

'I'm sorry about the baby,' said Kick, and ignoring what their respective ages would have been, added, 'I would have let him play football with us if he'd lived.'

'There'll be a trial and everything.'

Suddenly Kick turned and grabbed Billy's arm. He pointed towards the chapel up at the top of the sloping burial ground. 'Look, there're two blokes watching us.'

'Oh Gimbals! It's my dad. I'm for it now,' said Billy.

'Who's that with him?'

Frank Perks strode down towards the little group, his face wearing its usual stern expression. The three stood in silence waiting, wondering what he would say to them.

'I thought this's where I'd find you,' he told Billy.

'We're burying this old tin box,' Billy mumbled, hardly looking at his father. 'It's got her letters in it – from her husband.'

'You're not going to stop us are you?' Yvonne asked, looking worried.

'No, I think it's a nice idea. The police have told me all about it – everything you did. They said the letters aren't evidence - so why not?'

Billy was looking back up to the brow of the hill with its little funeral chapel. The tall stranger was still standing there, looking down at them, his lanky figure silhouetted against a silver sky. He raised an arm and waved. Billy waved back.

Frank Perks turned and followed his son's gaze. 'Do you know who that is?'

'Yes. It's Jacque Cadell, skipper of the Wellington,' Billy answered. 'It's him who should've got that medal, not Pearce.'

Frank Perks nodded thoughtfully. 'He wanted to come here with me. I went and persuaded the police to release him. I thought it's what you would want.'

'Oh brilliant, Dad.'

'That young doctor helped me to do it. We went to the police station together. Anyway they released him without charges.'

'What'll happen to him now?' Yvonne asked.

'I don't know. He's a free man,' said Mr Perks. 'The doctor says he can get him a place in a special RAF hospital where they treat burn scars.' He turned, looking back to the figure on the hilltop and released a quiet sigh. 'I don't think he'll want that, somehow. I think he just wants to be free and on the road.'

Silence fell over the group. Mr Perks shuffled awkwardly. 'Sometimes we never really know what we want, and more often than not we get it completely wrong. Like this – I mean this is all a proper turn out for the book, isn't it?'

'What d'yer mean?' asked Billy.

'My son, the detective. You really showed 'em, didn't you? I'm so proud of you, Billy. I'm proud of all of you.'

Billy thought his heart might burst. He fought back joyful tears, as his dad looked away, hiding his own.

After a moment, Mr Perks sniffed loudly and turned back to his son. He gazed down at him and winked. 'Do you want to come home now, son? Your mam's worried. You've been gone a long time. And d'you know what – I'd like you and me to spend a bit more time together. What do you say?' He offered Billy his hand.

Billy grabbed it and leaned into his father's body, hugging him tightly.

'Oh, and I brought you this,' his dad said, handing him a large paper bag. 'It's out on bail – Detective.'

Billy ripped open the bag, and beamed a great smile. 'It's my tuppenny hat.'

END

Glossary of Sheffield – eeze

Alreight	(pron. as in eight) All right
An'all	As well, and all
Aypenny duck	Halfpenny savoury meat ball
Ayup mi owd	Hello my old friend
Back-naks	Back gardens
Bob	Shilling (twentieth of an old pound sterling)
Bobbies	Police officers
Chabby	Toddler (also pron. chavvy)
Clemmed	Feeling cold
Dee-ad	Dead
Dee-in	Dying
Dint	Did not
Donkey-stoned	White chalk drawn edge to steps, as used in the wartime blackout
Dunt	Does not
Gen	Given
Laikin	Playing
Mardy	Grouch, sulking, whining
Mester (little mester)	Self employed cutler or metal smith, also the man of the house
Moant	Must not
Mun	Must
Nay	No
Neet	Night
Nithered	Feeling cold
Nowt	Nothing
Nowty	Poor quality, small, shabby
Owt	Anything
One-n-tuppence	A shilling and two pennies
Racked	Plodding of packhorse. (Racker Way, now called Rivelin St. is a 4000 year old road.)
Rantied	Rocked, wobbled, unsteady
Ranty	Children's' see-saw
Reight	Right, intensely, very
Reight badly	Very sick
Scroamin	Climbing, scrambling
Scutch	Smack, slap
Sen	Self
Shurrup	Be quiet
Sin'	Since
Sithee	See you, pay attention, observe
Skoyl	School
Snek	Latch
Tanner	Silver six pence coin

Th'art	You are
Thee sen	Alone, your self
Threpenz	Three pence
Tup	A ram
Tuppenz	Two pence
T'owd	The old
Watta	(pron. as hatter) Water
Waynt	Will not
Weshin	Laundry
Wunt	Would not

A Sheffield-eeze Ditty   (Speech exercise)

Oh weer reight dahn in coyl oyl,
Weer muck splarts on t'winders.
We've used all us coyl up,
An' weer reight dahn to cinders.
When towd bailiff cooms eel never fint us,
Cos weer reight dahn in coyl oyl,
Weer muck splarts on t'winders.

Translation

Oh, we are right down in the basement,
Where dirt accumulates on the casement.
We have used up all our anthracite,
And are right down to the residue.
When the landlord's representative calls,
He will not discover us,
Because we are right down in the basement,
Where dirt accumulates on the casement.

Anon.

240

Interesting websites for more about Sheffield

Sheffield tourism   www.sheffield.gov.uk/out--andabout
Rivelin Valley conservation group   www.rivelinvalley.org.uk
Art Galleries and Museums   www.museums-sheffield.org.uk
Hollybush Inn Rivelin   www.ealukmusic.co.uk
Pubs in Walkley   www.sheffieldpub.co.uk/pubs/walkley/
Tramway Museum at Crich   www.tramway.co.uk
Pictures of old Sheffield trams   www.cyberpicture.net/sheffield
Peak District National Park   www.peakdistrict.org.uk

Origins of Walkley

The name comes from the Anglo-Saxon for Walca's forest (Walcas leah).
At the time of the Norman conquest 1066, Walkley belonged to Waltheof
the Earl of Northumbria. After the battle of Hastings, Waltheof submitted
to William the Conqueror and was allowed to keep his lands. He later
married Judith of Lens, a niece of William the Conqueror. Though this
might seem a really smart move, it must be said that Waltheof must have
been a bit of a dope, for he joined a revolt against William, but was on
the losing side. Extraordinarily, William pardoned him, yet a few years
later Waltheof revolted again, and lost again. Of course, old William was
naturally a bit fed up by this, so he executed him.
Nevertheless, I propose Waltheof as the model for that well known
Sheffielder, Robin Hood, or Robin of Loxley. Just like Robin Hood
Waltheof's titles included Earl of Huntingdon, and Lord of Loxley – does
that sound familiar?
Waltheof's great hall overlooked Rivelin Valley, probably near the
Sandygate Golf Course. Well it is very nice up there and there's a good
bus route right into town.

Printed in the United Kingdom by
Lightning Source UK Ltd., Milton Keynes
142356UK00001B/47/P